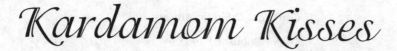

Kardamom Kisses

SHINIE ANTONY

Rupa & Co

Kardamom Kisses

shirie

For Dean, with oommas

Contents

Contents

Acknowledgements

Words fail me often, but there are times in my life I am glad they did not fail others. Like former gurus.

'Miss' Puri who very politely said, 'Try to avoid writing poetry in your Maths notebook.'

Sister Mary Rose whose response to my desire to join the nunnery was a very acidic, 'Feeling a little asexual today, are we?'

Ms Reena Bharathan, who taught me British History, but more importantly inspired me to put some buds in an army boot to enter a flower arrangement contest.

Dr Narendra Pani and Shankar P. who unfailingly feigned surprise at my errors ('It was you???') and Jaideep Bose who'd holler, 'Who the hell edited this story?' (Methehell, of course.)

Or 'sometime' friends Diana Sylvester, Chetan Bhagat, Urvashi Dev Rawal and Vivian Fernandes who said all the right things at the right time to the right person who repeated them to me.

Or even Deepthi, whose eyes sparked militantly whenever she stayed silent.

Part I

A Southern Sun

1

*I*T WAS AN UNIDENTIFIED SUMMER WHEN AMMA PACKED HER bags, air-coloured dreams and hurtled down here with us like coconuts *thup-thup* from a tree. The heat simmered on, turning to a crisp the plantain leaves we ate on, parching throats, skinned knees and even the nectar inside the earth-bound dangle of the bulbous bambloos lime, bleaching pillows and dreams alike until sunshine by the bucket had blinded us to other seasons.

It sparked Amma's hair into something flammable as she flapped foliage on the floor and called out to a brother, 'Etta.'

A hurried brush against the doll's cheek with my eyelashes—we called it the butterfly kiss—and I ran in with rumours of the outside world. 'It's drizzling.'

Amma gazed unseeingly at me; she never managed to wash the sleep out of her eyes. 'Too bright to rain. You know what they say...'

To pre-empt the frayed tale—a fox had to go down on hind-knee and ask his fiancée cat for a paw in marriage first; then, *and only then*, did glittery raindrops run down the sun-dappled sky like sequins on half-price sale—I nimbly skirted the nadu-muttam where lotuses bloomed blue in the water retention of a cemented comma.

'Too hot it is, too hot…' Amma's yawn merged with the water scalding my hands. Fanning brow with the veshti's gilt edge that forced flies to reverse into a skittish arabesque, and forecasting, 'The sun will froth over, if you ask me,' she wore on her placid round face the certainty of consensus while making small talk with self.

From the burrowing of slush-worms into the skin of our ankles to half-cut jackfruits on kitchen shelves, from the crackling spoons we shaped from dry leaves for our dolls to the fermented rice flour that made up all our snacks, with Amma's bosom suggesting a chest-centric solo act under her tunic and the reassuring discovery of it being split into two after all—everything seemed spherical as the sun. Even the night that sucked it down like a sweet, the sun in the sky with its million vermilion rays, was only the pitch black round of a mouth saying 'aah'.

Exhausting her quota of opinions on the ongoing weather, Amma allowed impatience in her next call. '*Etta*.'

Heeding the summons with a semi-nod this time, Velyammavan twanged the holy thread crisscrossing his bare chest and shunted down a languid gaze to his feet suspended on the elevated armrests of the low-slung chair.

'These feet of mine, they do not belong to me,' he meditated, referring to the nautical career that made a nomad of him. 'They are…'

'…gypsies attached to you,' briskly tightening the drapery of lungi at his waist, supplied his literati brother—the self-appointed 'putter of words in mouths'—our Cheriyammavan.

'He is a writer,' we told anyone who cared to ask, without specifying *what* it was Cheriyammavan wrote.

'Is it a sequel to the scriptures, Keshavan?' sceptics mocked as he dashed about licking stamps onto elongated envelopes. The postman, after Cheriyammavan had hounded him at home-turf during a particularly nasty bronchial bout, clarified in a disrespectful reprisal each time, 'No money order, Kochu Thampuran.'

Neither his growing anthology of rejection slips from the *National Geographic*, nor creative forays into contemporary flatulence hampered Cheriyammavan's literary image within the family. If there was a letter to be written, an application to be filed, a bill unpaid or cheque unsigned, he was our man, so that his faraway facial expressions were interpreted as a projection of the soul's travelogues and not the onset of siesta.

Velyammavan, on the other hand, freely emptied sentimental twaddle into letters that went largely unread owing to their length. In these, he dwelt so tremulously on the commonplace in our lives that we were hard-pressed to invent exciting extracurricular contests and non-stop academic wins to stick to our side of the bargain.

'My little angels,' he dubbed us, and we got the profile down pat—the wide-eyed, goddess-on-a-calendar expression—and though accessories like a sitar or conch would have helped, we had to consider mobility.

Cheriyammavan was the thinker and Velyammavan the doer, and sometimes their core competencies clashed in ill-rehearsed kalari-payattu mudras. 'Like setting fire to wet dung,' the latter would yell at Cheriyammavan's terminal tarrying. 'Pacha chanagam.'

His brother's back safely turned, Cheriyammavan winked at us. 'Call me PC for short.'

Both squatted down presently to sprinkle water on the plantain leaves from the brass tumbler's nozzle, activating

Amma to dash in and out to dot their leaves with pappadoms, pickles and sweet-sour ginger pulp.

Velyammavan rolled the chunky brown rice in his fist. 'No, no, don't learn,' he reproached his wife, who loitered in the kitchen with leisurely unintent, while Cheriyammavan pretended to chomp on his leaf and we tittered to humour him. 'It is a whole art, this system of serving! You have to know what comes after what.'

Turning to his ball-cheeked brother, he gasped, 'Hanuman, what have you done with my Keshavan?'

As spouse and sibling accommodated the slights with their characteristic aplomb and we children laughed with more gusto, Amma nervously tugged back hair—revealing a portion of forehead she painstakingly eclipsed with fringe—uncertain over the chronology of cabbage, cut into a million minuscule membranes and crushed with coconut, in the queue of morsels.

Velyammavan's monitoring of wife's watch on proceedings had him miss Ammooma's shake of head and Amma's subsequent frantic retreat.

'You are so lucky,' belched Velyammavan, rubbing his potbelly after the meal, which was routine repast to his brother, while we girls picked out raisins and blackened bits of coconut from the payasam like a headful of lice. 'You've earned it in your past birth, you scoundrel, this right to feast. Heavens have to collude for such destiny. Look at me, port to flea-bitten port.'

Cheriyammavan's throat transmitted static. Nothing he ate ever agreed with him and this abdominal disagreement rumbled out an airy kaleidoscope in his wake, like the trailing feathers of an onward peacock. Indigestion apart, he identified his brother's unnatural attachment to rural roots as delayed seasickness and he deflected the inevitable overseas narrations with blandness to play down any sour-grape syndrome.

'*Eeiii*,' Velyammavan would yodel to his wife for endorsement and she'd collaborate by manufacturing the saddest of sighs to indicate homesickness, sometimes interrupting a particularly mirthful anecdote to furnish the said sigh.

We'd prepare to duck as she was habituated to grab a passing child and press to chest in supplementation of the sigh, which meant being crushed between the coconut shells of a padded bra and two escapee breasts bobbing below like frisky kittens in a sack.

It was Badi who alerted us to that pong of sweaty sponge. At her behest, too, we hid under the bed that day for a numerological verification of Amma's mammary, though we hesitated to denounce outright the buoy in her bosom.

'Because of you. You didn't touch solids for two years.' She gathered me into her lap—the doll in my lap doubly secure in this lap in a lap as I giggled at the suggestion that I ever fed in such convoluted ways—retying the ribbon in my hair.

Basically, from what I could see, breasts were like a clock's hands—I had just learnt to tell the time—and Amma's were at 3.45 and Ammooma's one gravity-riddled blob at 6.30.

'You love Choti,' stated my pensive sister, having turned to solids at once upon birth. 'But Papaji loves me.'

'The uncles love me, too,' I pointed out, picking at the prickly heat spangling down my arms. I had no memory of Papaji, though Amma says he grabbed me at the hospital and sat for a long while with me on his knee, just staring at me stare right back.

'I kept telling him you are hungry, since you couldn't say it yourself, but he smiled tenderly and didn't put you down, not until *someone* soiled his clothes.'

My own smile condescended, until Badi pointed out it couldn't have been, well, him.

Velyammavan shook clingy droplets off the greenest leaf and tapped it once, twice before choosing a betel nut from the little copper-inlaid box on his lap, humming in prelude to a kacheri by us girls. Burying the nut in whitewashed leaf and then the leaf in mouth, he beckoned to us.

Solemnly, we shuffled in, a little nervous, a little vain; convulsively swallowing back the syrupy-sweet payasam threatening to stage a comeback into the mortal world. Our only brush with verbalised classical substances courtesy Amma was performed with suitable sobriety. Since his homecomings were spaced out by ten months, we trusted his memory's inability to locate our recital from previous hearings, happily mouthing the same lines, in the same raga, to the same thaalam, and any credit for the resultant rendering was entirely ours.

'*Maha Ganapati, manasa smarami…*' we began with the confidence of breaking no new ground, while Amma hovered anxiously and Velyammavan conscientiously imitated our hand movements, patting a palm lightly on thigh, fingers of the other hand strumming the diagonal poo-noolu. His wife's hand hooked inside the yoke of her nightie to home in on a breast and whir in tune with our now-slow-now-fast keertana. Cheek bulging with murkaan, he'd clang his eyes shut, refusing to open them long after we finished, and while his wife paid homage to his reverie by calling a ceasefire at her chest, we sat there on the floor holding on to our angelic faces and pinned-needled bottoms.

He flooded the spittoon with terracotta gargles eventually, enabling us girls to rise, stilling Amma's fluttery hands and re-igniting his wife's aeronautical ones. At such times, with chest going swiftly from 2.40 AM to 5.50 PM like the clock's hands had gone berserk, her face would break into a blissful smile and she never heard anything you said, just went into 'mmmm…' mode.

Attempts at conversion to a veshti or saree like Amma's and Ammooma's she stonewalled. Dispatching eyeballs into orbit, she maintained, 'Months and months in the ship I am fully dressed. This the only time I am getting to relax.'

And to scratch, too.

She claimed creepy-crawlies were the culprit and clapped furiously to send them to their heavenly abode between her palms. With her face, the planet around which buzzed the mosquitoes like a million moons, slapping herself at random was more cosmic masochism.

'Ah, Kutti has learnt the traditional kai-kottikali,' Velyammavan ridiculed the slaughter, while we followed around with a tin of tar, keeping a tally of the tiny carcasses.

He always called her Kutti, a habit from childhood since they were kin; in fact she was born fiancée to him as first cousin. Fifteen years his junior, she was his mura pennu in nappies, and though we had come along, bona fide bonny babies, she still appropriated the 'Kutti' tag in deference to a matrimonially pawned infancy long ago.

Later, to the accompaniment of Velyammavan's snores in the verandah, we respectfully laid to rest the bodies of the martyred mosquitoes in their tar morgue, per force conducting our postmortems under the most primitive conditions. Though the tiptoers around us spoke in hushed tones and kept a finger permanently glued to their lips in deference to Velyammavan's slumbers, our medical investigations seldom woke him.

'Sleep is a blessing from God,' he used to say, just before being thoroughly blessed.

Cheriyammavan took care of his ageing mother and one beleaguered sister, not to mention assorted nieces like me and triplet baby sisters who were the result of a last heroic coupling by Appoopan who allegedly never recovered this fathering fit at sixty and died soon after. Ammooma herself claimed to have barely recovered. Fortunately for her, Amma was opportunely back home to hatch her siblings.

An ornate picture of Appoopan in happier and, more importantly, alive days dominated the front verandah, which was also a sitting room for unwanted guests, like distant relatives of distant relatives, new vegetable vendors who were not familiar enough to march straight to the back door and Bengal-cotton saree salesmen who called Amma by name. 'Mangala,' they screeched, 'Mangala, see this Dhaka border,' and Amma flitted out at once to lie facedown amidst the myriad sarees.

'One wash and they run out,' Ammooma tut-tutted in passing.

But submerged knee-deep in a sea of gossamer dreams, with fabric light as the breeze brushing her knuckles, Amma's bemusement was seamless and, quite simply, she was transported. Young as we were, we did recognise her altered footing, the downright levitation when surrounded with the murmur of materials, the mystic throb in the motley bolts of silk. There was, in the descent of hush as she buried her nose in the rustles of zari or in her myopic peering into the hastily brought out mirror, a transcendence palpable even to us. Like it was really her soul trying on those sarees. And she looked up at us a million dreams, pleats and pirouettes later, all spongy and roseate.

'Not for her the usual feminine sweetness of smiles and intelligent nods, oh no. That would mean staying among husband's people and doing all those despicable female things! No, educated women these days, they need only to dress well.' Any malice in Ammooma's words, however, was worn out by frequent usage and the irrelevance of her daughter's response: 'My mind is so ill-mannered, it tells me to do what you tell me not to do.'

Later, when the skin of her face was no more shot with organza, there would be weak excuses for the extravagance— 'The girls can get long skirts made.... Or they can be gifted away'—punctuated by Ammooma's indulgent snorts.

Newly purchased sarees were kept overnight in the puja room where another picture of Appoopan leant against the wall, owing to a broken stand. Here among gods and demigods, he smiled relentlessly through incense and floral rot. His moustache, neatly divided into two, was like the wings of a bird readying for take-off, all set to carry on its back an apparently clueless nose.

'Ask him whatever thing you want,' Ammooma whispered to us, smearing our foreheads with sweet-smelling sandalwood paste.

This attribution of celestial powers to a late husband did not deter her from badgering her sons when *she* had a list, we noticed. My tiny aunts, though, spent long hours there with their eyes clamped tight. They, they'll believe anything.

My aunts.

They were younger than me, had eternally delicate stomachs in miniature echoes of Cheriyammavan's well-documented frailty, and sported uniform scowls. Of course, they have been known to smile on occasion. For instance, when Velyammavan and his scratch-specialist spouse were home for their annual stay, they beamed self-consciously— which in their case merely meant a cessation of melancholy.

Ammooma and Amma constantly pursued them with plates, exhorting, 'eat, eat', but they lay about like small sticks in the house, suffering from food. Even proximity to the kitchen during peak cooking hours induced nausea in them.

Ammooma said to us, 'Don't switch on the fan or my daughters will fly about in the room.'

'What a lie!' we snapped back.

Because we had switched on both ceiling fans and Badi had brought in the table-fan too, for good measure, but there they were, flopping firmly on the floor whence situated.

The aunts did nothing by themselves, needing our mother or their mother constantly. On bed they would sit up until Badi or I took them by hand and led them to the bathroom, put toothpaste on their toothbrush, pulled down their underpants and then pulled them up after they performed the only momentous task they could by themselves.

According to Ammoooma, it was proximity to Badi and me that unlocked their tongues. They were otherwise heard to utter only one word, 'Amma', which was also what they called their own parent. It was a word that had to be decoded as and when voiced, sometimes with urgency, like when they said it with bulging eyes, signifying the process of underclothes being soiled.

Other than their mother, no one set much store by their grey cells. Mid-August, when Cheriyammavan emotively re-lived 'India is free!' in the high pitch he reserved for the irrevocable, they unblinkingly chirped, 'Free with what? Free with what?'

I doubt whether the occasional blows we delivered on their heads were so stinging as to contribute to the permanently surly expressions; let's face it, they were just born that way. Still, when Velyammavan's suitcase was sprawled open and goodies were strewn about carelessly, they would line up against a wall and try their best to socialise. Tentative, unused smiles, suggesting more a collective snapping of the string in their underpants, were attempted until the suitcase emptied, after which they reversed and parked these smiles back in tiny dental garages.

Badi and I were the startlingly brown ones in the pack, but this won us obscure points in the form of adults shaking heads in sympathy. And when we clung to Amma, which we rarely did being sort of big for our age, it caused like comments on complexion contrasts. But as one tongue-clicker clarified, we had 'at least got height and straight hair from father's side', there being a stampede of blanched midgets with ringlets on our maternal side.

According to Amma, there was one more thing we had inherited from our father—his coconut-cream velichenna voice. But the less said about that the better.

'It has the effect of the Talkies,' Velyammavan murmured, sagging in his voluminous cloth-chair, leaving us unsure whether the reference was to Cheriyammavan's poesy or subterranean scatological oration.

'They no longer mime on screen,' was Cheriyammavan's petulant response. He moodily crumpled the parchment with his poems on it. 'Technology has advanced and so must we.'

'Yes, yes,' his brother agreed placidly. After decades of decoding celluloid silence, Velyammavan now armed himself against the onslaught of the Dolby soundtrack with imported ear-buds. 'But the unspoken is going to the dogs I say.'

Cheriyammavan visibly tensed, but lack of conviction over any intended slur to the arts had him emit an objective grunt.

'Has Amma had a complete check-up?' Velyammavan asked next in his faraway tone.

'Yes,' Cheriyammavan snapped.

Ammooma was taken kicking and screaming to the Mission Hospital in town just prior to her elder son's arrival. Allotted tests and sundry reports remained in the future realm of fantasy, but the sincerity with which she related the bluntness of needles against her crinkly skin and grapplings with narrow-necked test tubes in dim-lit bathrooms never failed to be music to Velyammavan's ears.

Her younger son, however, exhibited a touching trust in her constitution, and to that end resented the annual medical excursion thus thrust upon him and any resultant detraction of ennoblement.

Housekeeping and familial nurture fell in his portfolio and the whole year he trudged tiredly like Good Son Shravan Kumar, repairing residential ramparts, ensuring free flow of groceries, pecking food into our open cheeping beaks, and then for sixty days a year his brother came along to render these tasks trivial. We got our school uniforms from the uncle at home, but the pretty party frocks with satin ribbon at the hem came courtesy the other. Cheriyammavan naturally resented this lack of glamour, indeed a kind of glistens-only-in-the-dark existential dullness, attached to his domestic trajectory. Though he lingered passionately on the maintenance of compound walls and fairly fizzed at the mouth about green chilli pilferage, he knew, heart of hearts, that being widely travelled within one's own home entailed no fluorescent tribute. He was the saviour of the green guavas—painstakingly packing each ripening fruit in empty coconut shells so the bats and birds did not get to them—but super-heroism was not about putting animals on a diet, it lay, quite simply, in sibling rivalry.

Our home, in the dreams Velyammavan dreamt while cresting the high seas, was not this dilapidated brick structure in Ollur with 'Meledeth Illam' carved in crumbly stone like the drying sandalwood that dribbled down our foreheads. Instead, it was a palatial pathway in Paradise where we roamed about in bullion-bordered sarongs, blowing gently at clouds as Brahmanical soap bubbles quivered meaningfully all around us.

Great care was taken to insert a carbon paper between Velyammavan's visual imagery and our own otherwise mundane existence; to fall short in his similes was tantamount to blasphemy, and to that end we toiled peasant-like night and day toward beatification.

For sixty days a year we were inflexibly, non-negotiably and deeply *happy* for our Velyammavan since, as Cheriyammavan summarised, he had the more author-backed role in this family.

His stay saw Amma light the lamp daily at dusk, chanting,

'Deepajyothi parabrahma
Deepa sarva tamopahaha
Deepena saadyate saram
Sandhyaa deepo namostute.'

And then she'd turn amiably to us with one homily or the other, generally ascribed to the pious folds of the Bhagvad Gita.

In his absence, she just went, 'Deepamdeepamdeepam...' in fast-forward gear all over the house, palm shielding the aflame wick, managing to communicate ire in separate degrees of its development.

I wasn't what anyone called a good student; school was just a place someone sent me and I went because I was the cordial kind and could think up no alternative. Also, I had to cheer Badi on in all her battles, which wasn't so wise when she practised her martial claws on me though I ran fast, much faster than her; my legs were said to start from my neck.

Hours spent teetering along the tightrope path between paddy fields, with the delicious risk of toppling over into the mire; watching the tadpoles who, unknowing they'd never grow into fish, swaggered about like dignitaries in the en route pond; jumping on to high branches and swinging till my grip or the geriatric branch gave way; hoarding teensy-weensy bitter mangoes in my school-bag that lent themselves neither to exchange nor to eating—these were the upside. If the bill for this bliss was to be cooped up in a room for six hours at a stretch so that teachers got to collect their pays and pensions, so be it.

'The world is very, very big,' the geography master was habituated to intoning mournfully as he adjusted the mundu over his shoulder with twitchy modesty. He was the only male in the Benedictine convent, and unsure about his length of employment in a predominantly spinster habitat. He believed them when they told him the world was coming to an end, but dwelt bravely on the largeness of the same world for academic purposes.

'Volcanoes, earthquakes, storms, gales, plagues...' he droned, enlisting means by which the ground could be whisked from under our feet like a frayed coir mat.

An old crone of a calendar hung on the wall, probably from the days of the inception of the school, with all the months typed in minute print. It was backdated, but the crude painting in it was the only picturesque egress in the resounding bareness of our classroom. In it were three tiny boats sailing from an impossibly verdant shore, the waves a frothy silver despite the sloping spine of the sun, and an enormous net in a tiny fisherman's hand with the words 'Chinese fishing net' printed between the holes of the net, lest someone mistook it for a disproportionate balloon. The dhows each carried cloves, cinnamon and cardamom, wrongly spelt with a 'k', on their fluttery sails.

'They used to come back with gold,' he'd spasmodically spin the plastic globe on his table before adding morosely, 'when they did.'

I imagined those petite boats laden with gunny-bags and gunny-bags of gold paddling back on the back of the same laminated waves, those lit by the same slice of half-set sun, to the bottlegreen coast in the calendar.

Despite the shabby atlas pinned on class walls, despite the dizzying sphere on the desk, despite monotonous warnings about traders departing with the spice of life, never to return, I occupied a sunny mid-morn patch that year with not a hint of a larger world anywhere around the corner.

The globe, from where I could see, was tethered like a tame doe on a long, long leash and grazing off my eyelashes that summer.

2

THE DAY THEY CONVENED A FAMILY MEET ON CHERIYAMMAVAN'S eligibility had been a traumatic one for me at school. It began with the usual lateness: eyes prised open with crowbar, books playing truant and my share of nei-appams naughtily proliferating in the plate. Through the window I could see Amma scout for the sunniest patch to dry raw bitter-gourd chips. Single-mindedly, the postman watched her back and I decked the appams in layers to project lesser bulk in my plate.

Twirling around, Amma bounced her eyebrows tartly at the postman.

He stammered, 'G... Get that useless brother of yours married, that is what I came to say. Then he'll spend the night in his own home and not go around rousing hard-working men, asking for non-existent cheques addressed to him.'

'His bachelorhood is a tribute to Ayyappan,' Amma rejoined spiritedly. 'Not all of us can give up God for a woman now, can we?'

The taste of sun was on my tongue as I skipped to school where Sister Lucy's Lent-induced glumness at Assembly diminished only when she asked us to proceed, line by line, to the far corner and kindly roll up our sleeves for the *vaccine*.

Sister Immaculata, whom we per force called Sister Inoculata, scooted to the said spot, hands sheathed in sinister rubber gloves. She often took girls absentmindedly by their hands and idly tapped the inside of their elbows in search of The Vein. The other nuns, seven in all, congregated in a corner, dipping their veiled heads like penguins contemplating stale fish for supper.

My knees the consistency of strained rice, I desperately searched for Badi, but to no avail, and sure enough the insides of my nose began to go viscous, thickening incoming air, dragging the breath in with a tinkle, like oxygen wore belled anklets. Soon my nostrils would crackle with crust and I would choke and the whole school would have to stop everything they were doing to come watch me dribble and gasp for breath. I have entertained them thus before and, being an exemplary audience, they knew what came after what.

The warning lights—my nose walls seemed to collapse inward—were flashing, but I refrained from fussing for dissenters were unceremoniously being hustled willy-nilly ahead of others. That was when I remembered Ammooma's grand exhortation during prayers.

'Appoopa, Appoopa,' I passionately pleaded, desperately trying to conjure up his image, but not getting beyond the divisible moustache and flyaway nose. 'Save me somehow and I will believe in you until my dying day.'

When my turn came, I approached two nuns near by who stood chatting lightly on sacred matters, hoping they would have forgotten, or at the very least forgiven, my previous year's trespass of 'Lucy's got loosies' graffiti in the school's smelly loo. The subsequent inscription of 'Sister Lucy has no loosies' a hundred times on ruled paper firmly convinced me of my sin and the deeply chronic nature of her constipation.

'Please Sister, I have already been injected. They took me from home yesterday,' I lied bravely, breathing through my mouth.

'Roll up your sleeve, child, and show the mark.'

Flummoxed, I stopped breathing altogether. Then very, very slowly, I rolled up my school shirt's sleeve, fearing the worst, turning my face away, gearing up to act astonished at the utter lack of scars. I can say I dreamt it... Important people were always dreaming in our textbooks; just yesterday someone had a dream and we were to by-heart the *entire* dream he dreamt, or at least the first paragraph.

'Okay,' said Sister, passing me by, to the silly, howling girl behind me in the queue, and I saw the angry red mark on my arm right where it ought to be!

Blood was evidently thicker than water even in the spirit world and this realisation tuned my attention to family matters more acutely that evening. Cheriyammavan was past marriageable age we had surmised, and it was with surprise that we listened to others' contradictory views at the hastily held ancestral AGM.

'This girl has come to us. Lakshmi herself has come to us. We must not turn her away,' Velyammavan said, and then bellowed forth without a warning, 'Who made this tea?'

Amma quivered into the kitchen, her hands scurrying away like mice with the cup. 'I forgot, I forgot,' she chanted all the while, shredding cardamom seeds with vacant expertise from their pods, banging them noisily between the mortar and the pestle, wiping out the powder from under the pestle's bottom and adding it to the tea boiling merrily all over again in a matter of seconds.

Velyammavan, whose high-decibel yell was based on the mistaken belief that his Kutti of the four breasts' fame had extended her ham-handedness to his brew, sought to alleviate Amma's panic with hyperbolic praise. 'This is heaven,' he beamed, tediously attached to divine similes. 'Hot, steaming tea that goes straight to your soul.'

One of my baby aunts made a sour sound at that. Her soul had just been fed something to the gills and wanted to throw up for the sheer pleasure of it.

Cheriyammavan was heatedly registering his protest. 'You make it sound like some nubile goddess has swept off her lotus and come searching for me to devote herself to! What you mean is that her family is desperate to get her off their hands. This desperation does not augur well.'

'Just because he was celibate for so long, our Kesu does not want to be sold short,' Ammooma chortled.

'And he isn't averse to a bit of gold or realty along with chastity, on the grounds that chastity isn't built to last,' Amma joined in with a twinkling laugh, demonstrating her complete recovery from the tea tragedy.

'Yes, yes,' agreed Velyammavan. 'There is some rubber plantation and an entire estate in Wayanad in the girl's name.'

'Nutmeg is drying and the area too much of a slope to make any profit when I checked,' the bachelor listlessly dismissed. 'Property that can be overlooked.'

'Very few would agree to overlook your horoscope though,' thundered Velyammavan.

Cheriyammavan, whose horoscope was presumably riddled with celestial potholes, pooh-poohed, 'They can look all they want.'

'Don't be such a suicide bomber,' Kutti scolded affectionately, having just read the headlines in a flurry of scratches, leaning against the mesh door that separated verandah from the interiors. 'Why don't you at least see her once?' The mesh door gaped wherever the metal net had surrendered to manual administrations in an invite to mosquitoes and had a tendency to slide at will, like now, so that she slowly slanted mid-speech to eventually lie down on her side and ask, 'That's not too much to ask now, is it?'

Perhaps it was the uniqueness of the plea's horizontal rendition that had Cheriyammavan finally capitulate.

Vertical once again with the aid of six small ingratiating hands that were always on the lookout to invest in future gifts, Kutti smiled, directly eliciting civic sympathy. 'If not for big teeth, she is real beauty,' Ammooma always maintained.

Unfortunately for us, the area outside her oral arena was completely under Kutti's charge. The long hours that she spent in the ship library soaking up trivia were a constant source of discomfort to us. That was her only weakness, an addiction to facts like they were salted mangoes to be suckled all day long. In preparation for her presence, we did brush up on history and English grammar, but her grilling always managed to over-draw.

During mandatory visits to lesser relatives bearing small items of gifts like soaps, shampoos or perfumes, also to temples, the beach and shops, Badi and I were her designated escorts as Ammooma and Amma preferred to stay back and get on with their endless cooking. Sometimes we let her walk before us and affected limps, held arms or neck stiffly, causing passers-by to click their tongues in disapproval at the uncaring adult who walked ahead without a backward look at her crippled children.

But she was wont to suddenly stop walking on a pavement before a readymade dress shop to brandish her verbal weapon—'Quick, tell me, which is the longest river in India?'—causing us to straighten, miraculously cured, and allowing her to unleash upon us a steady stream of statistics that we painfully endured following an attack of acute muteness. I have heard Ammooma say she dropped out of her mother's stomach quizzing the midwife on the exact length of the umbilical cord.

On the appointed day Ammooma, Amma, Kutti, Badi and I set off in an old Ambassador car bought newly by Velyammavan and driven by Cheriyammavan, both natural front-seaters by virtue of their curriculum vitae.

The whining trio of baby aunts was happily entrusted to Dasamma. An old victim of Ammooma's fits of charity, Dasamma washed toilets for a living owing to the rock-bottom position of her caste in the deck of social cards, and sometimes got upgraded to babysitter, like now. Quite apart from the scars she owed her husband and his toddied bouts, she was in exotic possession of a leg swollen with voluptuous open-mouthed warts riding up the bulging flesh, regarding which there were conflicting reports.

According to Ammooma, it was a carnivorous comeuppance, 'all the eaten flesh—chicken, goat, cow, pig, whoever—settles wherever it wants'. Dasamma said it was from shoving her foot into sundry toilets to clean the extraordinary amount of shit people left behind. And Amma claimed it was merely a disease, which we disregarded due to its intrinsic insipidity.

For the trip Badi wore a gold bangle on each wrist, while I had to be content with pink plastic pearls around my neck. The route to Lakshmi's house was bumpy, but cushioned in Amma's lap, I could afford to praise the car's upholstery. Actually, upon Velyammavan's arrival we girls immediately adopted sweet dulcet tones and wide-eyed remarks designed to make him shower goodies upon us and then even after the gifts ran out, the engine of our fake cheer was up and running.

'These flowers look like real flowers,' I lisped, carefully converting any 's' in my speech to an endearing hiss. As it was, Badi was gracing Kutti's lap on special request.

Not to be beaten, Badi inhaled exaggeratedly. 'Umm, the smell of leather!'

'Rexine,' corrected Cheriyammavan inattentively, causing me to catch Badi's eye and subject her to the first superior smile of the day.

Lakshmi's father was standing outside the gate to personally escort each one of us into their house and seat us on wooden benches that wobbled.

'This she has done,' he said, pointing to a colourful paper stuck on the wall behind us in which blooms were painted freely and I itched to point out horticultural inaccuracies.

Lakshmi's mother chose to zealously guard the kitchen door from where she visually lanced us one at a time while a diminutive girl scampered about with jeera water. When she reached me, I stuck out a tongue and centralised eyeballs, so that she nervously spilt the lukewarm water on my hand and earned a personalised glare from her mistress while I innocently relocated eyeballs.

The mother cleared her throat and when everyone looked at her, she catalogued in tones ceremonial, 'The journey was comfortable? Did you have trouble finding our place? Can I allow myself to believe you are really here?'

Velyammavan replied that yes, thank her and thank God, we were spared mishaps, big or small, that we had just turned a corner when gamely loomed their homestead, and that yes, he thought it about time she allowed herself to believe we were there.

'We had to use force with Amma, though. She thinks sitting in a car means dying in a car,' he wrapped up.

All corroborated amusement except Ammooma, who chose to announce abruptly, 'She is staying with us.'

Going by Amma's rigidly held profile and tragic expression, she was the *she* referred to. 'Just clearing everything in beginning itself. We are very clear people,' Ammooma added.

Lakshmi's mother nodded and continued to nod grimly to indicate that she had already been apprised of the fate of Meledeth Illam's eldest daughter. 'What a waste of good youth!' she tut-tutted in a richly fruity voice.

'Do you want to hear us sing?' Badi enquired eagerly, interrupting the other's facial potential for warming to theme. After Amma's fate was revealed, and she looked down demurely counting up to fifty, we felt free to advertise our talents in the ensuing pause. Everything that had to be expressed on Amma's destiny had already been expressed ad nauseum, and we felt morally obliged to provide the commercial break, so to speak.

'In this entire universe,' Badi began and I joined, chorale.
'India is the very best, very best.
Little birds we all are,
This nation is our nest.
No religion teaches killing.
That's why I am singing.
India is a temple,
India is cathedral, cathedral...'

'Keshavan translated *Sare Jahan Se Achcha* for them, just like that,' Velyammavan snapped fingers to indicate the effortlessness while translator stirred uneasily as if to rebut.

Lakshmi's father clapped with his eyes, blinking rapidly to applaud such superior capabilities at linguistic conversion. 'Wonderful, wonderful,' he chuckled, jiggling his knees with uncommon haste. Then, intercepting his wife's sidelong glance, he stopped the knees mid-jiggle, letting them bang bonily into each other, adding lamely, '*Very* wonderful.'

Amma and Kutti followed Lakshmi's mother into the kitchen—they were always prowling in others' kitchens to fake familiarity and deduct snacks at source—determinedly making small talk, when there came an unmistakable clatter. Kutti, she was always crashing into something when at large.

I was just plotting a casual lunge at the refreshment table to scoop some freshly roasted cashew nuts when a collective silence alerted me to Lakshmi's arrival.

Bony elbows at ninety-degree angles in namaskaram, suddenly she was there by the door—half in, half out—with head suitably bent, throwing into relief an oil-slapped scalp with its braided sides padlocked into one central plait in line with her spine. Mere respiration on her part caused the double-shaded blue silk saree to shimmer around a disproportionately large pair of hips. Her eyes, set in concrete, were trained at the floor. She never made eye contact with anyone but Mr Mosaic and just stood there…breathing. Her father beamed at us. See, he seemed to say, she's *alive*!

Kutti tried to pat the top of Lakshmi's head, which was way up, then realising her relative resemblance to midgets, sat down with a smile as sudden as a road accident. The hearty cheer of Lakshmi's mother met Kutti's abrupt dental effort and the brightness and blankness were momentarily blinding.

'This is the boy, my brother,' Velyammavan presented with a flourish, while Cheriyammavan studied the portion of floor allotted to him. 'The day we row, crows will fly on their back. Ask us whatever you want to,' he exhorted loudly, with a monogrammed echo of his own, 'otherwise we will interview you. Tee-hee.'

By tacit agreement, all laughed louder than necessary for we had sensed that seen to be having a good time was more important than having a good time.

Cheriyammavan transferred his eyes from floor to Lakshmi and I truly wished he hadn't for they bulged like his bowels were on the move.

Adam's apple quite anchorless, he enquired, 'Have you been to China?'

There was a pause when everyone looked at everyone else.

'Chi Na,' repeated Lakshmi eventually, coming up with equivalent syllables.

'Not one from this family has ever been to China, not for generations,' her mother denied hotly from the kitchen doorway and her father stepped on the gas at knee jiggling.

'Very wise,' said Velyammavan with a judicious glower in his brother's direction, while Kutti, who had been hitherto sharpening nails on the old oak of the host's furniture, groped worriedly for the comfort of a breast, which she converted to a grappling with thali at the last minute.

She was fishing out the tiny marriage-locket from her blouse interiors with great presence of mind, when Cheriyammavan persisted, 'What about Australia?'

'Aus Tra Lia,' Lakshmi informed us without pause but with adequate consonants.

On the drive back home—with me unceremoniously dumped on Velyammavan's lap by Amma who pretended her legs were aching—matters were decided.

'I see nothing wrong with the girl,' he began without preamble.

'Ha,' exclaimed Cheriyammavan. 'Except Down's Syndrome.'

'Nice child-bearing hips she has,' enthused Kutti.

'When he asked her about China, I thought her water broke!' guffawed Velyammavan, then at a meaningful swish of Amma's eyeballs, he added vaguely to us, 'Her water tumbler, you know.'

Badi and I duly flashed smiles of trained neutrality while our minds straggled backward frantically for illumination; until they deliberately tried to throw us offtrack, we rarely bothered.

'The broker said she's twenty-three. Let's not waste *her* good youth,' Amma sniped.

Ammooma elaborately tugged at an earlobe, her finger hooking into its large, elongated gap where once upon a time some weighty jewel bogged it down. 'You notice that her mother is doing all the talking.'

'So?' Cheriyammavan asked.

'Not auspicious sign. Girls from homes like that…they tuck husbands under bodice from what they are seeing at home, that is all.' Then, at her son's exaggeratedly exhausted expression, she said defensively, 'That is what they say, what can I do?'

'You are too old-fashioned, Amma,' he proclaimed, in his first softening of the anti-Lakshmi stance.

'And she is *one* girl,' Ammooma said triumphantly. 'One child means she is never learning to share. Me-my-mine, she will go.'

Again, Cheriyammavan shrugged.

'That is the point,' Amma put in dryly. 'She is *one* child, so what her father has, it all comes to us.'

'To *me*,' her brother corrected absently. After which Amma enjoyed her vacant lap in complete silence. 'Anyway,' he continued, 'there is no urgency to decide.'

'My next trip will be next year. Why wait until then? I can extend my leave by a fortnight and go after the wedding,' Velyammavan argued.

The high-level talks carried on until Kutti trod the melodrama route. 'You know why I call you son? Because I have no children of my own. When the doctors told me I could never have babies, my first thought was, then who will look after me in my old age, when I am ill and bedridden? Now I only look forward to your children. I pray that they will look after me.'

'Lakshmi will bring children with her?' I asked, my mind boggling at an image of miniature bucktooth replicas in bright blue sarees.

'Who is Lakshmi? Her name is Kanaka,' Ammooma frowned.

'Her name is parrot,' Badi giggled. 'Aus Tra Lia?'

'Aus Tra Lia,' I replied obediently.

Back home, Dasamma greeted us in tears. The aunts kept absconding to the nearby paddy fields and whenever she managed to shepherd them back home, she failed to count all three of them.

'I am allergic to paddy blades,' she grumbled, picking up the edge of her saree to scratch the portly leg, fascinating us with its embossed lacerations.

'Edi, are they lost?' Ammooma asked, and we felt a momentary twinge of relief that they had finally been misplaced for good.

But before the prospect of never having to see them could sink into our collective conscious, Dasamma shook her head. 'They are still out in the field somewhere.'

Badi and I were dispatched to the site without delay, but since our unspoken pact consisted of avoiding them at all costs, we deliberately gave a rustling bit of skirt or a peek of flibbertigibbet ribbon the miss as our three troublesome aunts played peek-a-boo with as much finesse as poultry in the proximity of a vixen.

However, our pretence at misery suffered a major setback when upon return we found the truant three snug in Ammooma's lap, mollycoddled anew.

'Shouldn't have left them behind alone like that,' their mother sighed, picking out a weed from the nearest head, while Badi and I maintained a diplomatic silence.

There was a strange muted wail, like a newborn being slowly strangulated, and we all turned as one to Cheriyammavan, who was patting his stomach with an expression of exquisite relief.

'Okay,' he snapped his fingers and picked up the weather-beaten diary in which he scribbled his most private thoughts and then worried what to rhyme them with in leisure. 'Enough entertainment.'

'When will Thampuran pluck out the frog from his belly?' Dasamma shot at his retreating back and broke into her braying laugh, which always sounded like she was crying.

The aunts took turns to sleep on Ammooma's stomach. While one climbed atop triumphantly and settled for the night, the two others would lie on either side. What fun it could possibly be lying stomach to stomach with anyone was beyond my understanding, but the little aunts were deliriously happy with this arrangement.

Ammooma looked forward to the nights they fell about asleep here and there in the house, exhausted by excessive rest, their unstinting vigil before the radio—waiting for wee newsreaders to pop out of it—or just listening to everyone talk and absorbing the whirlpool of words. Then she would lovingly pick them up like they were delicate flowers, comb back the hair from their foreheads, comment on their resemblance to my dead grandfather or his equally dead mother, and deposit them pell-mell on the huge swing-bed. She herself would then curl up on the floor alone. If we asked her whether the cold earthen floor wouldn't aggravate her arthritis, she smiled mysteriously, a smile full of delicious freedom and a belly bereft of baby aunts, within or without.

The aunts, on their part, would cunningly fight sleep as long as they could to avoid just such a fate. The winner, you see, would clamour to flop down on Ammooma two nights in a row if the assigned member was drowsily dribbling into somebody else's lap. Worst was if they woke up during the transfer. Cheriyammavan tended to be rough with them and they woke up in his arms, sometimes upside down, with their readymade bawls and then Ammooma had to hush them up.

To test whether they had actually gone to sleep, we tricked them by saying, 'Oh, now is the time for all deep sleepers to pick up their left leg.'

Following a visible struggle over demarcation of left from right, up it would come, wavering in the air, signifying that the limb's owner was just a yell away from its perch upon Ammooma's stomach. We sometimes made them sing, too, this way, but since their modulation at the best of times and in complete wakefulness was not their strong point we did this only for a certain audience, the kind who could differentiate between pure cacophony and our own classical efforts.

During most heated discussions on Cheriyammavan's wedding, they snored softly into the shoulder of the person against whom they had been leaning when sleep axed them down, their drool leaving damp splotches. After arguing a point on the austerity measures to be adopted during the nuptial celebrations, Ammooma would bend down dramatically to pick up her dozing offspring, slouching exaggeratedly if she had lost the point.

Ammooma particularly opposed the construction of an in-house toilet, declaring the one outside—where we carried umbrellas in case it rained—sufficient for the family's use. 'If it was good enough for your father, it is good enough for me,' she declared, adjusting Appoopan's bifocals militantly over her head. She was always adjusting them away from her eyes, those glasses that blurred everything further for her but that she clung to in misplaced marital fidelity. 'Whoever heard of making filth inside the house? Guruvayurappa!'

Dasamma was deployed to help with the upcoming celebrations. Large cauldrons spat up hissing oil on little brick stoves in the backyard.

'No Namboodiri feast is complete without us,' Dasamma puffed up her chest, stuffing rice batter into cinnamon leaves so they filled the air with a subtly spiced sweetness as they steamed. 'This sadya will be the talk of the town, mark my words.'

As Ammooma's spy she intercepted construction workers of the budding bathroom on the pretext of handing them black tea in chipped glasses to keep a keen watch on the proceedings and provide updates.

'Another place for me to wash,' she'd sigh to us, after delivering architectural bulletins full of tiles and taps.

Her two daughters—Rukmani and Janaky—also moved in with us for the interim and were as pliant and biddable as their mother. Dasamma was happy enough when they joined in our games, but in Ammooma's presence she'd pinch the fleshy undersides of their arms and pretend to scold, 'You should know your place.'

Ammooma saw right through her. 'Edi, no need to show airs here. Remember the time I rescued you from the pond?'

Dasamma used to spend whole nights submerged in a pond during her husband's drunken bouts, for if he caught up with her, he rained blows on her till one of them passed out. Someone alerted Ammooma and off she had gone to save her. From then on Dasamma cleaned our toilet and Ammooma became her benefactor, enlisting extra toilets in the vicinity for her to clean and more people to advise her husband, who was half-way sensible when not within sniffing distance of an arrack shop.

Sometimes, as we bent over to watch the lotuses in the front room, her reflection joined ours azurely in the waters below. 'This is the bangle the house wears on its wrist,' she exaggerated to her daughters. 'Remember, I told you about it? Remember?'

The daughters, who were given to unexpected giggles like their teeth were being tickled from inside, abandoned all reserve at mealtimes. They made dynamic inroads into the heap of rice and hooking a finger to shave the leaf clean of anything remotely lickable at the end.

At night, Rukmani put my two dolls one on top of the other. 'In the morning, they will have babies.'

'As if,' I pretended to sneer, but woke up next morning with grandmotherly zeal to check. There really was a small furry object lying on the ground, next to them, taking deep breaths!

I went in hollering.

'It is a chick dropped by a thieving crow from some nearby coop,' Rukmani clarified.

Of course, I knew they wouldn't multiply, silly dolls! Babies came out of sachets, didn't they?

'Quick,' directed Dasamma, her hand gently curved around the squawking chick. 'Bring out a large vessel.'

With it, she partially covered the mutilated bird and tapped at what was now its tin roof.

'Don't be scared. You are safe now with Dasamma,' she cooed. Water and grain in small dishes were left near the sickbed, the makeshift roof still in place.

Toward dusk, ungratefully enough, it passed away, leaving untouched the food provided for it along with the treat of tender-coconut slivers I had thoughtfully added to its menu for choice.

'At least, it died in its home,' Dasamma said. 'And that's a luxury only the lucky have.'

Emerging from a personal inauguration of the new toilet, Ammooma nevertheless lamented robustly for the sake of consistency, 'Who listens to me here?'

Haphazardly settling the triplets, whose half a dozen hands between them were cramped with tugging non-stop at the shiny new stainless steel flush all day long, she then curled up in solitary splendour on the earthen floor, serene as a smoke-ring.

3

_D_OUBLY LIT, KANAKA MADE A LUMINOUS ENTRY INTO OUR lives with two photographers, from their side and ours, aiming their non-stop flash at her bowed profile. Not once did she hoist eyes during the proceedings so that in most photographs she appeared fast asleep.

'Right foot, right foot,' Kutti kept saying as if Kanakamami was playing hopscotch all wrong. 'Enter home auspiciously with right foot.'

'Yes, that makes all the difference,' Amma muttered, tolerantly holding aloft the lit up nila-vilakku, while her two sisters-in-law exchanged falsely hearty smiles due to their forward molars.

We scampered about busily in long skirts, the silk rustling after us, occasionally picking out stiff brocade borders from the sharp teeth of our faux-gold anklets lest we tumbled headlong into the proceedings, our jhumkis swaying miniature chandeliers from our ears.

'Photo,' Amma screamed, shepherding us into the open yard. Someone brought a couple of chairs. I had just seated myself with great care when Amma screamed again, 'As if it's for you!'

'I was checking it for comfort,' haughtily I informed Badi, who was shaking and twisting her body to contain unbearable mirth.

The photographer personally escorted Cheriyammavan and his new bride to the chairs, then handed them a tender coconut. Its eye was pierced, a straw inserted in quick coronation and both the bride and groom were exhorted to hold it between them and bow in.

'More, more. Bend more,' the photographer screamed, it being very important to scream at weddings.

We were then arranged around the garlanded couple, but Amma delayed us all by flying into a rage at my curry-dipped sleeve.

'It is okay,' Velyammavan soothed. 'Only a photo, Mangala.'

'I have to send it to *him*,' she said. To Papaji she meant, and I had this sudden vision of my grandly framed picture hanging preciously in a palace, and assumed my most princess face.

Post-wedding, Kanaka, now officially our mami, clung to some old woman in her family and cried loudly while her father and sundry relatives looked on proudly at this display of domestic loyalty. The five of us huddled in our crumpled Kancheevaram and watched her teeth bob in and out with every sob. We did not voice then our fear that may be our meanness, much lamented by our mothers, was transparent and causing this mighty reluctance on her part.

While Kanakamami sat on the freshly made bed, one of the triplet aunts collapsed at her feet. At least we thought she had fainted, but she was just 'resting' she clarified when poked.

There were a lot of questions being asked of the brand new bride: where did she study? How much did she study?

Had she studied at all? However, all had to be satisfied with a shake or nod of her head. And when I explained pointedly to her a contradiction in the nods, she just nodded all over again!

'Three petticoats,' exclaimed the resting aunt from below the bed. She had lifted the new aunt's saree hem and counted the layers underneath.

Instead of lauding her for her arithmetic preciseness, Kanakamami began to wail once again until Dasamma bustled in, wearing the pattu saree Ammooma had gifted her for the occasion; Ammooma had a trunk full of incidental treasures from her frolicking days with Appoopan.

'Let me see the new bride,' Dasamma came twittering importantly.

Kanakamami at once removed palms from eyes and shrank from the outstretched hands. Dasamma stepped back, folded hands into chest and burst into raucous tears, which sounded surprisingly like she was laughing.

Ammooma rushed in with a cup of steaming tea to pacify the bride, but hiccupping, Kanakamami clarified, 'I drink only coffee.'

And she entered the kitchen for the first time clutching tightly a pre-marital container. Measuring the chicory into a stainless steel bowl, she decocted efficiently with downcast eyes. Cheriyammavan was soon converted to caffeine so that mornings and evenings she agitated in the kitchen to make two glasses of coffee. She'd then blow back the creamy froth off his glass, lips pursed like she was kissing its rim, before handing it over with much jangling of bangles and a quick furtive upward glance. Then they'd both sip and sigh like they had received a blood transfusion.

'Tea she'd have to make for all of us,' Amma commented, and Ammooma shushed, though her eyes danced.

Handing a hefty tip to Dasamma over and above the wedding feast charges from a small knot in her mundu, Ammooma sighed. 'These old women,' she muttered, though they both seemed equally elderly to me. 'Carrying whole rivers in their eyes!'

Dasamma just sniffed and quivered her breasts, which she could do at will owing to their corpulence under the frayed cotton covering.

'Teach us to do that,' we used to beg Dasamma. Usually breasts just *sat* on chests—the gagged little things—till they jumped off eventually in search of the navel like Ammooma's. But Dasamma's pendulous assets could be burped like babies if slung over a shoulder.

'Grow them first, you dwarfs,' she would tell us. 'Eat breast food.'

When we approached Ammooma for the said diet, she shooed us away. 'You want your sides to ache with flesh?'

We did, we swore, but to no avail. Our breasts were starved that summer.

Ammooma hoped that marriage would placate her younger son's grumbly metabolism, ground his fantasies and do away with that saintly air of his over having to look after a large, extended family, while we girls were determined not to let the event disturb our routine in the least, and decided therefore to ignore the freshly minted aunt. What upset us was Velyammavan's departure.

He came close to us at the gate, kiss-close to our upturned faces, charging the air with cardamoms. 'Write me for whatever you want. No need to consult Mangala.'

We put forth our cheeks one by one, for he always kissed us while going. Cheriyammavan's bidi-propelled breath, not to mention his intestinal vehemence, and Amma's tightlipped, odour-less whispers made us connoisseurs of air, so to speak, and these kisses, anointed with the aromatic promise of more visits and more presents, filled us with warm, sweet anticipation. This was just between him and us, a conspiracy of whispers and hushed secrets as he bent and we stretched to make the best use of air known to us yet.

Very unlike the brutal administrations of aged women who came visiting, clucking over us 'poor little children', kneading our shoulders and exhaling noisily, vacuuming our face inside-out with an exhibitionist whoosh. Foreheads coronated with their spit, we then ran in search of soap and water.

Velyammavan's kisses, on the other hand, were an invention exclusive for us, marking time, ripening us, smelling of foreign soaps and shores, of exotica. A doorknob really, beyond which was riches, the babble of real life, a world of adventures we couldn't even begin to imagine. Each year, during arrivals and departures, Velyammavan bent to us conscientiously thus at the gate, and we smelt the sun on his breath. It went to our head, catapulting us into his arms, clamouring for more and more kisses until it was a carnival of kisses.

Amma and Ammooma, who always pulled us back from such naked displays of emotion, indeed clicked their teeth and tongues, exclaiming for a touch of levity, 'what these girls won't do for gifts', dabbed their eyes surreptitiously with veshti-ends. Dasamma stood at a discreet distance to sniff loudly until our departing aunt went and stuffed some money into her palm.

'Look after them all,' the aunt would say. And then it would be Cheriyammavan's turn to sniff as he was our official caretaker.

It was a moment tinged with pleasant hysteria, of some nameless grief thudding in our chests along with the promise of nameless ecstasies.

Then, with a host of last-minute instructions on car maintenance, the continuance of our classical vocal training and nostalgically charged backward glances, Velyammavan walked out with his wife.

Sunlight and the scent of spice wafting warm along our skin and spine, we stood at the gate in dual layers—adults behind, children scalloped in front—blowing kisses at each other in turn as if pollinating air with Velyammavan's farewell, unable to brake the momentum of the marathon kisses. Even the tiny aunts were aired at the kissing ceremony though most gate-related activities were banned to them as, barely discernible to the naked eye, they were slight enough to filter out of the bamboo gate without anyone noticing. Ammooma lived in constant fear of misplacing the microscopic trio, and a general dread haunted them since birth anyway, so they got used to being locked up during celebrations, festive occasions and impromptu crowding.

'Say ta-ta,' Ammooma directed them.

Raising their hands obediently, squinting at their eldest brother, they sang-songed, 'Ta-ta.'

That year was tricky for me in more ways than one. I had failed a second time in the fifth standard and no one was prepared to explain it away for me any more. I was the tallest girl in my class, and when I loomed large during the morning assembly or PT class, I cringed with shame. Everyone called me Mangala's Failed Daughter. It also caused Papaji to poke long-distance fun at Amma and her inability to bring us up 'properly', so that instead of pulling me into her lap, she was always pushing me out of it.

'No more babying,' she began to say.

Cheriyammavan was away a lot, to inspect the Wayanad land he received in dowry. Sometimes Kanakamami accompanied him, and sometimes she lurked behind sullenly in her room.

'I have written to Ettan for an urgent loan,' he told Ammooma. 'Spices don't pay anymore. I am thinking of clearing the plantation and starting a resort. Tourists can have a holiday at minimum prices. There are always the foreigners to be milked; scatter some fauna in the flora, throw in a safari on a full-moon night, and they'll hang out their tongues. As long as there's rotting kelp in our backyard, we can play tour guide.'

'What does your wife have to say?'

'It was her idea,' he said after a pause.

But Velyammavan's reply enraged him.

'Says it is a foolish risk to take. If he doesn't want to lend, don't lend, but why make fun of my enterprising spirit? Not all of us can have fancy jobs with nary a care for mother or sibling.'

Amma and Ammooma dared not voice an opinion on the matter, but Kanaka's condolences were a foregone conclusion. The couple seemed to shrink into each other in sympathy like a being with two heads and eight limbs.

'When he comes on leave, you explain face to face,' Ammooma tried to pacify.

He only grunted. 'His NOC I no longer need, thank you very much.'

'No mention,' Ammooma automatically answered.

I must have inherited Cheriyammavan's dream of being elsewhere—he wrote to various magazines about snowfall or mountain peaks he never saw or stood on, respectively —for instead of school I found my feet turning toward the railway station near our house one day.

There I studied the timetables, the arrival and departure timings painted tantalisingly on the wall, black on yellow. Ollur was not a big station. In fact, most trains disdained from even stopping by to dislodge passengers, as if this was too down-market a destination, and just rushed past without a backward glance to Thrissur where the station wore a more pedigreed look. I feared somebody would pounce on me and promptly frog-march me home. Nervously, I watched people alight from a passenger train, waiting for a familiar voice to say, 'Aren't you Mangala's youngest, the failed one?'

No, no one saw me. So the next day there I was, back again. This time I intentionally lurked closer to the ticket counter. With bliss I learnt that there were tickets being handed out just to tour the platforms. I did not have a rupee though, so I pretended I just wanted to know the rates, but when I told him that the man at the window repeated, 'One rupee,' as if he was trained to say just that. One rupee. One rupee.

I got it without any trouble. I only had to ask Badi. She was very elder-sisterly that way. I only had to look disturbed and talk of failing all my life and never having seen Papaji and she would give in to any reasonable demand.

Once I got the ticket and was out on the platform, there was no turning back. My feet itched to jump into a train. I would wait until the guard had finished waving that green rag, I told myself, and then walk briskly toward the moving train. In slow motion, I'd secure a foothold and then suddenly I wouldn't have to move myself, the train would be doing it for me!

I devised a foolproof plan. I would go to Ernakulam Junction and then come back immediately as I had the return ticket too, stamped into the onward ticket itself. It was with a slight tremble in my foot that I stepped into a train alone for the first time. The compartment had only two families and each thought I was with the other. When I shrieked loudly going over a noisy bridge, I caught them exchanging indulgent smiles. The whole journey took two-and-a-half hours only.

After that first time, I grew bold and travelled at least once a week. Even Badi, whom I usually took into confidence for the simple reason that I just had to tell her everything, had no idea about my new itinerary. It got easier to hide things from her after she abandoned me in the primary school and joined a higher-secondary one. Since my journeys were made during non-peak hours, whole compartments were at my solitary disposal and I could be anyone I chose to be.

After shying away from our ramshackle Ollur, most trains shuddered to a stop only when they reached Chalakudy. The platform right outside my nose pressed against the metal windowpanes would be a little crowded, but surprisingly very few people actually got on to the train. They all wanted faster trains. At Angamali, men in lungis shouted 'ice-prooooot' piercingly into my ears. That was usually a cue to sip from my water bottle for the sight of gaily-iced sticks magically parched my throat. Then, when the train set out again, this time for Alwaye, I'd fish out my tiffin and examine the contents. If I liked, I ate; if I didn't, I donated to a beggar I liked. I would decide beforehand. For instance, let there be one with a blue shirt. Of course, sometimes no such beggar appeared as shirts per se were at a premium with them, let alone blue or red ones, and I had to chuck the food out of the window. And if I did that when the train was moving, it flew back at me like spit, especially sambaar or chutney. Semolina upma and lemon rice were the best bets for dumping, just plopped flat on to the tracks and lay there like dead.

Twice a week at least I journeyed thus, away from the tyrant teachers and textbooks that exposed my inferiority to the whole world, meanwhile actively campaigning for an early wedding. But Amma was adamant, saying the police would handcuff her and put her in jail if I was married off at such a tender age. 'Give me a few more years to arrange it,' she said, while Ammooma muttered I was like my father after all.

Marriage, I was sure, would free me from the burden of books and marks, of report cards and stage fright. Besides, like a Kanakamami, I would be able to walk around with a smirk and all that jewellery.

My favourite pastime on Sunday afternoons was to stare at her sleeping form. We children had long since given up on her as a potential playmate, but her devotion to personal grooming fascinated me endlessly. As she slept with her saree end carefully spread out on the pillow next to her to avoid crumpling, breasts lolling this way or that on her sunken scoop of a chest, my attention was solely focused on the intricate pattern of a necklace or the sharpness of a bracelet. Every finger was be-ringed and there were gold anklets and toe-rings on each foot. She unfailingly appeared alarmed when she woke while shifting positions and caught me staring unblinkingly at her.

Such was the profusion of the festive metal about her person that when Cheriyammavan took her to a dentist soon after their marriage, I expected her to return with finely filigreed gold-belled braces on her teeth. But they returned rowing about her age. She had blurted out her real age when the doctor insisted that years played an important factor in reining in recalcitrant teeth. Her age, we calculated using up all of our fingers, was a year older than our elder aunt, Kutti! But Kanakamami illustrated no euphoria when informed about her lead in the age-of-aunts' race.

The upshot: teeth continued to stay that way and she with us. On weekends she locked herself up in the room and changed every single piece of ornament on her person. I waited for her to re-emerge so that I could feast on those radiant adornments, my eyes no less sparkly than the gem in her nose. It was her treasure chest that originally set me thinking about marriage. Once when I touched the rice pearls embedded in a choker, she pushed my hand away. Then sensing my hurt, she promised airily, 'You like these? Take it with you when you go to your husband's house. Okay?' Happily, I set about planning my own wedding.

The three aunts were on Ayurveda treatment for their terminal stomachaches, and every evening they unfailingly hid themselves to dodge the daily bitter dosage. Badi and I were on the self-assigned righteous task of flushing them out. It did not help the aunts that their nieces were a step ahead of them. A night that had started out particularly harmless, with the same pranks and final submissive screams of each freshly medicated aunt, turned sinister with the arrival of a late-night visitor, Cheriyammavan's arch foe, the postman.

'Telegram,' he said succinctly, adding loudly, 'Not money order.'

Ammooma began to mutter to herself, a sign that she had a lot on her chest and that it would soon be on everyone else's chests. All Amma primly said, after they saw off the postman and Ammooma went sniffing to bed, was that Kutti had gone to meet God.

'So did God send the postman?' Badi asked, but there was no satisfactory reply to this.

We rushed to Kanakamami for an explanation. She sat on her bed, walking her fingers up and down the bedstead's rosewood panelling.

'Jumped into the sea. What use is all that so-called beauty and fairness now, you tell me?' she counter-questioned. 'Can it make you swim?'

'But why?' we were baffled.

She shrugged. 'May be he pushed her.' Seeing our shocked expressions, she laughed merrily, 'Can't you take a joke? See, Choti, my father sent me this ring.'

Automatically, I bent to look at the new bauble.

'I have asked him for toe-rings with diamonds,' she confided. 'Something with a North Indian design, in meena perhaps. Also, those charmingly menacing snake-headed Bengal bangles of five sovereigns each.'

She had told me that lesser gold content meant you had to remember to remove the item before you slept. If you wanted it for daily wear, it had to be a bit on the solid side. And also about filigree, those trickster net patterns, which not only cheated you out of the precious metal, but also stored lint and dust where no brush could reach.

All five of us sat around the bed, dipping eagerly and curiously into Kanakamami's box. And there was plenty to keep us occupied. It was only when one of the triplet aunts fell headfirst into the box with eyes shut tight and mouth ajar, that we realised how late it was and stumbled back to our respective beds.

Next day Amma said that Velyammavan would arrive soon and that we were not to mention his dead wife under any circumstances.

'Not even if we are ourselves dying?' confirmed Badi, who liked to get these things straight.

'Yes,' said Amma unfeelingly, 'just die quietly in some corner without disturbing anyone.'

This time he came sans any fanfare, kisses, and more significantly, without any presents. He lay in his bed silently most of the time, getting up only to eat from the tray that Amma took to him. Cheriyammavan and he rarely exchanged glances, let alone conversation regarding the various ports and their allure.

This time round the elaborate stage-managing of rapture was given the go-by, too. Baby-talking adults didn't ask us girls, 'Look, who is here?' and we didn't have to shyly simper for kisses.

Kanakamami's vague dissatisfaction with the arrangements blended in neatly with this newfound freedom; we giggled when she muttered that anyone could see he was drunk.

When guests came, they were led tip-toeing to his chamber, where a glimpse of his supine form could be caught. From the doorway, we could spy two large feet with cracked heels and then a huge mound further on, which was his back or stomach depending on which way he lay when he passed out, and then like a small disembodied dot, his head. Visitors would stand around the bed like he was a VIP corpse, look at him and say loudly 'so sad' or 'poor man' before bidding a subdued farewell.

Their conversation provided us some insight into the event, though we were careful enough to appear more devastated by the recent tragedy and less vulgarly curious.

'She wanted him to have a second chance in life, that's why she killed herself.'

'A uterus choc-a-bloc with fibroids, no place for baby.'

'Woman without child is woman waiting for funeral pyre,' encapsulated an elderly relative whose wife was even then in the throes of labour pain and therefore unable to travel.

'We saved Amma's life,' Badi exclaimed, though Amma gave no hint of this enormous gratitude she owed us.

To supplement excitement in her humble way, Badi kept a toy piano belonging to the baby aunts under the bereaved bed. The trio had ruined it by playing it collectively, a multiple concert the miniature organ could not abide for long without throwing up its strings. At Badi's behest, I'd lean against the bed, dangling my feet in the air and then stealthily step on the keys with my toes under the bed so that a pained and prolonged squeal slowly rent the air.

Velyammavan himself was impervious to the hidden playback music, but guests visibly started at the sudden intrusion of this otherworldly sound, especially since we kids always stood impassively by.

'Choti,' my sister would ask innocently in the darkened corridor outside his room, skilfully spraying the minuscule vial of attar hidden in her fist. 'Do you not feel as if Kutti is actually *here* in the room?'

I'd nod gravely. 'I can even smell the jasmine buds in her hair.'

And they would all hurry out, remembering bus-timings or vaidyan appointments, not waiting for Amma to serve her signature tea.

Of course, we personally never doubted that a manifestation of Kutti's spirit wouldn't squeal so much as quiz, 'Quick, tell me how many days since I died?'

Badi, by virtue of being decision-maker, was ranked deity amongst us. The triplets never dared to cross her even if they thought she was completely wrong, completely mad or completely both. She cast herself in stellar roles in the in-house skits produced by her, with me in second lead. As extras, the triplet aunts had a multiplicity of roles to choose from, but forebore from expressing satisfaction.

'Mangala!' Badi screamed. Her Papaji we thought impressively formidable.

As Amma I flitted about cooking, buying sarees, slapping forehead and saying I couldn't live with him or without him.

Occasionally I got to scream too, though Badi demanded that my voice break and I cry in the midst of it all, which rather set me back. High octaves came to me with difficulty.

'They are in separate places,' Badi explained to our aunts, who never put their heart and soul into enacting the domestic help or doorman. 'Amma and Papaji can never be together because she came here, understand? And she came here for who?'

'Us,' they'd say solemnly, and then spoil the show by shoving me into Badi's office-returned path.

'They are star-crossed lovers, meant for each other but never together,' Badi explained patiently or impatiently, whacking or not whacking them. 'Like...like the hook and eye under Kutti's blouse.'

In the yard behind the house, where we played every evening, the little aunts watched fascinated while Badi and I practised acrobatics.

As we turned cartwheels or somersaulted clumsily, the aunts eventually stopped affecting poignant boredom and basked in reflected glory, because over the wall neighbourhood children would peep, comment, applaud. Not that we ever let the audience aunts forget their place.

'You can never join the circus,' a rebellious aunt once dared us from her placement on the wall, swinging a scrawny leg in mild insolence.

Now we had changed our minds about joining the circus only because Badi pointed out that they would begin with making us clean the elephants' potty, sort of at the bottom of the ladder. I mean, we all dreamt of an avatar, but not as Dasamma!

I jumped down from Badi's shoulders, holding a stick in my hand. We had been trying a new act, but either Badi was not big enough or I was not small enough, for when I clambered over her, she felt too soft and insubstantial and I just had to jump down, though she kept saying, 'I can hold you. Don't worry.'

We were already feeling frustrated at our failure to go through with this new feat, and now the taunt.

'Should we tell them?' Badi asked me.

Sucking at the salted spool of tamarind tucked in my cheek, I waved a restraining hand. 'Nah, I don't think so. They can't take it, they are babies.'

'What? What?' they chorused in a gratifyingly bewildered voice. Sometimes I wondered why God had bothered to give them three separate mouths when they spoke with one tongue.

'The circus people are not interested in us,' said Badi, making me wonder what she was up to. It was no secret; I wanted to fascinate circus managers everywhere.

'But,' continued my dependable sister, 'they want *you*.'

'*Us*?' they bleated, identical eyebrows taking flight.

'Yes. For the magic shows, you would be so useful. They can kill one of you realistically on the stage and then show the other one to the audience and say "*Magic!*". Anyone in the audience can come to the stage and kill you any way they want to, with anything they want.'

'Like that big rusty axe Dasamma uses on the firewood, Badi?' I pitched in helpfully.

'Anything,' Badi repeated with underworld menace. 'Since they can do it only twice, they said they'd charge very high tickets.'

'Somebody will miss us!' they cried in unison, faces eaten up by their huge, advancing eyes.

'You know what Dasamma says.' I imitated her wheedling tones, 'Too many girls in this house, too many.'

'No questions will be asked,' Badi confirmed.

'But Dasamma loves us,' they wailed with wobbly underlips.

'She *says* she loves you. Anyone can say that!' we scoffed. 'She has two daughters already, we are two girls and you are *three*. She'll gladly kill a girl or two, especially those whose pee she has to mop up the whole day,' Badi explained.

Threatened by death from inside the house and now out of it, the aunts went back to being the respectful souls they used to be. Not that they were intrinsically irreverent; many a battle outside the domestic diameter was won for them by none other than us. Plus, they could name-drop; we were reconciled to being traced back to them.

And we *never* allowed anybody else to call them Sambhaar Pieces.

When Cheriyammavan attempted to usurp the title, we stalled by the simple expedient of affecting deafness. We had spied his stress when he was saying something he thought irrevocably hilarious, usually around adults, and when no one laughed, he'd busy himself clowning with his poo-noolu— by conversions to a cowboy's gun-holster or a hush-push lady's hoity-toity bag strap—re-tying his loosened lungi or rustling the day's papers in his hand as if he expected a spray of hidden news to break loose. Truth to tell, we were to blame for his self-image of stand-up comedian. Stationed behind him when he entertained stray visitors or relatives, we'd make faces— contorting lips, grimacing, pretending to puke or choke, nodding or shaking heads contradictory to his speech—so that the audience first smiled, then submitted to full-blown merriment. Cheriyammavan, misunderstanding their mirth, claimed comic talent.

'I heard Dasamma is opening a dosa-place. She said send me the Sambhaar Pieces, I have to make sambhaar everyday...' he'd quote in lieu of a joke.

And when we continued to comb our dolls' curls or chew pencil-ends preparatory to solving homework puzzles, he'd clear his throat, bang knees together, go on banging them, making the lungi eventually lose its grip over legs or waist so that he got to stand up, turn around and tie it tighter. When he was at a loss for words he either rearranged the blinds over his hind limbs or worked a spade urgently into the tapioca plant in the verandah as if we were having tapioca for dinner.

Lungi was his willpower dress, we've seen him hitch the tip up in the air with a synchronised flick of wrist and toe before submitting himself to the seriousness of headlines. 'Ha-ha,' he tried again, shaking the vernacular daily. 'Look at this. An old hag found dead in train.'

I pricked up my ears.

'Heart-attack. Clutching a ticket for four stations away. No use, eh, buying tickets into future?'

'Sambhaar Pieces can travel on one ticket,' he said, encouraged by my weak grin.

'Yes,' agreed Badi to shut him up as he was apt to play his private wind instruments if thwarted too long. 'Since they are all in a sambhaar, they can. In one big vat.'

Ammooma pretended to take offence. 'Different in every way, aren't you, my little steamed puttus?' she'd say, quickly adding, 'Steamed in diverse coconut shells, that is.'

Amma would look up from her legless throne, the grater on the ground, wipe sweaty face with shoulder since coconut occupied both hands, and throw a scraped shell at her mother's foot in response.

It was just as well Amma and Ammooma eschewed the nickname or we'd have had to abandon it altogether; the christening wasn't noticeably underlined with affection.

At night Badi put her hand out of the window and pretended to be yanked by a monster. 'Oooh, he's eating me up,' she howled and I tugged her frantically from this side, causing Sambhaar Pieces to scatter about in confusion, expecting to be eaten up any minute.

But Amma spoilt it by walking in and announcing, 'There's a monster out there with loose motions. Has he been eating one of you?'

Badi was the one who brought to my notice Cheriyam-mavan's increased need for afternoon sleep. Indeed, he returned from his shop for a nap most days, but I had not thought it odd until the frequency was pointed out.

Nothing escaped Badi's eye.

'Are you thinking what I am thinking?'

I gave a cautious nod as I really wasn't thinking anything yet.

'And that is?'

'He is getting older and needs to rest more?' I suggested.

Badi snorted to convey her superiority. 'Want to find out how exhausted he really is?'

'We can always tell him we want him to read us a story and lie down with him.'

'You will spoil all the fun with your stupidity.'

I dumbly followed her directive, which was to scoot into the scene of crime while he swallowed a hasty lunch with Kanakamami, climb on to the wooden cupboard and hide behind her two big trousseau boxes kept there.

Thankfully, Badi had cleverly got it cleaned the day before, so that my one allergy sneeze arrived much before they did. Then we heard the hollow gold bells chained around Kanakamami's ankles clang against each other.

Chum, chum.

'Aiyyo!' she exclaimed with great urgency.

Badi and I had an eye each stuck between the narrow vertical space between the boxes and witnessed her external teeth bite him all over his neck. He then lifted his lungi sideways, parting them like a frilly curtain slowly, his thin legs straining and trembling like Ponni's goat when it tried to jump the fence. Then Kanakamami fell backward into bed, limbs awkwardly splayed as if she had just fallen from a tree.

Badi drew a sharp breath and covered her eye glued to the stage. As an afterthought she shifted that hand to my eye, shutting it effectively. Since my other eye was directly pressed against the box, momentarily I saw nothing. By the time I managed to dislodge her hand, the stage was empty and we had had a narrow visual range to begin with. Rotating my visible eye all around the space available before me, I rolled it to extreme left to glare at Badi. How dared she!

But before my glaring but mute eye could effectively take her to task, there began a mewling sound from the region of the bed. It was Kanakamami's voice, but in a most peculiar pitch. 'Aaah,' she said, then in all the accredited vowels, 'Oh. Oooh. Eee. Aii.'

'Forgive me,' said Cheriyammavan in a subdued voice after the intermission, a lapse of time during which we blackly anticipated detection, 'it is my eating habits—no meat. I am not strong like other men.'

Then, inexplicably, he burst into tears.

'So that is how babies are made,' I remarked with sufficient import later, though Rukmani had already apprised me of the one-on-top-of-the-other arrangement as prerequisite to reproduction. Cheriyammavan's bleak cry in grand finale suggested a measure of pain in the process I'd rather not dwell on.

'It is disgusting,' bit out Badi. 'You'd think they would be over all this by now.'

'If they have been doing this…thing for the past seven months of their marriage, where are the babies, Badi?' I couldn't help asking.

'They wouldn't be able to do this anymore if the babies came, stupid.'

'Then why are they doing it?'

But she stalked off. It was just like Badi to perplex me and then discount me. After all, I was small, I was stupid and I kept failing in school.

At dinner that night I kept my eyes averted from Kanakamami. I knew if I looked at her, giggles would spill over and then everyone would say oh, tell us what is funny, especially Sambhaar Pieces who would give their right arm for a laugh without questioning the possible use of three malnourished right arms to anyone, and I would have to make up something on the spot.

'Ammooma, can I have another pappadom?' Badi asked. But when Kanakamami, whose proximity to the papaddom jar prompted her to pick one and offer, Badi changed her mind.

At bedtime Badi told me she would never eat anything from her hands again. 'She is so dirty.'

Kanakamami with all her bangles and chains was tiresome and clangingly noisy, but she bathed daily, I attested, knowing full well that if anyone was dirty in this house it was I. It was almost a year now that I had been granted permission to bathe myself, but I only splashed water on all visible parts of me behind closed doors.

'She needs a dip in a deep, deep pond,' Badi muttered darkly.

'How deep?' I wanted to know.

'Deep as the deepest well.'

'Stop whispering,' ordered Amma, switching off the light and getting into bed with us, effectively ending our in-depth analysis on hygiene. She could be relied upon to pull rank always.

4

TRINJALAKUDA, THE BLACK LETTERS ON A YELLOW PAINTED background read. The platform teemed with tensed people peering intently at their wristwatches.

'I called up and they said train is arriving in fifteen minutes. Now it is one hour. One hour! Why they are lying I want to know,' someone was saying.

Perhaps they liked to see the platforms full of people, I thought. A station can't bustle with coolies alone.

Whilst I wandered up and down the platform, waiting for the return train to arrive—for I had graduated from the crawl of the comatose passenger trains to the gallop of Express trains with their minimal stops and hasty interludes at stations—a woman appeared out of the blue and asked me if I was lost. I said no and darted to another platform from where I saw the woman talk to a Lucy-like man. When I returned to my platform, the man walked up to me casually, 'Mole, are you lost?'

I shook my head and asked him, 'Are *you* lost?' May be we could turn this into a discussion on all the displaced people everywhere in the world.

'I work at this station and my job is to help lost people find their way. Are you from here?'

I nodded. There was obviously something not quite 'here' about my face, courtesy Papaji.

'Where are mommy and daddy?'

I thought fast. If he worked for the station people, then he would have the police on his side. I could just picture Amma's face when my principal and the policemen frog-marched me back home.

'They are in the bathroom,' I said, pointing to the green woman painted on a wall. Near her nose was written in uneven letters, 'TO LET'. Someone had scratched out the 'I'.

'Both of them are there?' he was enquiring when I ducked and ran to the Green Woman. Taking refuge in a bathroom had seemed a good idea when the man had been asking about daddy and mommy, but the smell and a horrified glimpse of the mess afloat in one of the cubicles had me wishing I was outside. There was the rustle of a nylon saree as the station woman who spoke to me earlier came in.

'Ei, so you are hiding here,' she said playfully, smiling like she was on my side, like she hated Maths and Social Sciences, too. No, there was that sternness, a tautness in the smile that belied the stance. This woman was no well-wisher; she was the one who caused mysterious heart-attack deaths in compartments, the one who manipulated helpless tickets into early arrivals. The sea must have smiled at Kutti, too, before she jumped.

I could hear a train thundering in. It was mine, I just knew it. I looked at the woman fearfully. Perhaps it was the proximity to the toilets or may be it was the sound of water dripping from a tap nearby, I felt first my panty and then my school skirt drench.

The woman shifted her gaze from my eyes, looking down between my legs to complete my humiliation. The train made impatient sounds, like it was thinking of leaving. Suddenly I rushed out, past the woman and the man, toward my beloved train just beginning to chug away without me. I ran as fast as I could despite the bunching up of wet cotton between my legs, shouting, 'I have a ticket, I have a ticket.' I never thought the train would attempt to leave me behind while I held the ticket. I had reached a door and miraculously a leap landed me inside the moving train.

I sat on a seat nearest to the door and tried to still myself. My heart was thumping as if I was still running and my nose was dying on me. Suddenly I didn't care if I never saw another planet, another place, another city in my life.

I just wanted to be home.

An attack of full-fledged asthma followed. Amma and Ammooma sat by my bedside, gratifyingly at my beck and call.

'Take her to Hyderabad,' Ammooma suggested.

'No fish is going to enter my daughter's throat. Not while I am alive. Not even in the name of treatment.'

'You can watch her struggle and say this? What if the cure is working? And Mangala, her father eats fish or no? She is half her father or no?'

As if on cue, the fisherman who trawled our street cooed, 'Hoooey, fresh mackerels, fresher sardines.' His 'hoooeys' were like dog-whistles; they crossed roads, pierced walls and shattered mud pans.

Cheriyammavan chose that moment to show off his worldliness. 'In Japan they eat fish just like that. One minute fish is swimming and the next minute it is inside your stomach! Shashi it is.'

'Shashi not once eat fish,' argued Ammooma.

He shrugged. 'Not that Shashi, Amma. Another Shashi.'

It took a couple of noisy pants from me to provide them with refocus.

Around that time two of the Sambhaar Pieces developed fever. Not to be left out, the third affected it.

I overheard Ammooma telling Amma, 'Something frighten them.'

'What does not frighten them?' Amma sighed.

The doctor, who probably knew the triplet aunts as well as his own children by now, did not suspect any psychological depth, and merely prescribed paracetamol.

'I told you it was nothing,' Cheriyammavan said. Actually it was his wife who had said that, but by now it was understood that either he would begin a sentence for her to end it or she would start for him to finish.

The illness furnished the baby aunts with license to loll about simultaneously atop their mother. That night they lay like pups in various puckered postures all over poor Ammooma.

'We have to do something about their fear,' Dasamma said the next day, nibbling absently at a broomstick.

'They all go hide in pond like you?' Ammooma mocked, unwilling to hear the mildest criticism of her belatedly born trio.

'Take them to the temple ulsavam and let them walk under the elephant's belly. Rukmani did it, you know. She'd shiver and piddle just hearing her father's voice and the poojari suggested she crawl under the elephant's belly. Now you see her, no? No shivering, no pissing.'

Meanwhile, my heroic return to school was somewhat spoilt by the immediate onset of summer vacation. Velyammavan had begun to stir. But when he began to narrate every minute detail of our late aunt's life, sedating him was passionately considered. No more prostrate, he stood vertical and verbose before us, nauseatingly and unstintingly sentimental. It was like our dear aunt took his pacifier with her; we so began to miss his sprawled and silent form on the bed.

Ammooma and Amma were the only two who allowed him to ramble, letting his anti-lucidity drivel wash over them like certified anecdotes. Since there was no announcement of a prize for the best listener, we felt free to unashamedly remember other, more important jobs whenever uncle launched his rockets of marital reminiscences. Not that we had not liked Kutti. Far from it. She had been more aunt than Kanakamami could ever be, never having looked archly to her left and right like Kanakamami whose eyes never met yours head-on. But I guess we bid goodbye to our late aunt around the time she jumped into the sea. Now we were given to idly wondering about her mortal whereabouts.

'Her heart must be part of fish waste,' Badi idly informed.

'What about her teeth and hair?' one of the Sambhaar Pieces asked.

'Oh that will be sold as dentures and wigs,' Badi declared carelessly, and the baby aunt looked suitably appalled.

Apart from this vicariously gory curiosity, we had nothing to offer by way of genuine obituaries. Sad stories about her kindness and clairvoyance regarding her own end met with our strong disapproval.

'Must have scratched her back against a post like bears do and then, splash, no post, only litres and litres of seawater,' Badi opined. It was so easy to imagine this that we stared at her open-mouthed a full minute before swinging our necks to Velyammavan's wedding photo in the verandah, where his bride stood against him at a seesaw slant.

When Kanakamami began her campaign of Displacing Dead Aunt, we were therefore with her all the way. People died and dead people were useless. Making us children carry the heavy sandalwood garland for the late aunt's monstrously framed picture further alienated us. The only bright spot had been when Badi and I dropped our share of the garland in a premeditated move and the three anaemic aunts tottered under the sudden weight of their burden. Velyammavan frowned at us, his distrust distri-buted evenly among us.

He was no more the jovial passer of parcels, he was not even the calm, benign presence in the guest bedroom. He was this nasty, smelly man with uncombed, scary hair that stood like a misplaced crown on his head. And he lived with us.

Kanakamami had nothing specific against him until he told her mistily one day that his own wife always cleared the *entire* table. This was a direct dig since she only cleared her spouse's platter over and above her own—an advice she imported from her pre-marital home. Now that her grievance was real, she sought our support and we gave it because it was vacation time, we had nothing to do and a man who could be entertaining us was frittering away precious hours.

The alive and annoyed aunt soon started to assert herself. At first she confined herself to comments like, 'In my house, we never grate pumpkin.' 'This? My mother just powders it on the grinding stone.' 'We always mix the masalas when the oil is lukewarm,' etc., angling for platforms to demonstrate her superior culinary skills.

'This is *our* way,' Amma shrugged, but Ammooma handed the ladle to her younger daughter-in-law with a sycophantic smile, condescending to 'issues' the youth needed to get out of their systems.

In due course Kanaka elbowed out Amma and Ammooma from their traditional holds on the pretext of being nice to them, solicitously shooing them out. She decided the menu, the quantity of rice to be cooked, portions to be served and went out to buy the vegetables and groceries herself. When the pipe in Ammooma's room began to leak, it was

Kanakamami again who took charge, kind enough to call her own family plumber.

Her first decree banned lesser beings, including Dasamma, from entering the house. Dasamma's loud guffawing cries and Ammooma's interference ensured that she continued to sweep the courtyard, clean the outhouse toilet and consume leftovers sitting cross-legged on the kitchen threshold, half in, half out. It had taken considerable cunning on Ammooma's part to soften the blow for Dasamma, who nevertheless sniffed loudly whenever Ammooma rattled loose change.

Dasamma's revenge consisted of dropping the 'Thampuran' while addressing Cheriyammavan. 'De,' she called out if she approached with broom and he was at some intersection in her path.

Cheriyammavan, whose thinning hair necessitated a cross-cranium combing technique, scampered past Dasamma with nary a squeak after she once circled him, asking, 'Tell me why your hair lives on the other side of your head.'

The inhouse toilet was cleaned personally by Kanakamami, and by default came to be used exclusively by her and Cheriyammavan.

Her father came a-calling to consolidate the takeover. 'Your mother sent me,' he explained to his daughter.

Fuelled by her recent redundancy, Ammooma played tour guide with alacrity while we girls chaperoned since there was something unsettling about the unfamiliar coyness in her smile to a man nearer her age.

Surveying the vastness of land around the house, he forgot himself in a spurt of temerity, 'Six acres! Who will look after all this when the elder son is gone?'

Back home he instinctively ate only those sweetmeats that his daughter made with her own two hands. Amma's unni-appams lay like abandoned orphans.

Complimenting obscurely, 'Once Kanaka-mol gets into the kitchen...!' he reclined in Velyammavan's armchair, going jiggle-jiggle with his knees.

He patted a little aunt's head and though the other two found urgent tasks to perform near him, he gave no indication of noticing them or their heads. Perhaps he thought there was only one of them and that he had finished with the head-patting ceremony and was now in danger of breaking his own record at jiggling to clear what he in all probability considered the onset of double or triple vision.

Before he left, he handed his daughter a paper-wrapped box, which she quickly took to her room and when we asked her if it was something edible, she made a face. 'Only if you like bitter kashayams.'

The triplets, who had just recovered from their meaningless, and in one case entirely imaginary, fevers, were too intimidated to fall sick again. They knew it would be a strict 'get-well' regime this time. When they whined about food being too bland or too spicy, she frowned nicely at them so that they quietly retired to their room after an unwanted meal and threw up with minimum fuss in solitude.

The ordeal under the elephant's belly loomed large, too, scaring them witless. But the more they appeared to be scared, the stronger was Ammooma's resolve to go ahead with the act.

Ammooma and Amma, now relieved from their daily routine, sat idly in the sun and stroked the cat, no longer an enemy as Milk Protection was Kanakamami's subdivision. At first they felt redundant because they were always stressing how 'she' would tire of all this bossing around.

'Silent cat breaks the mud-pot,' Ammooma grumbled against the lack of a notice period.

At my naive, 'Who are you talking about?' she misled, 'Our Dasamma.' I went back to combing my doll's hair so that they would return to their gossip, forgetting about me and my ability to hear. I was wondering how to introduce the topic of a pet dog...

As if conjured up by the misuse of her name, Dasamma appeared at our gate.

'Where is your broomstick?' I asked her impudently, running away.

I went to the backyard where the Sambhaar Pieces practised recreation. They immediately wore their customary scowls when informed of their foe's arrival and continued with their ditty half-heartedly.

> *'Amma and Appa went to the fair*
> *Both came back without any hair*
> *For, at the fair, they had got lost*
> *And, my oh my, seen a ghost*
> *The ghost said, "let me eat you"*
> *They replied fast, we are but two*
> *At home we have twelve children*
> *Come eat them, just tell us when.'*

'Now,' I yelled and chased one of them. They scrambled grimly for they played this game only because it existed, not in the least because they enjoyed it.

'My babies,' shouted a voice above the din. It was Dasamma come to do her fawning bit with my aunts. Now they scattered with more sincerity despite Dasamma's heavy wheeze assuring them, 'I saw you being born with my own eyes. Won't you give your Dasamma one little kiss at least?'

She held one squirming aunt by her blouse-tail and watched disbelieving as she continued to wriggle. 'Mole, it is me, Dasamma.'

'Don'tkillmedon'tkillme,' was the frantic response. 'Iamreallyaboy.'

'It is the fever,' I explained after the incoherent protestor had vacated the vicinity.

'Poor things. Not strong mentally. After all, brain matter divided between three.'

I nodded understandingly till she turned to me slyly, hand on chin, 'Edi, all Sardarjis look same to me. I worry how you go recognise your father?'

'That's simple,' I told her, registering the slur of being provoked to reveal the non-existent meetings between Papaji and us that Amma tom-tommed about in vain to maintain propriety. 'The man who looks most like me is my father.'

The elephant had four of the fattest, blackest and hairiest legs I had ever seen. Badi and I stood heroically ahead of our cowering aunts, who had replaced the hum of muted weeping with shameless howls.

'It stamp us. It bite us. It eat us,' they cried. Ammooma's eyes were watering too, but Dasamma was influential enough to arrange matters speedily with the poojari. He came grinning and broke into his spiel. 'This is God's own pet, Eirawat. He do magic and wipe away tears of terror. One walk under its stomach and you are cured of fear forever.'

With great force we shoved them under the pachyderm from one end and with equal force they were pulled wriggling from the other end, a lot like threading a needle. Three times this was done and we had almost dislocated shoulders, shoving them in and out.

'Now wait for Eirawat to...relieve himself,' the poojari smiled. 'For that will show that fear has passed on to him, then from him to out.'

Two hours later Eirawat deigned to oblige with the needful and a Sambhaar Piece leapt athletically into it in a mis-calculated attempt to miss it. She goggled, ankle-deep in the yellow-brown splotch, looking very much like a small, but well-fertilised member of the plant kingdom.

'Now you are cured,' the poojari declared, discreetly accepting the bribe of coins and plantains that Ammooma offered via Dasamma.

'Now you smell,' Badi and I lost no time in correcting.

They came back home more frightened than ever before to reveal their fright.

Badi underwent a mysterious transformation thereabouts. A commotion that was later called celebration ran claw-foot past us and I was, shame of all shames, clubbed with the baby-aunts.

'She is now all grown up,' Ammooma said, mystifying us, since Badi looked not a whit less diminutive to us that morn.

Most irritating of all was Badi's self-inflated reaction to the fuss.

'I can't run,' she stated importantly. 'I can't even move. If I tell you why, you will faint.'

Naturally, we were collectively willing to lose all consciousness.

Though I faked knowledge of the event, somehow baby-aunts knew the truth of my ignorance by Badi's uppity demeanour with me, mortifying me into seclusion from them as well as her. They had developed their own lisping codes and I was not prepared to pick any role other than the leader's, but for them Badi was still boss, albeit in absentia. Being a sidekick would have ruined my budding career as a miscreant.

Kanakamami's defection, too, unnerved me. When I gushed over her gold, she nodded quickly to get rid of me, then pulled Badi in by hand into her room, the one that smelled of sandalwood and was redolent with rubies and mysterious jewelled-vowelled baby-making rituals.

In the mornings, they'd sit with their heads together, fists pressed into mouths to suppress giggles, and they had the same visual trick: a quick dart to the left, then right, irritating in its haste to escape detection.

'You are mere children,' Badi informed us loftily, leaving us with no weapon to defend our youth for our age would always remain less than hers, and Sambhaar Pieces stared at her with shiny eyes, deeply content with their inferiority in every field, including age.

I had secrets and now Badi had her share of secrets, too. I shouldn't have been feeling all high and dry, like the kitchen rag Amma rinsed and dried alone and isolated on the highest twig of a dry jackfruit tree in the backyard, from which lumber was snapped for kindling. The giggles Badi shared with Kanakamami completed my humiliation, it was like she had stood on a podium in the Town Hall and announced on microphone her indifference to me.

There was in her smile, her eyes a certain creeping slyness that forbade me from flinging juvenile accusations of neglect at her. In Amma's careful application of warmed oil on her hair, in Kanakamami's acceptance of her aid in the kitchen, in the wide berth both uncles accorded her, they all meant one thing: she was special. In what way, I wasn't sure, but special she was, more than me.

More and more I began to crave canine company.

'No, Choti. No dog until you are at least fifteen years old. I look after too many children as it is, I cannot run after a dog as well.'

'But Amma,' I wailed, 'I will look after it myself.'

She laughed unkindly at that. 'My answer is *no*. A dog means extra work. It will need to be walked and it will need to be fed meat. Can you imagine that? Meat in *this* house! And you are too small to look after even your dolls, just look at them. So filthy.'

Surreptitiously, I covered the doll's ears. Sometimes Amma was like that. Stubborn. Refusing to see reason. Too caught up in her sarees and cooking and with her ironing and with her sewing and with her scolding and gossiping with the outside world to be a real mother.

I read out aloud from my schoolbook, where hundreds of happy families frolicked with their respective dogs. Any home was said to be incomplete without a pet, but Amma greeted my factual outpourings with an uncaring 'hmmm' like Kutti at a scratch-post. I quoted dog-owners who swore their canine housemates ate only vegetarian fare. I reminded her how I missed Papaji. Usually this worked and owing to its potency Badi and I kept it as a last resort. When all else failed, we remembered our father in very heartbreaking and innovative ways.

But Amma said I should just pray to God for a dog, God being to her what Appoopan was to Ammoma, the ultimate red tape. Like I said, sometimes Amma did not know how to act like a mother. If you did all she said to do without a squeak, she was composed. Cross her and conditions applied.

Post-vacation, I had thought I'd return to the same class, but a personal visit by Sister Lucy soon provided perspective.

'Now she has to write only two papers as she has cleared the first part. She need not attend school this year at all as she is just repeating the year. It might be better if you coach her at home,' she imparted, the solar eclipse on her face partially lifting at a me-less school and its graffiti-less toilets.

Amma snorted when she left, 'Comes here to check my marriage story. She doesn't believe I am married at all. I don't believe her marriage story either. God's got too many brides about, if you ask me.'

'Hush,' bade Ammooma. 'You are married, so is she. I am thinking if this Marx man is married.'

Then Badi made a semi-comeback to 'the children set', starting with me. I did go all snooty and pretend to be too busy to acknowledge her bored greetings—we had this game where the Sambhaar Pieces stood with their backs jutting out and I ran up to them from a distance and rammed an outstretched leg into one jutting back whereupon the other two would fall about giggling before queuing up in suspense for the next kick—but by and by Badi let me snuggle back into our exclusive club of two. I was determined not to allow her bonding with Kanakamami to be an awkward area; I did mind losing her as a pal, but Badi's return was precious, more precious than Kanakamami's gems.

The crack between us I tried hard to cement had me nodding when Badi contemptuously spat at bus stops, 'Men!'

I'd spit, too, 'Men!' not knowing why they deserved a tribute of saliva for standing at bus-stops and looking to the left and right of the road as if such a large thing as a bus may just go past without their noticing.

'I hate them,' she said.

My pre-paid concurrence had me nod vigorously though I had begun to query the dubious pleasures of ageing, keeping such doubts to myself for fear of playing right into Kanakamami's ladled hand.

Badi's abhorrence for anything masculine next entwined itself around Velyammavan's bent frame. For some reason, she imagined he stared at her all the time. Pushing out her chest, she asked me, 'Can you see anything?'

Unsure of what response she sought, I gave a half-nod, which I changed to a shake of the head when she squeaked.

'No wonder the old man is always eyeing me,' she declared. 'You won't believe what Kanakamami had to go through, even when his wife was alive and living in the same house.'

'You'll die,' she said when I made no move to quiz her. Somehow, I sensed not knowing was self-defence, though she waited a full minute for me to ask for my untimely demise.

5

THOUGH AMMA OFT GRUMBLED THAT AMMOOMA OVERWORKED her, it had been more for the benefit of those who speculated about a daughter's indefinite return to her pre-marital home. 'Even if I am dead and laid out on a mat in the front room, she will say, Mangala, see who all have come, make tea quickly.'

And Ammooma would roll her eyes. It was like a game they played. But after the kitchen was wrested out of their control, they struggled with leisure, a monstrous snake made of empty space. But soon it was like the snake swallowed them and they lay in the belly like swallowed preys must, motionless and benign.

Now they sat around happily chattering all day, either to each other or with sundry relatives who popped in out of domestic curiosity or marriage proposals for our eldest uncle, who was now the eligible bachelor in the family.

When Kanakamami found that all her machinations to gain the upper household hand had not only resulted in her getting precisely what she wanted, but also in the other family members not pitching in their bit, she frowned again. And when she frowned in her husband's presence, it never failed to reverberate in furrows on his forehead.

'I want to hold a family meet,' Cheriyammavan lip-synched.

'Are we to be there, too?' Badi queried on behalf of the under-developed.

He looked at his wife and with an imperceptible shift of her aggressively blackened eyebrow, permission was granted. 'Yes,' he said, 'if you want.'

'Why don't we begin it with a prayer song?' Badi suggested.

This time Kanakamami's eyebrow rested while her tongue did the needful. 'No, Badi,' she said firmly, ex-friend or no ex-friend.

'Come, come, Kanaka,' reproached Velyammavan. 'It is a family meeting, after all. We must invoke the blessings of the dear departed.'

'Yes, Etta,' she agreed, but her teeth barely moved from their perch on the lower lip.

'What about a nice show by us then?' I asked, for I danced very well, everyone knew.

'No,' she said in a higher pitch.

'Why not?' Velyammavan enquired idly. 'They are such gifted artistes.'

I smiled modestly at Badi who smiled modestly back.

Finally, it was decided to merge the cultural event with a semi-hymn. After this the serious meeting would start, which we could attend but not interrupt verbally or by bodily functions. Since the conference would commence the next day, we were not left with much time on our hands for rehearsals.

Late afternoon Badi hummed several songs to me, preparatory to selecting *the* song, and I indolently watched the road beyond her. It was really a lane masquerading as road and meandered impertinently onto the main road where buses, even state transport buses, stopped by. Into our road only private cars came and that too only one at a time as otherwise it spelt traffic jam in the narrow confines. Rarely did we have to press up against the prickly henna hedges along our wall, which extended all the way up to the real road, as some vehicle tooted down on us. When this happened, of course, we were thrilled enough to pretend to faint right before it, causing the driver to let his primal personality emerge. Ranting and raving, while we held our heads and mumbled, 'soda, soda, oooh!' he'd dig into his pockets for coins and realise that he was on the wrong path, a cul de sac so to speak.

On this road our car was an incidental celebrity, with its blistering hot metal exterior and superior honking system. Velyammavan used to let us sit in the car and toot the horn to our heart's content. Then one of the aunts revealed a singular lack of toilet training right on the front seat and the practice was discontinued.

'Choti,' Badi rebuked, 'You are not listening.'

'I am,' I protested so violently that she was mollified. We believed that there was no such thing as a half-hearted lie and though Amma eulogised Harishchandra's bone-deep honesty, converts were few.

There was no need to go through entire stanzas, I told Badi, but she insisted on singing everything she knew, very precisely from start to finish, so that my attention wandered again.

The fine sand in the courtyard, swept regularly by Dasamma, reflected the upper outlines of the house. The red tiles sloping down both sides of the spikey roof were tanned colourless in the profile below where a dimming sun cast the washing on the roof as shadowy waves in the sand. I sensed the presence of rain before it actually pelted down, obliterating the sun and thence the sifting silhouette of our house on the sands.

'Badi!' I squealed.

'You liked this one? So do I! The earlier song...'

'It is raining!'

We watched as Amma and Ammooma ran out in one orchestrated move, former dashing out to the courtyard to rescue the clothesline, while latter ran out to the gate on which some cotton bed-sheets, no doubt urine-stained, were draped. But the raindrops outsmarted them and managed to get some serious drenching done.

'They were almost dry,' Amma lamented on her return, arms full of a jumble of multi-coloured clothes.

'There is one here that belongs to everyone,' I commented. Indeed on a closer inspection we found that each member of the family was represented in her arms. Nothing that belonged to Cheriyammavan or Kanakamami though. Their clothes occupied prime drying position in the verandah outside. Earlier, during monsoons, our school uniforms used to be hung there. This year, of course, I would have no uniform.

'Choti is seeing too much,' Ammooma stated pessimistically.

We were told in no uncertain terms that we had to let Sambhaar Pieces participate in the cultural event, too, which had Badi and me initially considering cancelling the whole thing, but then we decided to be magnanimous.

'You will stand here,' Badi informed the rebel aunt. The other two, the sickly ones, were to stand at the ends, so that we stood from left to right, one sickly aunt, me, rebel aunt, Badi and leftover aunt. Now the song we had selected was:

'Spicy little thing,
I'm spicy little thing.

Chew me, then sing,
Ah-ah-ah
Chew me, then sing,
I am just a little
Spicy little thing.'

We were to sing this three times over and the last time we would drag out the last line and then each of us would rapidly name a spice like pepper, cardamom etc. in rapid succession. We were also to hit a hip—each her own—at the 'ah-ah-ah'.

I did raise some preliminary objections, 'Spicy Thing? Badi, we have to sing something divine, not about, uh, kitchens and things.'

However, Badi was sure no one would notice the alteration in our invocation.

Then Cheriyammavan asked, 'Who is conductor? You know in western orchestras there is always a conductor.' He showed us a magazine where a pony-tailed man stood with hands outstretched, airing his armpits.

Badi ordained she would be 'conductor'. The three aunts had never heard this term yet, indeed had not heard most terms yet, and giggled hysterically when Badi lifted her hands to 'conduct'. The aunts who stood on her either side got a physical retort at once and wasted precious rehearsal time unnecessarily with their howling. The rebel one always beat her fist against her chest in lament at the slightest provocation and the sickly ones felt compelled to imitate.

'I was only conducting,' said Badi innocently. 'You have to stand a bit away from me.'

The three aunts scooted away as far as they could and thereafter lent suitable sobriety to the occasion.

The aunt in the middle was to be the 'Spicy Thing' of the song, Badi decided. I had serious reservations about the choice as I was well aware of my own talents and did not want them underplayed. But when the Spicy Thing costume was aired, I decided that my outer beauty needed as much advertisement as my inner one. Now it was the turn of the rebel aunt to demur.

'But I won't be able to see a thing,' she protested, staring at the brown gunny bag that Badi had procured for the Spicy Thing's couture.

'You do not need to see anything,' we asserted. 'It is your voice that is important here. Remember, you are just a cardamom that sings.'

'More like a peanut that pees,' I mumbled under my breath, to rub in the deglamourised garb.

With great reluctance, Rebel Aunt donned the Spicy mantle. The two side aunts had to go high-pitched at 'ah-ah-ah' in the song, which came up very often, as we were planning to sing the same stanza again and again to hoodwink listeners into thinking it was a song of reasonable length. Approximately fifteen 'ahs' apiece would come their way, I deduced. When we came to, '*Chew me, then sing…*' Spicy Thing was to twist this way and that while Badi and I pretended to grab and eat it.

Next morning, we strapped Spicy Thing to the potty for an hour to evade unseemly accidents. Then we lowered Spicy Thing into the sack after slashing two circles in it for her feet since we did not fancy physically lugging the aunt around. Then we tied the upper end with a thin rope, letting the cloth on top roundly fan out a bit, like a gay parcel our surly postman had just delivered.

'I can't breathe, I can't breathe,' Spicy Thing began, copying my anthem, but we pointed out the multi-holed nature of the fabric and Spicy Thing calmed somewhat.

'Art is not all glamour, you know,' Badi admonished.

We led Spicy Thing down the passage to the drawing-cum-dining room, where the sofas and chairs had been arranged along the wall in deference to our performance.

Badi pushed us each into our places and pressed us down by the shoulders as if to sow us there.

'Good morning, ladies and gentlemen,' she said, showing off as usual when the audience had assembled. 'We are here to attend Kanakamami's family meeting,' she added, only to have Kanakamami interrupt with, 'Hmph! It is your uncle who called this meeting. Not me.'

Badi imperiously turned to us, with both arms ready to thresh air, 'Start.'

'*Spicy little thing, I am a spicy little thing…*' we went joyously as Badi windmilled her arms like she wanted to get rid of them forever.

When we grabbed Spicy Thing for a taste, it wriggled forcefully. The other aunts were going ah-ah-ah in all seriousness when Spicy Thing made an unrehearsed bid for freedom, so that Badi had to stop conducting and manually pinch its arm amidst all the pretend pinching. Spicy Thing obligingly went totally limp, so that when left alone, it sagged to the floor. After the song, we stood gracefully at the same spot, waiting for Badi to stop waving her hands and accept the accolades.

'Why she not getting up?' asked Ammooma in a worried way and we noticed that Spicy Thing was still slumped in a heap in the middle.

'It is over,' we yelled, prodding it with a foot, but Spicy Thing gave a little wriggle and continued to slouch.

'Untie,' Ammooma ordered.

When Cheriyammavan unpeeled the sack, aunt's chemise-clad body showed pink dots all over. Again the doctor was summoned, much to Kanakamami's irritation, who insisted that ant bites could be solved with a dab of cold milk.

'Yes, you will say,' agreed Ammooma. 'One less burden for you, if she is gone.'

'I am not one to shirk responsibility,' said her daughter-in-law, front teeth all agleam, 'as long as they are *my* responsibility.'

'Are you not their elder sister?' Amma intervened righteously.

'Aren't you?'

'But I have been married out of this house.'

'Then why,' asked Kanakamami triumphantly, 'are you still here? Aangla marichal naathoonde kaneer kanano?'

A loud gasp emerged from various throats, titillated by the morbid vision of Amma applauding Kanakamami's widowhood.

'You have no husband and you don't want others to have a husband either!' Kanakamami encapsulated triumphantly. 'And you,' she said, looking at Velyammavan, 'what are your plans, if you don't mind my asking?'

'It seems the meeting is already under way,' he noted, winking at the enlarged and garlanded picture of his wife, who smiled fuzzily down at her own quadrupled breasts. 'My plans are a bit private at the moment.'

'You mean to say, you won't tell me as I am not part of your family,' Kanakamami moaned, magnetically attracting a husbandly arm around her bony shoulders.

Spicy Thing, rapidly receding into Sambhaar Piece, issued forth a piteous moan.

'My daughter is lying on deathbed and your wife is talking of property!' bit out Ammooma.

'Did I open my mouth about this house being ours?' asked an indignant Kanakamami.

'Oh, so it is your house now, is it?' questioned Velyammavan. 'Haven't you told her some fundamental facts?' this to his brother. Someone had meanwhile let the doctor in, who poked the spotted aunt randomly with a stethoscope, his eyes never straying from the tableau before him.

'Is anything the matter here?' he asked Ammooma, who hovered around him.

'You tell. Doctor is you or I?' she reproached.

'Oh.' And he bent to aunt again, this time with a more medical expression.

'I know you are the elder brother and that after mother this house is supposed to come to you. But you must realise by now how poor I am. I will never be able to buy land and build a house. You, on the other hand, are blessed with a wealthy job. No encumbrances either,' Cheriyammavan delivered in a sensible voice.

'So what do you suggest?' asked the other uncle in a pseudo-soft voice.

'If you can buy my Kakanad land off me and build a comfortable house there, mother and sisters can move in with you. Since you are not home most of the time, you won't be disturbed.'

'We, disturb! Mangala, are you hearing?' Ammooma shouted.

'Measles,' shouted the doctor in turn.

'Oh God, where do I go with my daughters?' Amma cried plaintively.

'Where I go with my measled daughters?' pleaded Ammooma, not to be outdone in the melodrama department.

Immediately all the Sambhaar Pieces, sensing somehow that their well-being was under threat, wanted to lay claim to their favourite siesta spot and began to crawl up Ammooma's abdomen until she had to physically push them away.

'Come now,' soothed Cheriyammavan, 'no one is asking you to leave today.'

'Legally, no one can ask them to leave tomorrow either,' Velyammavan's voice was categorical.

'What about the day after?' Badi piped up. I wanted to be clever, too, and say something along the lines of yesterday being really out of the question, tee-hee, but as always, by the time I had played out the line in my head to perfection, conversation had moved on.

'You and your wife can leave this very minute if you like.' Velyammavan made it sound like a playful invitation.

'This is the respect I get in this house,' Kanakamami told the doctor. 'This is the thanks I get for keeping my mouth shut most of the time.' Technically, she couldn't keep her mouth closed at all, what with all those teeth in there trying to be out here, but the doctor let that pass.

'When,' asked her brother-in-law in his newly invigorated voice, 'have you ever been silent on any topic?'

'Shall I tell you? Shall I tell them, Ettan?' she asked generally. She must have nodded for her husband, because the next minute she was accusing blindly that her jewellery box had been invaded and that things were missing. 'Did I go to town about it?'

'What was the biggest thing you lost?' someone enquired.

'Is it that serpentine chain that lies against your belly heavy as tapioca for tea?' Velyammavan asked with simulated concern.

'Why you look at her?' Ammooma asked the doctor, who had rolled up an undotted aunt's sleeve. 'Leave her, she is not ill.'

'It is my elaka thaali,' Kanakamami said hesitantly.

'Who precisely are you pointing your finger at?' Amma asked, and incredibly Kanakamami's travelling gaze stopped at me.

'Choti?' Amma's voice trembled. 'You think my Choti robbed you?'

'She was the only one with access to my box.'

'Elaka thaali you say, eh? The moving chain, so called because of its tendency to move. I say it has walked out on you all on its own,' Velyammavan put in.

My knees resumed its previous consistency of strained rice and now threatened to buckle under me.

As if suffering from a fit, Amma began to rain blows on me. 'You robber! You have taken after your father's side after all.'

I did not mind as everyone else ran to my aid, holding her by her flailing arms. She really resembled a goddess in a picture then, with her manifold arms, one striking the air, the other circumventing Velyammavan's neck, a third hand gunning for me. Her shrill voice, however, arrested the departure of the doctor, who had been reluctantly inching toward the door.

'How do we know you are not hiding it yourself?' Ammooma addressed her daughter-in-law.

'I knew I wouldn't be believed! It is my own fault that I was so careless with my ornaments.' Kanakamami struck her forehead a couple of times, but it was her husband who flinched. There were fat-hot tears waddling down her cheeks by now. 'Ask her,' she pointed at me. 'What was she doing in my room last Friday afternoon instead of going to school.'

'I don't go to school nowadays,' I mumbled with a guilty look. Indeed, I had crept about in her room on that day, spurred by a spurious hunger to rummage for the box her father left behind. I had been sure those were sweets, not kashayam as she claimed, and I had been right. But saying that would only confirm her accusation and my guilt.

Saved from Amma's striking hands, I sank against the wall. At last all my wicked deeds had come home to roost. The train jaunts, the deliberate missing of school, my report cards, fights with little aunts, faking own baths: they had all been recorded unseen!

A baby aunt had succeeded in climbing up Ammooma's hip halfway and was fighting all attempts to be dislodged when Badi moved sympathetically toward Kanakamami.

I was stupid, I was small and now I had no sister.

Velyammavan was busy the following day getting property papers settled. He told Amma and Ammooma that they did not need to worry, but they looked faintly anxious until he cleared matters over breakfast the next day.

'The house is still in your name,' he told Ammooma. 'But the first nominee now is Mangala. Then it is me. He is scared, the boy, that I will remarry and spawn a dynasty. That is why he is wriggly as a caught fish.'

Cheriyammavan, when apprised, was neutral. 'Mangala was given a dowry at the time of marriage. We do not owe her a share,' he said carefully. 'She is the responsibility of her husband's family.'

'You well know her predicament. When she married against his family's wishes, she did not expect incom-patibility.'

'Neither did we expect her quick return,' Kanakamami piped in, walking out of the kitchen.

'Good morning Kanaka,' welcomed Velyammavan jovially. 'I almost did not recognise you without all that burgled jewellery. Will you be regaling us with another home-made taandavam today?'

We children choked on our idlis at this.

'I am not surprised your wife committed suicide,' she snapped.

'Well, I am,' he said chattily. 'However, you are too young to be analysing anyone's annihilation. After breakfast you should go to some gold showroom and while away your time there constructively. Are those idlis for us?' he asked her innocently. 'Incidentally, how many sovereigns exactly was that thing you lost? Can't promise you an exact duplicate though.'

'Eight.' She threw the steamed white globules into his plate and stood primly behind her husband's chair. 'He says I must have misplaced it somewhere. So that won't be necessary.'

'What do I get?' cut in Cheriyammavan, pressing his finger into the soft idli until it came out of the other side.

'The Kakanad land is still yours. It is an area earmarked for great development. Soon Kochi will be too crowded and the highway goes straight through. There are flat-builders I hear who take on the construction cost for you. You could bargain for two facing flats.'

Cheriyammavan lifted his finger, the one with the idli around it, like a sudarshan chakra. 'That is it? I sacrificed my life to look after the family and this is what I get in return?'

'You also get to keep your wife, her nutmeg estate and any immobile jewellery left with her,' his sibling meticulously maintained.

Kanakamami fluttered, but then thought it best to maintain her feminine vigil behind her husband's chair. 'You had said the day you brothers row, crows would fly on their backs,' she accused instead.

Velyammavan surveyed her gravely. 'Crows will fly on their tummies or their spines, it is entirely up to them. One really mustn't interfere with raven flight schedules.'

'In effect, you are throwing us out,' Cheriyammavan stated flatly.

'In effect, you walking out,' Ammooma responded. She looked a bit tired, like she had not slept the whole night.

After that, the idlis were consumed in complete silence. When Cheriyammavan and Kanakamami eventually vacated the room, Ammooma sighed, 'Always, always doing drama. Any need?'

'And why add curd to chutney?' Amma enquired pedantically, dipping a pristine idli into gunpowder masala.

They were to be exiled officially only in a month's time, but odds and ends belonging to them were carted out sporadically. Kanakamami pretty much abdicated the kitchen to the stand-by queens, but she did return to hand-pick anything that may belong to her, to confiscate from a kitchen shelf the rasam powder or tender mango pickle that her mother had personally concocted, to scrutinize some land-related papers left next to the tap.

Their retreat was represented in the strategically closed door, behind which Cheriyammavan and Kanakamami planned their departure, their garments militantly drying in the verandah, the absence of their dirty linen that was hitherto flung into the common dirty-linen basket, and in the public avoidance of even Badi.

'My fate! Elder son widower, younger one henpecked. How long he wear that newly married face of his?'

'Uneasy lies the head that wears the same pillow two nights in a row,' Amma murmured. She oft took refuge in the incomprehensible owing to her own experience in matrimony, which she considered vast. 'It can't last, this infatuation.'

On the verge of turning over and revealing my wide open eyes, I changed my mind. It could be fun to be presumed asleep. I was not far wrong. The conversation centred around Kanakamami and her selfishness as usual. There was a pause while each ruminated over what the other had provided by way of fresh insight, masticating and digesting slowly to draw out the pleasure.

'She look so innocent,' Ammooma said suddenly, and I imagined them gazing tenderly at me. 'In wedding photo,' she added and I realised that they were still harping on Kanakamami's exterior since I was as yet unmarried. If only I had a dog for myself, I would not have been so lonely. But I knew Amma; her No was always No. What was the next best thing, I wondered. Then I knew it. A cycle!

'Leave it,' I mumbled as if in sleep. 'Don't touch my new cycle. It is mine, *mine*.'

'With a tongue sharper than coconut grater's,' commented Ammooma, who could be a bit deaf. 'Those ever-smiling teeth of hers! Nothing but syrupy fangs.'

'Go to sleep, Amma,' Amma told her mother with a sigh. 'And you too Choti.'

There was an increased vacuum in my life. When other children got up early, marched to teachers and their canes, I lay in bed, pretending to sleep late and make it appear a treat. Now Amma began to groan all over again, 'What shall I do with you?' More to the point, I wanted to tell her, what would I do with myself. The station was no longer a viable option, Sambhaar Pieces were to begin school this year, no dog licked my heels, and Kanakamami's jewellery box was now no more open to me. If only I had a cycle!

It was Velyammavan who came up with a solution. 'I can take Choti with me for a voyage,' he said.

Badi, who had been sipping her milk, stated flatly, 'She won't come, you know.'

Why had she said that or even thought that? Of course, she did not know about my thwarted penchant for travelling or the amount of time that would be available to me once she left for school.

'What do you say, Choti?' he asked.

'I... I have to think, Velyammavan.' For having spied the forbidding look on Badi's face, my 'yes' was a pinned butterfly.

Badi beamed at me and picked up her schoolbag.

It was the first day at school for the Sambhaar Pieces and they were understandably agog with confusion. Amma already had to change an aunt's knickers.

'There is nothing to be scared of,' she assured her sisters, lest they decide to relax their bladders all over again. 'You will make a lot of friends.'

After Velyammavan had trapped them in his car and driven away with them sticking their wide eyes to the rear glass in a row, Amma turned to me, 'They are too timid. Asking me if Dasamma will be waiting for them in the school. I told them yes, she will be there. Just to comfort them.'

When Velyammavan came back, I was evasive. At lunch I affected sleep and while everyone else slept, I ate. At four in the afternoon, Badi was back from school and I could tackle her regarding this golden chance in my life.

'Do you see him as a fairy godmother?' she asked instead. 'Stupid. Can't you see?'

I couldn't, but was loath to admit to visual handicaps.

Badi sighed loudly. 'Come here,' she jerked my hand, dragging me to Kanakamami's room and knocking tentatively. The door was open and swung back on its hinges to reveal Kanakamami reading a magazine and clothes spilling from various bags on the floor.

She looked at us coldly.

'Choti doesn't understand...about Velyammavan.' Badi said in a small voice. 'You know he wants her in the ship with him.'

'Oh, yes,' she smiled, snapping the magazine shut and placing it on the bed beside her. On the cover a man held his hands out to a woman who was laughingly looking the other way, her backside drawn too large for the body like Dasamma's filarial foot. 'You want *my* help?'

Badi nodded as if under tremendous strain. 'She is my sister, after all.'

'It is a secret, Badi, *our* secret, I thought I told you that.' Kanakamami was stern. 'But seeing that you have seen fit to tattle anyway, I have no choice but to let Choti into the secret. But you,' she turned to me severely, 'will you be childish like Badi and let the cat out of the bag, too?'

I grimly showcased negation.

'It is like this, I had just had a bath...'

'You were going in for your bath,' Badi attempted to correct.

Kanakamami continued like she hadn't spoken, 'Your Velyammavan saw me—I was not fully dressed, you understand—and he, he hugged me.'

I looked back, aware of a keen sense of anti-climax.

'She doesn't understand,' Badi grieved.

'What did he do?' I asked, suddenly thirsty for facts like my dead aunt had been.

Kanakamami patted a dozing breast. 'He pressed me. It is not done, don't you see, Choti?' She then shook me by my shoulders. 'I am his brother's wife, I am almost his sister, I am married to another man, he cannot go around touching me when he feels like it. Do you understand?'

Her voice, like the magazine woman's bum, was growing disproportionately big, so soothingly I said I did, I understood because I was maturing all the time and life was getting clearer by the minute. I did manage one intelligible question. 'Why don't you tell Amma?'

She snapped her fingers; I had hit the nail with my query. 'I do not want to divide a home, that's why.' Then she brought her face close to mine, her eyes boring into mine intensely, giddying me, 'This is the truth.'

'So, Choti,' Velyammavan squeezed my shoulder affectionately, back to releasing the aroma of cardamom and imported mint toothpaste instead of alcoholic fumes into my face. 'Why does my favourite niece have to think so much about going away with me?'

Amma glanced at me sharply, having sensed my withdrawal. 'She must have already packed her bags.'

There were just two more days for his leave to end, I didn't know how I could gracefully reject the offer. I mean, everyone knew I was going to be deadweight here at home. I had to be fed, shod and watered. At the ship all this would be done for free. I could see glamorous, exotic lands I had only read about. I could save myself from turning into another Cheriyammavan, dreaming and rambling on armchair or pot, pretending to be tourist.

Plus, with me out of her hair, Amma hinted, she could find some small job for half a day until the Sambhaar Pieces managed to find their way home from school.

Owing to Amma's fear that I would fall out if left unbolstered, I lay in the middle. By unspoken arrangement I turned baby when it was just the three of us. Badi was reading a comic book and Amma was thinking aloud on the contents of my suitcase.

'Underclothes, warm clothes and all your...'

'Amma,' Badi folded her comic book. 'Choti is not going anywhere.'

Amma threw her a distracted smile. 'I know you will miss her, but this is all decided. Perhaps next year, you can go, too. Then Velyammavan can explain all the new maths to you.'

The fan came to an abrupt standstill. Sambhaar Pieces were known to inch up from behind walls, stretch a stunted hand and switch off fans and lights, all in the name of sport. But no childish cackle followed, no little feet scurried, so it must have been the power people, who unfailingly did this when it was unbearably hot. It was a kind of research to see if people could actually melt into sweat, Velyammavan had told us. At summer's end they came to tally human puddles on the pretext of checking the meter.

'And better get used to missing each other,' Amma continued, the cessation of ceiling fan making her voice louder. 'Our Choti wants to get married right away, which means she will be out of here before we know it.'

'You don't understand,' Badi scrunched forward, allowing her oily plaits to swing down on the pillow in her lap, her breath rustling the pages of the book she had trapped between her face and the pillow. 'She cannot go with *him*.'

'Badi is eating the comic!' Amma shrieked. 'She is a goat.'

Impatient at this determined note of gaiety, Badi snapped, 'Send us to Papaji if you are tired of us.'

A shortlived silence and then—bam!—as suddenly as Badi had yelled, Amma had slapped her, jostling me between them.

Badi convulsed back onto the bed, the pillow and the comic book still over her face. She was saying she hated, she *really* hated Amma, but her voice was somewhat muffled.

I looked at Amma. Amma was looking at the fan when suddenly Badi swung back to her haunches on the bed, hissing, 'He is a *man*. And he will do things to her. Any mother can see that.'

'What...things?' Amma's voice had gone dead quiet and I hoped the comic book would absorb Badi's reply, but no such luck.

'You know, what he tried to do to Kanakamami. He's always staring at us with the strangest eyes and sometimes he...touches us when no one is looking. Ask Choti, she knows.'

Amma turned to me; only her chest moved, in and out as she breathed. My options were limited, she couldn't see that though. I felt invisible, insubstantial and a curious ambivalence toward myself, the self that was inclined to interrupt, interfere. So I just sat there *breathing*; up my nose and down, not saying anything. Nobody believed me, anyway, I was thinking. I am small and stupid and said to steal.

Badi slowly sat up again, pages of the book sticking wetly to her mouth. Amma swallowed, leaned forward and gently wiped the stuck pages off her face.

At that moment the power people decided to postpone their experiment and let go of the fans. With a mighty creak, the blades began to rotate again, slowly at first and then with gathering speed, pushing the thick air round and round between them.

Badi turned over and looked at me triumphantly. I turned to my side, so that I did not have to look at her anymore. Yes, I loved her, but right then I hated her.

'Choti,' Velyammavan called out, bent on all fours. 'Come, sit. You used to make me a horse when you were small.'

'She is no longer small,' Amma pronounced, her eyes tightly fixed in her face. 'Why don't you get yourself a wife? It's obvious you are missing married life.'

He looked up at Amma. He had to look up since he was still at ground level, like some post-modern coffee table carved from human flesh.

'I said you need your wife,' Amma repeated, since he had made no reply.

'Yes,' he said slowly, sitting on his haunches, like baby elephants at the circus did before the ringmaster. 'I suppose I do. It is no secret.'

Ammooma butted in, 'No use talking about second marriage, Mangala. He won't agree, how much I tried. He is trying to be hermit and live in jungle in future I think.'

'I am not interested in his future. Only in the welfare of my children, who happen to be girls, unfortunately.'

Ammooma quickly shepherded us children out of the room, so that we had to lean against the door to hear the rest.

'Do you think I am cheating you out of anything?' he asked in a reasoning kind of voice.

'I am not talking property or inheritance or family share here. That is not the only cheating there is of women.'

Now Ammooma's exasperated voice boomed, 'What you talking about? Spit it out straight, girl.'

Amma replied, 'I am ashamed of my brothers,' and burst into loud sobs. These were punctuated by louder sobs on our side of the door as one of the triplet aunts trapped between me and door grew panicky about respiration and the rest of the conversation ceased to be audible thereafter.

Soon after that Velyammavan vanished without farewells or those specially flavoured kisses of his.

For the short while before he left, there was a ban on our movements, which included strict instructions to scoot double-quick if he came socialising.

'Come here,' Velyammavan had gestured to me. He bent to my ear and I swallowed, thinking he was going to grill me on my role in his newfound familial status. But he only asked, 'What can I get you this time?'

Something big, I was wistful.

'Ah, naturally, the spectacular,' he had nodded understandingly. 'But you know the spectacular is for mundane people. It is for the boringly ordinary so they can get away from the dreariness of their lives. Not for us.'

Which meant, I guessed, that nothing was coming my way. 'Why is no one talking to you?' I dared to ask since no gift was on the line and braced myself for Badi-like disdain of my immaturity.

'Grown-ups play such games sometimes,' he said after a while, which was as bad as the disdain in that it explained just about nothing.

Then he left and this time we were careful not to set up a dual-frilled farewell committee at the gate. There were no affectionate admonishments, no impossible prize announced for academic excellence and no small voices chirping ta-ta.

6

KANAKAMAMI RETURNED FROM HER SEMI-RETIREMENT WITH a deep look of suffering drawn like a transparent veil over her face and Cheriyammavan still hovered around her like she was a fragile parcel marked 'this way up'. The hovering was official. 'I do not know what you may say to her next and upset her. Remember, she has left her own home to make her home with us.'

'He is a dog,' Ammooma muttered and I took great offence, mistaking her comment for a compromise with me. I still wanted a dog, you see, and what good would tying up Cheriyammavan to a post in the front yard do?

'Eldest children are innocent,' Ammooma maintained deep in her heart and on the tip of her tongue, 'They are kadinjool pottan. But the second sons, you have to beware them.'

But when Dasamma reiterated the same wisdom of first-born innocence, Ammooma shooed her away. 'Eldest-youngest nothing! In the end, sons are sons until the day they marry. Then every man turns pottan.'

Dasamma tried her diplomatic skills on Kanakamami too, divining somehow her complex rivalry with our dead aunt, who had been fair and had had a definite bosom, however itchy. Dark and flatchested, Kanakamami secretly relished

Dasamma's pronouncements against her sister-in-law, but with a suitable tch-tch full of respect on her lips.

'Breasts like deadweights on a donkey's back,' Dasamma dismissed while Kanakamami went tch-tch.

By and by, dust settled over the recent disagreements and Kanakamami's martyred expression began to slip now and then. Long confabulations late into the night between the adults concerned us not in the least as we children were busy welcoming the monsoon.

There was self-drenching to be done, clay to be kneaded into pots and pans, ripe mangoes to be suckled, various versions of newspaper boats and kites to be launched in the sea and sky, respectively, and a grown-up's watchful eye could only cramp our style. Hence, we went about our business as they went about theirs, little knowing that the two businesses could touch toes eventually, could dovetail, that the polite words spoken, the goodwill and wishes around us were all an act of impossible jugglery.

Three perfect months followed, days filled with barely remembered activities, conversation and routine chores, dragging the stole of pleasant mindlessness in its trail.

Dasamma grumbled that inflation warranted a raise.

'Thankamma said she'll pay me the same as you,' she told Ammooma. 'As if! I told her these people my own people, not to mention old customers. How I ask them to pay more? But my rates have moved on, oh yes, they have. So she pay me double of what I am getting here.'

'They eat meat,' Ammooma dismissed, as if our lentil-based use of toilets was somehow more light-hearted work.

Hunching over masses of petals plucked fresh from our yard and stolen from nearby gardens, stirring them occasionally as if we were cooking up a floral broth and not creating a pookulam, we were biddable and pliant as the flowers we fingered.

Butterflies and burning lamps and burgeoning bananas tricked us into the shortest Onam ever; a blink and the coconut milk in the ada-paayasam had curdled and the petals had dried into a handful of manure, but that was nitpicking.

The sparkling pookulam of the previous day turned pyre for a princess, played by an aunt with a marked lack of majesty, to make up for her Spicy ordeal. We collected twigs in firewood for the regal corpse and had covered her till neck with timber, swathed her small face with red gauze and when Amma found us frantically rubbing stolen matches, aunt had almost caught fire from the noon sun.

I did catch words, meaningless words I stored up for my mind, which was a vast warehouse on the lookout for something to store.

'Best before makara velakku, Mangala. This year I have to go to Sabarimala, I already promised Ayyappan.' Cheriyammavan's piety overheard and broadcast by me drew only a grunt from Badi.

'Now he will have to sleep in another room from Kanakamami. Ayyappan is not one for hanky-panky.'

And I clamped down the swift rise of my eyebrows. Badi was forever hinting mysteriously, but I knew that questions brought no straightforward answers from anyone. Waiting to grow up was ordeal enough.

Even when Dasamma visited us one day with crocodile tears swimming up her cataracts, we failed to be alarmed. And there really was no need for alarm because I was growing up fast and was almost grown up when Amma caught me to her, explaining that she had to live here forever, but that Papaji was lonely for us and that we may have to go and keep him company once in a while, one by daughterly one.

Kanakamami sat with us in the fine sand of the courtyard and casually praised Papaji's family in her first attempt at reconciliation with me, her warmth at odds with the contents of the conversation.

Wordlessly, Cheriyammavan fiddled with the rudraksh beads around his neck, his brand new 'Ayyappan' dhoti flapping blackly around his ankles, obstructing his foot at the accelerator as he drove us that day. He had no compunctions about using Velyammavan's vehicle. 'He owes me,' he had told us when we girls—eager for free rides anywhere—had asked him.

The aunts had wept up a storm at the gate; they were left in Dasamma's care for the day once again with a strict warning not to invade the nearby paddy jungles and were suitably wilting under the resultant pressure of now having to raid the fields just for rebellion. We had set impossible examples for them to emulate!

Inside the high-court premises, Badi and I played Feet-Out, a reflex game which consisted of jumping on the other's feet after several misleading flexings of knee; the one whose feet were squarely jumped upon was loser. Ammooma and Amma sat close together on a cement bench and Cheriyammavan and Kanakamami were sipping tea from smoky glasses. They were all staring at the gate and Badi fooled me with sudden backward looks, causing me to be footed-out constantly. When Papaji was finally spotted, Kanakamami and Amma rushed animatedly at us with some final advice.

'He is a good man and he will look after you very well,' Kanakamami vouched with a falsetto lilt.

'When you are asked whom you want to be with, say me,' Amma counter-vouched pointing earnestly at herself as Papaji, turbaned in loud pink checks, reached us. He examined us unsmilingly—I looked away just before he reached my eyes, a ruse I learnt at school when teachers brimmed over with trick questions—and then vanished into a room with Amma.

So that was Papaji, I thought, with more curiosity than premonition.

'He does not look like a singer,' Badi opined, disappointed at the well-fed visage of our parent, having imagined a delicately built man with long tapering fingers.

Not taking my eyes off her feet—Badi's a cunning devil, see—I gleaned, 'You do not remember him, do you?'

She sniffed a sniff of defeat and jumped squarely onto my feet.

We could barely see them as the room was very crowded and everyone in it seemed to be talking at once. Then, after I had been slowly and steadily footed-out for twenty minutes, they returned with a stranger between them.

'Badi, Choti,' Papaji called in an authoritarian voice. 'Come here. This uncle from the court wants to ask you something.'

Court Man cleared his throat. 'Disha Ahluwalia and Drupa Ahluwalia, your parents, who have lived separately for seven years, desire to make this separation legal.'

'Which does not mean anything,' Amma anxiously put in.

'So,' continued Court Man in a louder voice, throwing her a displeased look, 'the law has decided, in your best interests, that you will both live with one of them, keeping each other company. You have to decide whom you want to live with. Column one, Sumangala Namboodiri, and column two, Kedar Ahluwalia. You girls can choose.'

Both Badi and I did not speak, chiefly as he had not specified when we had to make this choice.

Amma gathered us to her tightly, saying, 'Their place is with me.'

Simultaneously, Cheriyammavan said, 'Mangala, it's all decided,' and Papaji shouted, 'Don't confuse everything now. They are small and can adapt.'

How did being small make our need for Amma any less, put us out of her column? I wondered.

'What has he offered, Mangala?' Cheriyammavan asked in an undertone. Amma's whisper failed to mollify him. 'You can't live on that, plus bring up two children, that too girls. That's way too less, bloody singing Sardar! His word has never been the best part of him, Kurup's orapu it is, nothing we can trust! Best to let go, let him take them to Delhi, you have to think of a new life.'

He turned to me urgently, his rudraksh beads swinging brownly. 'Tell them what Velyammavan did to you. Velyammavan is her other uncle, you see,' he explained to Papaji.

'He went down on his fours and asked her to ride his naked back. Shameless is all I can say!' Kanakamami put in, when I had not spoken a word.

'Mangala, is this true?' Papaji asked. 'Is this true?' he asked Badi and me.

Kanakamami put an arm around Badi. 'Don't be scared. This is the time to speak up, molu.'

'He's not been himself ever since Kutti died,' Amma mumbled.

'Badi?' Papaji's voice had risen.

'Y...yes?' Badi stammered.

His demeanour glacial, he asked, 'What exactly **did** he do?'

I clung to Badi's hand.

'Yes, what *exactly* did he do?' Amma asked desperately, albeit belatedly, replacing her previous preference for haziness when it came to details.

'Isn't it enough she has suffered because of you, must she suffer all over again in public like this?' Papaji neatly turned the tables against her, though she had merely echoed him in the matter of queries. 'And you call yourself a mother!'

Bristling, Amma sundered our hands, holding them in her own, tugging us hard so we tripped and fell against her. 'They are mine,' she was screaming hoarsely. 'I delivered them, looked after them. They are not your babies. I just lied, they are not yours at all. Oh yes, I slept with all those men you suspected me of sleeping with.'

Papaji rushed at us, 'Everyday ice cream, films with long-long songs. There is a television in my house, just for you. There is Daadiji, Guddi Mausi, your cousins, aunts and uncles, all waiting impatiently to see you, play with you, love you.'

Amma declared authoritatively, 'Your mother is a congenital idiot and Guddi,' she threw us an earnest glance, 'Guddi is not really anybody. Just a slut who lives with him, a blood-sucking leech he wants to marry.'

She pulled at one end and Papaji pulled at the other, causing inertia in the middle where Badi and I stood with linked hands so that we hardly budged, bewildered by the facts of life in such minuscule capsules that stuck in our waterless throats and the tears streaming down Amma's face and Papaji's loud pitch. If someone clicked a picture of us right then, we'd have looked like that family planning advertisement: 'Hum do, hamare do.'

'They are Punjabis, Mangala, *Punjabi*s. Do you get that? They are mine, they have my blood running in their veins.'

'What about me then? What about my share of the blood?'

'So what do you suggest? Cut them in two down the middle?'

At that point Amma put up a theatrical hand to her head and fainted, which conveniently all.

'Hasn't eaten all of yesterday, foolish girl.' Ammooma clucked over her.

Cheriyammavan hastily took out a suitcase from the back of the car.

'Come,' Papaji ordered us, extending a hand to Cheriyammavan.

Cheriyammavan pounced on Papaji's hand and shook it warmly. 'You are doing the right thing. The right thing.'

Papaji, whose extension of hand had been for the suitcase, gave an embarrassed cough.

'You are taking pieces of our heart with you,' Kanakamami told him tearily. 'Be gentle with them.'

Surprise at being parts of a great human organ silenced our tongue and while we grappled with it all, she fell upon us. 'I will not say farewell. I will *not*,' she emphasised. At the gate, she clasped me in her arms. 'Choti, don't forget this aunt of yours.' As I struggled against her granite chest with all my might, she aimed a damp kiss at my forehead. A timely tilt of my head got her a mouthful of hair instead.

'Here,' she said to Papaji after she had anointed Badi too with her spit. 'They are yours now.'

Despite the novelty of Amma lying bang in the centre of a crowd as if in her bed at home, we keenly observed Papaji transfer our suitcase into another taxi against which a portly woman was leaning in an exhausted manner like she had tried all the doors and failed to squeeze an entry. She moved away lethargically at our approach.

'Myself Guddi. Yourself?'

Wordlessly, we stared at her. A fishbone seemed to have walked out of her throat to strangle her as pendant. There were other bits of bleached metal—platinum, we learnt later—twisted around her fingers and wrists so that she seemed almost shackled. On her part, she politely pretended we were just what she expected.

Papaji picked me up and then promptly forgot to put me down, so that during the car ride and later at the airport he kept me on his lap, humiliating me beyond belief by the seating arrangement. Only Kanakamami returned my wave cheerily from the rolled-down window. Cheriyammavan and Court Man were knee-deep in talk. Ammooma was bent over Amma, still stretched out on the ground with feet up and bare in the air, sort of in goodbye.

At the airport, Badi drank coffee from a Styrofoam cup. According to Amma, coffee was digestible only by adults, so when Guddi Mausi asked, 'Will you have coffee, Disha?' Badi jumped up. She was so dying to be big!

'What about you, Drupa?' raising eyebrows she turned to me, taking our addiction to caffeine for granted, something to do with our mother's southern blood vitiating our veins.

But I hid my face in Papaji's shoulder where I was still hoisted against all dignity. Badi then unwrapped the banana fritters Amma had packed for us, but before she could bite into one, Papaji cleared his throat.

'Throw them,' he decreed. 'They must have rotted.'

Guddi Mausi wrinkled her nose, looking askance at the oily snack like they were bits of fried python. 'Not a summer snack, *nai*?'

'It is coconut oil,' Papaji apologised.

In the plane I was duly unpeeled from laps and belted into a seat of my own at last, right next to Papaji. I promptly turned my attention to the window through which filtered in the most blinding brightness so that the glass pane appeared aflame and I had to shade my eyes.

'Stop snivelling. She is as good as *dead*, do you hear? I am all you have now,' he snapped, forcing down my hand and handing me a comic book.

I opened the comic book in which the Sun God's sunflower-yellow face was wreathed in crayon smiles, quite unlike the explosion in the sky that the eye couldn't meet. I stared into the pages till the bile rose in me. Then retching, I spat out a saline puddle. When the plane taxied, the puke tilted, reshaping its oblong liquidity into an encircled diameter with frothy offshoots of sunbeams and by the time someone stepped into it, my sun had soured.

Part II

A Specific Winter in the North

7

RADHA'S HIND LIMBS SNAPPED A RUBBERBAND AROUND Krishna's knees while sarees flowed over Draupadi's shoulder in endless seconds sales and Sita sat cross-legged in fire with the inscrutable smile of the urinary-infected; the three coming together on the canvas in a mythological joint venture to hammer home the Purity Point.

'Relax, it is only an internal check-up,' the doctor murmured.

Drupa bent to clamp down on the gloved hand that delved down determinedly to her groin. Together they appeared to be grinding fresh flour out of whole wheat in an old-fashioned chakki, bobbing round and round as neither gained upper hand; his delving, hers blocking. For pure recreation, long walks on beaches beat internal check-ups hollow any day.

'Appoopa,' she chanted by habit.

Already a eunuch had flagged her down with claps in broad daylight last week like she was a cab. 'Beta hoga, beta. Don't forget me then.'

'A hijra,' Kedar had explained to Choti when a sari-clad eunuch waylaid them once, 'is both a boy and a girl. A hijra is a...Birl.'

'Am I a Birl, Papaji?'

Drupa had run to the chemist and checked her pee, known then that it was true, she was with beta, though it had galled her to be the last to know. God knew, having the baby was no option though the Birls assured her a standing ovation despite her betrayal of the Birlhood by breeding. She had been a Birl in name only!

When she was ten, Guddi Mausi had pointed at the first little black and white TV set Drupa had ever set eyes on and told her in very, very tragic tones, 'That woman will never get her virtue back again. Purity, once lost, can never be regained.'

Guddi Mausi, current choreographer of the 'Save what's left of the Purity' campaign, slumped in the corridor, drowsy head flopping to ample chest. Despite the rightness of the latest little Ahluwalia, thoroughly illegitimate, being sent on his way, it wasn't an easy snooze, not when she kept changing the dramatically casual excuse she planned to mouth for any friends or foes who might wander in here and wonder—Vaahe Guru— why she was lounging about in an obstetrics ward at her age!

Steps echoed along the corridor and she sat up with a cranial jerk that rattled the tassels on her henna-red plait. The spiky stilleto heels of Drupa's sister, whose terminal thinness sent fresh shockwaves along Guddi's well-padded nerve-endings, soon emerged. They propelled into sight a deadpan Disha who picked a bony arm out of her pocket to point vaguely at Guddi's feet, 'Pairi pauna, Mausiji.'

'Jeendi-re, Puttar,' Guddi beamed at her waif of a step-daughter; so starved, poor thing, her ass had fallen off somewhere.

'How is Drupa?' Disha's pout grazed Guddi's dimpled chin, which the girls had long ago christened 'Baby's Bum'.

'Giving his medical examination,' Mausi informed, unfailingly exchanging gender pronouns. The exact nature of her widowhood baffled new acquaintances when she soulfully claimed to miss her 'Her'; but to old friends, a reference to 'him' would've only produced a mental picture of Kedar in a skirt. She counter-asked absently now, 'How is Dave?'

Plucked eyebrows levitated and a delicate shrug released eau-de-cologne trapped in armpits. Disha passed most queries on spouse.

'You smoke and smoke and can barely stand!' Guddi grumbled, preparing to leave.

Disha tucked the lit cigarette behind her ear as hibiscus to execute impromptu an impure form of Flamenco, swishing an imaginary skirt. Guddi's groan and eventual departure had her lean against an antiseptic wall and blow languorous smoke. A passing nurse admired the mural she thus made; the streaked hair, the lycra skin, the peekaboo nipples ready to be rung like doorbells. Where Drupa had all the sartorial sparkle of an old maid, Disha was the centrefold; she highlighted the humdrumness of other women with the bright plumes of her daring. The nurse watched the wraith by the wall and quite forgot to point out that smoking in hospitals was just not on.

Lying in stirrups inside, staring at meaningful portraits of chastity on the wall as poke, poke went the quack, Drupa was well aware of the Purity leakage in progress. Her family had rallied around, of course, declaring Emergency, for it was a collective shame and therefore a collective cover-up; mourning less for the foetus, more for her innocence. Nothing keeps in this sly winter heat, least of all me, Drupa sighed. She remembered the garish painting in her geography classroom, where the setting sun cast its own shadow in the waters so that another sun seemed poised to rise right under the setting one; the two suns blocking each other from rising and setting, respectively. One had to give to make way for the other, so here she was.

She had balanced a tube full of fresh urine—like a village woman fetching water from the well—down the hospital's sanitised corridor, conscious only of mild curiosity and a dismantled hair-do. Then the routine report turned up with its clinical verdict and her eyes had widened to 38-D cups while her lung lost its usual bargain with air and a chill ran down her legs as the tube tilted and the trapped pee flowed out. She hadn't wet her pants that bad since…years.

The displacement of Badi's hymen had been merely a loss of virginity, but this, what Choti had organised, was loss of virtue. The former had nothing to show for it except a stinging slap from Papaji and an outraged gasp from victim. But this was beating the jungle drums, a social announcement that hormones were gung-ho, wreaking visible damage with the whole world for an alibi.

'Breathe deep and slow,' the doctor ordered.

Drupa tried to obey to disprove the old adage that doctors made the worst patients, but her wandering eyes snagged at the dustbin where wet membrane from a leftover MTP lay winking.

'My vagina is burning,' she said.

Though she had come to a hospital far, far away for anonymity and the doctor who probed her had no idea of her own professional qualifications, Drupa knew he knew she was unmarried. She had seen too many nervous girls not to know whom she resembled right this minute. Perhaps he knew she was a doctor, too, a gynaec to boot, for who else but a gynaec said vagina with a straight face.

Still, there was this temptation beating up her temples to find out what books he read, fiction or non-fiction, what kind of movies he enjoyed watching. Did he catch the new offbeat ones with their Hinglish diction or the hard-core Hollywood ones on their post-Oscar strut? And last but not the least, did he go for baggy underwear like hers? She was single and, barring the current location, reasonably interested in meeting the right man.

But she knew he'd wince. Say the cottage slathered with bougainvillea and a feline creature sunning on its red-tiled roof can never-never be. Tiled roofs leak, cats carcinogenic, bougainvillea too plebeian a bloom and had she enquired the rentals for cottages in the countryside lately? Men were practical that way.

'Breathe,' he commanded again, oh, so masterfully.

She swallowed, hard-boiling to the toffee Amma used to get her the rare times she scored a perfect ten in her test papers, cut off in glitzy paper fans at both ends, candied in her own exhalations. When even oxygen got on her case and she had to apply for anticipatory bail at air headquarters.

Within fifteen minutes she was out, the medical termination of pregnancy scheduled for the next day, after which she could return home with squeaky-clean insides.

Everything matched in the room allotted to Drupa—the curtains, the carpet, the floor tiles, even the walls were a seamless bandage-white—the room seemed to have broken out in a leucodermic rash. Even as Drupa experimentally sniffled as prelude to a good cry, her sister sauntered in, a large ivory medallion lying on her sweater like a blob of milky vomit. She affected great astonishment at the skull decorating the pristine white sideboard.

'Yeh aapke bachche ki maa banne wali hai,' she informed it, gathering her multi-coloured hair into a ponytail with the air of tying a ribbon around rainbows.

At Drupa's look of irritation, Disha put up a pair of peacenik palms. 'But seriously, must this skull travel everywhere with you?'

Drupa shrugged. 'Not all of us can fuck the nearest man to feel at home.'

'Yeah, much easier to hang a scenery.' Her habitual pout bracketed by two sunken cheeks, painfully acquired by hunting down every last wisdom tooth, Disha was rhetorical, 'They'll make you numb, right?'

Drupa nodded, not wanting to set off another moral lecture. Numb she already was, thank you.

'I hate abortions. That's why I had Daler. Me, I'd rather have the baby.' A senior citizen in the Republic of Amour, Disha regularly paid taxes in the form of botched contraception and abortions. She patted a paper-thin midriff allowed to peek out despite the razorblade slash in the air, the muscles on her bony arms quivering and settling in what seemed a trick of light.

'As if I have an option.'

Disha fished for a fictional something in her suede handbag, the overhead light squatting vermilion on her head like she had applied sindoor with a Parkinson hand. Into the bag, she confided, 'You of all people know that the baby isn't Dave's.'

Oh, my God, I'm doomed to listen to everyone's debaucheries now, panicked Drupa, but managed the semblance of a smile at sibling, she with the dreams of posthumous lab-duels over her exquisite skeleton.

'Oh, I almost forgot.' Disha dashed into the corridor where she had left a bag full of fruits and flowers, which she then proceeded to arrange photogenically on the little side-table with her own two calcium-deficient brittle hands. 'That's why I insisted on calling him Daler.' Her other children were called Dorothy and Deborah, names that warmed the cockles of Dave's call-centre Anglo-Indian heart.

'I hate lilies,' Drupa declared abruptly. Nobody could deny her a floral prejudice!

All the self-help articles Disha read in magazines and all the new-age therapies she paid for had honed her sensitivity enough for her to guess, 'You're mad at me.' Then recovering with a sniff, 'It wasn't something I could mention over aaloo parathas and ask everybody's opinion about. Hey, listen, I'm having a baby, only it isn't anyone's you know. It'd be towed away like those fancy cars at the no-parking outside Palika Bazaar. Dave would've killed me,' stated Disha, who truly feared only osteoporosis.

Drupa rolled her eyes. 'Where *is* my Jiju?'

'Rock-climbing,' Disha peered studiously at the medical chart where a woman, in uncanny resemblance to Velyammavan's late wife, dipped to her own breast in a mammogram.

'What I don't understand is why he leaves you alone all the time! You can't be left unmanned even for a minute.'

'I do have the average marriage, you know,' was Disha's snooty response as she worked open a window on its rusty hinges; instantly, the wind was served chilled in room service. 'I know all there is to make a marriage work.' She put up a manicured palm in mock-holiness and intoned in singsong voice, 'Cross eyes at your man, but never legs. And don't ever go, "suck *that*?" when up floats his dead sardine.'

'First-born but secondary in every other way, that's how I feel,' she had snarled at Drupa once upon a time, frightening the younger girl. 'Why did Velyammavan ask you on his ship trip? What made you so special? The poor little child laying nice-round eggs in her report card! No daddy, no marks, on top of that an oxygen mask on head. What about *me*?'

This was during the first bewildering week with Papaji when everything looked spanking new and strange. Diverted by novelty, they remained disoriented by the determined familiarity expressed by the fluctuating folks around them, a populace they felt no kinship with yet.

With happiness a calculated average, the girls were hard put to balance their internal audit with bliss. There was only one rule here, under no circumstances were they to mention Mangala at all. When Disha in high fever once burbled for Amma, Papaji struck her hard across the face; he, who never raised his hand, especially not at offspring he hadn't seen in a long while, and he didn't glance once at Drupa when she burst into muffled sobs.

Guddi Mausi had dragged him into another room, heatedly chastising, whereupon Drupa chose to choke and wheeze and warrant a dramatic dash about town for an air specialist in Kedar's mint-fresh 'Choti di gaddi'.

'Breathe, breathe, beta,' Kedar exhorted in the backseat as Guddi routinely jumped red lights, occasionally rolling down the window to roar at cyclist or pedestrian, 'Baap ka raasta hai kya?'

Delhi roads were wide but at intersections they gnarled into jalebis in hot oil with drivers blinking colour-blind eyes, jamming horns and accelerators to rip past the traffic rigmaroles. Guddi made haste, one foot fatly on the accelerator, flipping the vehicle expertly under a vanilla-white moon. Besides, there was Kedar's cacophony to contend with whenever the car paused.

'She has stopped breathing,' he wailed while his wife ran right into a vehicular beehive. Cars from all corners converged as if for a hurried conference, at the centre of which two cars faced each other, one with its bonnet open coyly like it was being French-kissed by the other. After the illegitimacy of all drivers had been established, the party broke up amidst much tooting of horns. But their own private party continued when a lamppost seemed to detach itself from its moorings and shuffle unto them just in time to catch the car's rear wheel. When Guddi gingerly got down to inspect the damage, she looked not at her car, leaning against the lamppost like a dog with urgent bladder, but the immediate presence of a policeman. Men in uniform were all right in erotic fantasies, but up close they irritated her with their narrow interpretation of the law. 'Law!' the girls were used in less panicky times to the scoff from Guddi, whose Foofi's son was a law student and from whom one idle afternoon she had imbibed all she never wanted to know about the judicial system.

Inside the car, Kedar ignored the lamppost and their vehicular socialising with it. 'Breathe,' he reiterated montonously.

It was not that she could not breathe in as he dreaded, Drupa would have explained if he stopped shaking her head as if testing a coconut for maturity, it was the outgoing air that posed a problem, stuck a pebble in her throat.

That night, as Drupa struggled with each retiring breath, Disha had maintained an elder-sisterly watch.

Disha called her now. 'In the likely event that you don't tell us when your discharge from hospice happens, at least take a cab. And for God's sake don't haggle when you reach home.'

Duly, dully, Drupa obeyed despite the discharge being entirely voluntary. In the early morn light, she peered at the passing of familiar lanes made unfamiliar by discomfort and darkness. She realised, having emptied her mind of all thoughts pertaining to self, how the tenses mixed in the Capital's landscape. No particular tense, present or past, was preserved for a passenger's perusal. Willy-nilly, personal bank balances waved themselves from unauthorised marble minarets beside old crumbly domes where the homeless appeared almost surreal in the pearly light. Just before her destination, which she muttered inaudibly to the driver, the cement pavement abruptly gave way to a pedestrian puddle of blood and bones where police mapped out an accident site with chalk. Glass lay shattered ahead of the PCO van but Drupa, too exhausted to gasp at the remains of what used to be somebody, was just glad to be home.

Daadiji had taken them on a dawn tour, too, when they were children, to acquaint them with their 'true heritage', their roots.

'Nahi, puttar,' she turned down Kedar's offer of his Maruti car. 'Mendak ni chaheda meinu.'

Manfully swallowing his ire, for like most men who possessed a driving licence he had felt labour pangs in his mythical womb upon the Maruti's delivery, he suggested, 'Tussi woh jeep hire karlo-ji.'

Sitting in the backseat of the rented jeep, the girls often sensed a remoteness emanating from their grandmother, a bit like the breeze blowing in stray dubious whiffs from the tapering lanes outside.

'Better late than never,' she sighed, periodically peering at them from angles of short notice to accommodate the advance of long-sight.

Just when they were sure she was watching the advent of the dust-dry landscape en route to Karnal—the merger of the tarred highway with marathon fields of mustard, gesticulating blades of glinting gold instead of the pitch-black tar in the sun—the girls caught her eye, trained unerringly on them.

'Like God's picture in a room. Wherever you go, those eyes never leave you,' Badi groused in Malayalam, so that Daadiji went mistrustfully, 'Unhh? Unhh?'

The girls huddled b'twixt the plastic clingfilm on the seats and the airpocket that hit their solar plexus every time the driver braked with no warning when cyclist or pedestrian played king. The village they reached late evening had a tractor hulking by most doors and corn ears ripening in most fields.

'Punjab has always been prosperous,' observed their grandmother with pride, dipping her matri alternately in freshly churned butter and milky-sweet khoya. On the walls hung green bouquets of spinach, mint, mustard leaves and cowdung.

They nodded uncertainly, eyes smarting from the turnips cooking in a tureen next door. That night they slept under the stars. In the morning Badi shook Choti's shoulder under the quilt, almost dislocating it. 'Wake up, the old woman's asleep.'

Leaving Daadiji with mouth ajar as if addressing someone sternly in her dream, her drool irrigating pillow, they explored hastily the surroundings, aware of the servants lurking within earshot in the house. They leaned into a deep well in the field and basked in their boomeranging voices.

'Amma,' they shouted into the deep clandestine cavern, waiting impatiently for the tinned echo to spiral up a secret for their ears only.

'*Amma.*'

Daadiji either excruciatingly fawned over them or completely forgot about them depending on indigestion or glasses; the first at times whipped her age-ripened whimsy into 24-carat insolence, and the second was often abandoned atop her head.

Aunts in all shapes and sizes fed them refreshments in all shapes and sizes from fowl to lamb, dewy-fresh from the Jama Masjid area.

Uncles, in the evenings, were drunk enough to fall face-first into chicken curries while their wives merely laughed and dipped rumali rotis into the spilt gravy on the table with a frightening on-the-rocks insouciance, their plates rapidly resembling mass graves with exhumed remains.

Badi and Choti, their eyes and nose watering from biting too many red and green chillies, were aware of displaying some form of culinary cowardice. Accompanying Guddi Mausi on her monthly pilgrimage to stock up spice from a wholesaler in Karol Bagh, they'd meander through the maze of masalas, peep into sacks, pick up black or brown seeds and sniff delicately. There were huge black cardamoms unlike the gentle brown ones back home, which Guddi Mausi bought in bulk and stored in airtight containers in the kitchen. Sucking gooseberry murabbas as special treat, they'd affect an olfactory surrender to the mystical ambience of the warehouse.

'Condiments on kitchen shelves are a true indicator of prosperity, especially those pickle bottles with white fungus floating atop. It is like saying, we have enough to eat without licking at these,' the girls were told.

'Masalas are the key to immortality,' Guddi Mausi guaranteed, gazing intently at stacks and stacks of fennel seeds and peppers, going deeper and deeper into the labyrinthine shelves with pickled everythings, only the amplitude of her backside lagging behind at sharp turns to serve as visual guide. 'They light the fire in our belly and preserve our internal organs, so they last longer...like pickles.'

Blandness in food was misconstrued for blandness in character, but the girls couldn't, no matter how hard they tried, adapt to naked chillies overnight. They offered no theoretical antipathy at the table, but stomach linings retaliated with cramps and gastroentrities.

'Not drinking enough water,' Daadiji dismissed, unwilling to admit that tastemaker reigned only when it decentralised, not doused, disdaining the bland khichdi served up for the kids from the kitchen. 'Look at them! Ganga flowing from one nostril, Yamuna from the other.'

Peas huddled in urgent conference along their plates, spinach pooled like drying dung and potatoes with kheema in a tight clinch were accorded due privacy; cutlets were not cutlets any more, but patties with meat paste they realised. When it came to gastronomic feuds, Drupa and Disha charged in the opposite direction, fuelled by egg in ears from spitty whispers of well-fed cousins.

This lack of bravery relegated them to the second rung among their latest cousins and a faulty Punjabi diction secured the lowly position. The day Papaji and Guddi Mausi arrived with them in Delhi, the airport had been taken over by the Ahluwalia clan whose younger members ran amok in trolleys, their throats hoarse from being aeroplanes. Only the elder sons of each family sported 'Sardar' headgears; the rest of the masculine race was allowed to ripen naked-headed.

'Beta, these are your brothers and sisters,' Kedar had announced in a choked voice.

'He means cousins,' Disha whispered to an open-mouthed Drupa, whose cheeks were pinched non-stop and whose skin, unaware of the dermatological disasters in store for it, was a moist maroon with attention. Soon Drupa was hoisted on a shoulder.

'Say tea-pot,' a tiny relative addressed Disha, who was trailing desolately after the festive disappearance of her sister around a corner.

'Tea-pot,' she told the playschool dropout.

'Keep saying it.'

'Tea-pottea-pottea-pot...'

'She wants to go to potty,' he snickered and the festive procession halted to usher a reluctant Disha into a wash-room. 'Don't be shy, beta,' they kindly told her.

The significance of the noon hour—'it is 12 o' clock'— and most Sardar jokes escaped the girls totally at school, leaving them helpless to defend what they did not identify with but could not in all honesty deny.

'It is the legendary Sardar supervisor. At twelve, he galloped up on his horse, to check the work done in the days of yore,' an old uncle let on. 'That's history, by the way, not me rambling.'

Outnumbered and too stupefied, they took a while to come back. 'Malayalam. Say it either way, back to front, it's same,' 'Kerala, not *karela*,'—the incoherence engendered less pride on their part and more teasing on the others'. Accents were beaten to a pulp, camaraderie flung back on their face and their late aunt was freely referred to as 'Bitch'.

'What can I do?' Tej had asked Kedar in seeming innocence when the latter's daughterly delegation cried its lungs out. 'They are the ones with an aunt called Kutti.'

And when he left, Tej stuck his tongue out at Choti, 'So, Droo-be? Kedar ke keede...'

Even Kanakamami at her severest seemed so dear then, when they hunched under quilts and slept with their rumps sticking up, trying in sleep to preserve the remnants of an identity they remembered for a long while into that cataclysmic chill. When the wind was still and the waters seemed to lap nearby somewhere, then the touch of seaweed slimed their fingers and tears and dreams made everything soluble.

Late mornings brought yet another aunt to their door with skinless almonds soaked in silver bowls or saffron-softened milk in tall frosted tumblers, whispering, 'Kundi khol do, beta,' but they rarely rustled up a giggle between them even though Badi dutifully uptilted her posterior. Obscene translations had lost the power to comfort them.

Kedar and Guddi took to sleeping with them, acting like two solid bolsters at both ends of the four-poster bed with no deadline for sleep, no school the next day if that was what it took to exorcise memories, to shore up a displaced sense of security.

'Papaji,' Choti's thin voice trembled in the dark, without any coherent thought in head except the need to recharge audio decibels.

'Hmm?'

'Do we have to learn Hindi now?'

'Beta, that's your mother-tongue, isn't it?'

'Mother?'

'I mean, it is your real language.'

Badi, advancing awkwardly into full-blown adolescence and conscious of her lack of age-related cuteness, dared to intervene, 'But it is no fun!'

'No fun?' Kedar echoed, sitting up in bed. 'No fun? Listen to this. Dastakari, dastana, dastakat, dastak, daastan, dast, das: they are all words sitting within words like those wooden dolls you have. You open one, bang, pops out another.'

'How so, Papaji?' Choti could be relied upon to provide cues.

'Because, my nanhi rajkumari, they mean handicraft, gloves, signature, knock, fable, diarhhoea and the number ten!'

Burgeoning awe was duly articulated.

Choti stammered, 'Will I...I also become a singer when I grow up?'

'Anything, beta. You can be anything,' Kedar swore, washing his car, throwing bucketfuls of water at the Maruti's back like it had just defecated on the road.

'And can I be anywhere?'

After a pause, Kedar acceded. 'Why not? Would you like to sing something with me right now?'

Badi and Choti were in a fix. They felt they had already learnt all the songs there were; now it was just a matter of singing them. Then there was their sense of loyalty. 'Cheriyammavan has already taught us *all* the songs in the world,' they said in a small voice.

'There must be something he left out,' Kedar snapped. 'Hear this.

> *'Ka-ka kale bedon,*
> *Oon hei kya?*
> *Haan-ji, haan-ji teen boriyan,*
> *Ek maalik,*
> *Ek Maa-ji ke liye.*
> *Ek us gali ke Munne ke liye.'*

'Ba-ba black sheep!' guessed the girls, missing Cheriyammavan with more might.

It was their weeping that inspired one of his pop hits, the one with the bhangra beat in the background. To their general doubts on paternal love, he had vouched emotionally, 'Of course, I love you. Sooraj ki pehli kiran se, dharti ki antim parath tak.'

They were bewildered enough by the literary lavishness when he then reiterated it, edited it and ran around repeating it to Guddi and others till they all agreed these were first-rate lyrics.

Amma was unspoken realm, but the tears they shed he acknowledged with a tight jaw or ungrammatical Urdu poetry. When accused of her maternity-deficient demeanour, Guddi was plaintive. 'Arre, Mangala is the ISO-9000 certified mother. Labour pain-walee.'

Once when they had whimpered round the clock, Papaji finally gave up. Flatly, he decreed: 'Holidays you can meet that woman.' He always called Mangala 'that woman'.

Deliriously, they got out the calendar in their school diary and began to mark off the days, in a tearing hurry to march right into March, not speaking once to each other of the upcoming miracle, scared of dispersing the magic headed their way by premature vocalisation. They declared a ceasefire with their warring cousins and tapped their feet patiently for the ice all around to thaw into a beautiful day.

Papaji's promise made everything bearable for a short while, this forced crawl under the elephant's belly. They dashed up the terrace holding the crinkled cotton or silk strip of his turban at both ends, both pretending to be butterflies with unusually long wings, holding it up to dry so that when Papaji wrapped it around his head, he'd light up, 'It fits my head just right! Dried to perfection under a sun set in the sky just so.'

Apparently, not everyone could dry a turban with quite that perfection. It was an art, and his daughters knew it as if by instinct! Papaji would painstakingly examine their fingers by the brightest light to see whether there was any magic hidden there, anything that perfumed his cloth-crown in their handling. Despite his public praise, thankfully they weren't inundated with requests for turban drying as they had feared.

It was the Getting Used To season as the girls learnt to interpret Papaji's poetic fits, to secure paper and pen when they felt a fit coming on, to adapt to black salt and coriander garnish, sweet instead of salty buttermilk, they even got used to the shifts in Guddi's abdominal power centre, when occupants of an ill-fitting bra jostled for space with a galloping paunch.

Dreams imploded Diwali sparklers in two pairs of eyes, percolated snatches of Antakshari songs on their lips and between them, the two sisters were able to rustle up a semblance of interest in the new family milling around them as they waited out that winter.

Soon after that Choti was made to taste nectar, literally. There was a big do, not unlike Badi's mysterious one earlier, with relatives and friends infesting the place, simulating tender glances at Choti at what was her Amrit Chakna. 'Now she's a proper little Sikhni!' they exclaimed from time to time as she sat motionless in a chair.

'Drupinder Kaur, the five Ks are now yours,' Guddi Mausi solemnly informed Drupa, throwing a burly arm around the younger girl. 'Kesh, kanga, kripan, kada and kachcha.'

A bracelet of stiffened silver was shot down her wrist, a comb and rapier were added to her person, but it was the baggy underwear drooping to her knees that decided Disha.

'Hmmm...' she went, quite unable to hide her delight at the divine exemption. 'Hmmm...'

And when lice crawled all over the girls' scalps, a barber came home and sheared Disha, but Drupa suffered DDT powder and other pesticide on her head since her hair was never to be cut, *ever*.

Enviously, she watched the breeze ruffle Badi's hair into raven ribbons taking flight and asked balding Balwinder bua, who was undergoing chemo at AIIMS, 'Who is your hair-stylist?'

The wicked witches in Guddi Mausi's stories were all uniformly white. The dark princess always won the fair prince, harking back to which Disha flew all over Delhi with tail on fire, looking for a fair prince to call her own.

Her relatively lighter shade had ensured her kathak classes and a diamond nose-pin early in life, but it wasn't until she formally entered the marriage market that she took a lens to her hide. Being fair in the family wasn't fair enough, she discovered. When cousin Rupali tied the knot with a Kannadiga she met at IIM, the refrain went, 'She says English gushes out of his mouth like water from a brook. When the babies come, words can be taught, but can complexions come out of the pages of a book?'

The ensuing marriage melee, with sundry relatives of groom swelling the Claridges reception room happily but sootily at the seams, led to this newfound respect for an old-fashioned philosophy: fair was fair. From hereon, swore the more nubile members of the Ahluwalia clan, they'd shed their skins, marry and multiply determinedly away from what was their dim-lit parking lot in complexions.

That was why Disha happily alighted on light-skinned Dave, whose naturally blond hair was sallow like 'freshly laid turd' as Daadiji observed at the wedding.

But then Daadiji had never been known for her poetic bend of mind. It was the vast property in her name that had been her main attraction, for Daadaji had been handsome but broke when he contemplated marriage. Since he attributed his penury to the chaos of Partition and assets being purloined, his confession of her dowry's appeal was tinged with the pathos of a glamorous past.

To this end, his Sikh sensibilities managed to ratify Daadiji's premarital Hinduism, even converting her religious past into one of pure womanly devotion with mythological references galore to deathless fidelity, which he hoped would then spill over to his wife's and daughters' dealings with the opposite sex. Consequently, she oft alluded to a great-aunt who had committed Sati—an act highly commended by relatives of the deceased—as down payment in respectability for generations.

With a finger on her husband's pulse, Daadiji circumspectly hinted that the said lady had been first tricked to oh, just look up at that, and, caught off guard, nudged into her husband's funeral pyre in a smoothly orchestrated shove and then held down by manly hands so the ritual wouldn't suffer.

'But howji?' someone would ask, knowing full well Daadiji's itch to take centre-stage.

She would promptly get up and throw out both hands at a peculiar angle, twisting waist out of gear, and push air with all her power. Then she'd enact the hapless victim, widen eyes, oral orifice, jut forth hips at an angle—for the victim had been allegedly expecting Daadiji's aunt/uncle at the time—and zigzag across the room with arms flailing to the softest spot on the carpet.

Then, relenting at Daadaji's perplexity, she'd rekindle the feminine facet by adding, 'Bi-ji laved uncles' burnt hands with neem paste.'

Their children were used to her ranting, 'Let's go to Lahore and inspect your land records right now,' at each marital spat, lending some credibility to their suspicion that Daadaji wasn't averse to a bit of fiscal fable. Upon his death, however, they too freely spoke of ancestral acreage across the border, alas, never to be recovered so that their own children, in turn, felt the indefinable security of faraway funds. It was a heritage they felt free to pass on, taken into account its low-cost capital.

It was during a walkathon in Lodhi Gardens that Disha met her Prince Charming. Weekends she dragged Drupa, huffing and puffing, along the flowered pews and old monuments, her channel-surfing eyes on each male face in the crowd mechanically treadmilling against her.

'Remember what all halwayees say? Mithai ke saath, dabba nahi thola jaata. And your mithai has too much dabba on it.'

'Jogging...makes...the...uterus...slip,' Drupa would gasp medically.

'If it falls out, just skip lightly over it and carry on.' And off she'd sprint ahead in her effervescent Nikes.

Drupa would gladly collapse on a patch of grass nearest to her ass while her sister's perky one, encased in branded track-pants of exclusive pastels, swished past pretty as a sunset.

And here, among the sweating and panting populace battling their fat cells and neuroses, one nondescript, windswept dusk Disha stood aside and Dave stood aside and the next weekend they both stood aside and Drupa ambled up purely by chance to witness the twenty-four carat idiocy on their countenances during a dust-storm when, with mud in mouth and eye, they stared unblinkingly at each other.

'Like a scene from an art movie; girl meets boy in swirls of dust. Dilli vich luu, dil vich luv,' Drupa described later, with a gossip's flair for the dramatic. 'How does he look? Like the only son of Hrithik Roshan and Tom Cruise.'

Some energetic dates and a million goofy grins later they announced their decision to unite in holy wedlock. He was tall, fair and fit and Disha could spy themselves in mirror, mirror on the wall, well-toned shoulder to well-toned shoulder, the silver-foiled couple envied by all.

Daadiji only ever referred to Dave as 'that half-breed mongrel, who neither belongs home, nor to laundry-man.' The allusion was made so often, so spontaneously, that it merited a short form of its own: mongrel, half-breed, dhobi, all samples of the abbreviated synonyms. But that was behind his back. To his face she called him Sona, Makhan, Jamai Raja and other such kiss-ass terms. By being so categorically fair-skinned, he had won no ally in the family, only evoked a latent envy in their joint beige bosom.

'Darling, nothing vulgar,' tightlipped, he warned his new bride when Daadiji offered to throw them a wedding reception to counter the stark Christianness of the nuptials. He did not particularly trust a woman, however antique the vintage, who pumped his hand, up-down-up-down, with the most radiant of smiles as if drilling for oil while wishing him a Happy Good Friday.

'Daadiji, it cannot be a happy Good Friday,' Disha had hissed.

'Why, puttar, when it can be a good one?'

Daadiji felt particularly defeated in her own white-by-default weeds in the Gol Dhak Khana church during the wedding mass—widowhood had its unpleasant side—and the confetti she perversely aimed at his kanpatti had been the absolute last straw. She now strove, albeit belatedly, to appease religiously muddled forefathers frowning down from the sky at the absence of an Anand Karaj. A great-aunt who committed Sati and then this inter-caste indiscretion!

'I was not allowed to celebrate Kedar's marriage. At least, let me celebrate his daughter's,' she cunningly implored. 'There will be everything, from needle-sharp basmati to daulat ki chaat. By everything I mean *everything*.'

Kedar wondered when his mother would remember that his marriage to Mangala wasn't the more valid of his marriages just because it produced offspring.

'My son's fate!' Daadiji expostulated softly, but explosively, a long-sighted eye pinning down her daughter-in-law. 'Leave the pickles alone, Guddi,' she scolded as if playfully. 'Aren't you...?'

'I don't bleed thirty days a month,' Guddi replied good-naturedly, the barb about barrenness bouncing off her.

'Pickles lose their bite, you know,' Daadiji turned to Drupa, who had trouble segregating her menstruating days from non-menstruating ones. 'Remember that when you make pickles at your husband's place.' It was understood even in those early days that the dandy Disha dragged home would not deign to suck on small, sour things.

Drupa, by virtue of her general joblessness, was deployed to ensure that vulgarity stayed out of the process. Convincing their grandmother of the cost-ineffectiveness of a live band with goateed DJ, floral vehicles, lehangas dripping with glass and silver for female guests, chaat stalls all over the hired lawns and keeping her sense of tradition untrammelled taxed Drupa's diplomatic abilities to their hilt. That she still managed to appear unemployed was mere testimony to her deep sense of personal worthlessness and nothing to do with her career as an anti-vulgarity crusader.

'Darling, how lovely,' Dave delivered with gritted teeth as he shook hands with a large section of gaudily dressed humanity on an overbright stage and generally cursed the coincidence of Diwali falling on his special day. Disha dazzled in a vermilion salwar-suit cut on a traditional bias, her dupatta old-fashioned with bootties dripping like shooting stars all over, and was ravished by her own reflection.

That night fireworks had exploded in the sky, luminous and loud, and the stars in the night sky were banished by the synthetic brightness of ladees and bottle-bombs, fountain sparklers and chakrees that went boom in a tizzy. Ten days later the cosmic cacophony was reiterated for Guru Nanak Jayanti and Dave still couldn't put in a word edgeways. Guru Nanak's birthday, he learnt to his dismay, would always follow Diwali by ten cracker-riddled days.

Except for the inflection in the various 'Darlings' uttered by Dave, there was little to indicate marital discord. In fact, Drupa feared at her disposal a whole theatre of nuptial niceness, conspired to lull her insecure, nail-biting spinsterish soul, to pooh-pooh the erosion of natural courtesies in what was turning out to be a really long marriage indeed. Animosity had slipped out of the sleek, shiny counterfoil and now wouldn't fit back into its cover anymore. Round and round they went, going back to the outset, from the time their eyes met that first time, and he criticised the very way hers had met his.

Initially no one gave this union more than a year, causing the couple to coochie-coo determinedly at social gatherings, conducting clashes entirely in vibrating undertones, and, living with them temporarily, Drupa had found the tight-lipped endearments disconcerting to say the least. Love meant accusing him falsely of arch glances at a 'loose' cousin twice removed, and then forgiving elaborately when voices had reached a glass-shattering decibel, babies had shrieked, neighbours woken and passions assumed reasonably afire atop a creaky bed.

Late mornings found Disha arranging flora all over the house in various vases with cell-phone tucked firmly into the skeletal hollow between shoulder and ear, cooing trendy endearments.

Drupa once woke up to a clattering noise thinking, this is it, Dave had thrown his darling wife down, favourite vase and all. Violence forked between them, arching in the air and sparking on strangers in their midst, though he stridently attributed all pending decisions to insha-Disha.

Halfway into her second pregnancy Disha had anyway lost sight of the noble racist goals that had propelled her at the outset. All she wanted was the house, the car, the anything, and to that end she executed bearable sacrifices; no more polyester salwar-suits, no down-market haggling with roadside vendors. Chunky kundan nose-pins—she had a considerable collection—she threw like the bouquet over shoulder after her wedding at sister dear and Drupa was sorely tempted to pierce her nose if only to gain an extra nostril to breathe with.

Meanwhile, having worked a long thigh-revealing slit in her ivory tusker of a wedding gown, Disha angled for her ounce of romance. She set off a crafty system of indigenous demand and supply on an MoU based on sulks and satin-slips, and, fortunately for her, Dave's adolescent ardour had been honed by dog-eared imports of *Victoria's Secrets*. Which came first, Drupa often wondered, his suspicions or her infidelity? Whichever, suffice to say that Disha strayed, and mightily, from the straight and narrow path prescribed to all pativratas. This roused husband enough to rain blows or, which was more the case, gather her scrawny neck in two strong hands and squeeze, ranting and raving, interpreting her as 'chootiya', finding 'cunt' not evocative enough on the tastebuds.

Horrified, the family had congregated at first whack, all except Kedar that is, who had by then joined the ranks of the deceased and may have slapped her himself, given half a chance.

'Dump the Angrez ki aulad!' Guddi Mausi exhorted with flared nostrils. 'He was brought up on fairy tales of the other cheek being turned.'

But that was the first time Daadiji accorded Dave some respect. 'He is a *man*!' she said admiringly, stirring her blood-clot red pomegranate drink with a finger, the dry parchment of her cheek glowing, going back for the umpteenth time to when her own spouse had smacked her hard on the head for letting the crocheted veil drop at a gurudwara, unintentionally unlocking her libido.

Meanwhile, Disha decked herself deeper in coyness. 'I feel loved,' she batted her eyelashes, with a smile that ran like laxative across her pinched face.

Full of shit, was the general consensus, which was consistent with her weekly purgative sessions, Sunday to Sunday almost if one cared to keep count.

'Not enough grain in the gullet,' was Guddi Mausi's verdict.

Manipulating expertise creamy-smooth from spouse to the man on the street with a talent for manoeuvring fidelity in all technical correctness, Disha had managed with enviable élan, out-staring her brutal husband until he dropped his hands from her neck in defeat. High in her firmament of gin and fun, her first-world face framed by hair straight as lampshade tassles, she moved freely among the designer stores until her uterus went and blew up on her like a self-strapped bomb.

The girls produced by this union—Dorothy and Deborah—were curiously lacklustre, with lank tresses and a complexion pockmarked pinkly. Dave called these freckles 'just like his darling Boston aunt's' while Daadiji asked, 'small pox hasn't been eradicated, ki?'

Only Daler, born on a chilblained Thursday in December, had that supersmooth alabaster Aryan skin you could pinch scarlet, the blood just an organza membrane away. Though they pretended to chastise him for his uncommon colour and marmalade cheeks—'Saala gora'—the family touted him as their new mascot. They were saying, 'This is our bright future.'

'I plan to settle abroad,' Dave declared in general, holding his daughters, while his wife hurriedly sampled national goodies of the manual kind. 'India has *nothing*.'

Drupa had happily ascribed to the area outside the arena as voyeur. Outside, she had been outside until her tampon turned tail.

'It isn't...Dave's, is it?' Disha had interrogated one midnight, having phoned to confirm the parentage of Drupa's impending baby.

She wasn't the least bit entertained by Drupa's answering guffaw. 'This is truly an MTNL moment,' she trilled, dipping into the bowl of papaya slices provided for their abortional sap. 'One can't romance, not even in the most desperate of one's fantasies, someone who evinces such keen interest in the consistency of his offspring's stools.'

An affirmative silence followed, for Disha had enough trouble bedding her own husband. 'Then who?'

At the other end of the phone line, cradling the skull secured from a medical college in kleptomaniacal bravado, Drupa sealed her eyes with wax. 'No one.'

And she had hustled herself right into the grey land between married and unmarried by sampling conjugal goodies before they were offered to her on a joss-stick-studded platter.

Damn.

It wasn't her fault she wasn't in an average marriage like Disha, she wasn't an average girl in the first place. Hers was a dishevelment that failed to fuel fantasies of rumpled beds on hot summer nights, just an honest to goodness lack of hygiene.

Even then there had been enquiries. Like the time when slightly drunk and principally purple with imported make-up professionally plastered on, she had really let go at a baraat, magnetically drawing a mildly rich Sikh who braked in his balle-balle solely to applaud her pendulous pelvis.

Brighty Singh even twisted his handkerchief into an indescribable monument and went down on both knees since he was on the bulky side and a single knee made for a wobbly pulpit. 'Here is my Taj Mahal for you.'

An erection that at once brought to Drupa's mind the grimy debris beneath the glassy-eyed Yamuna River purely from an environmental point of view and quickened no obligation to profess undying love in return.

Disha, hard-pressed to pardon Drupa's mauve visage ('ummm...blue like Lord Krishna'), with sweat rivulets unearthing real skin tones in their wake, faked delight at this upstaging. 'You have begun to give out that smell, Choti. Now the men will come drooling.'

Alas, a false alarm! The men who approached were few and exerted admirable control over their saliva. Brighty Singh of the baraat crumpled his kerchief like the Municipal Corporation's heartless demolishing of illegal constructions and went his way when he sobered down. Suitors asked sensible questions and beat sensible retreats. No fault of theirs, no fault of hers, but she was just not going to get married.

She wore glasses set in concrete for one thing, visibly carried an inhaler for her asthma as well as the cigarettes that gave her the asthma attacks in the first place, and had hair that hailed from a beguiling widow's peak only to end at one, too. Facial features huddled haphazardly so that she possessed one of those unfortunate faces: average when animated, but in repose the countenance of a clown. Throw in teeth straight from Transylvania, a chin expecting twin chins, simian eyebrows, acne, and the adipose overdose almost got upstaged. Drupa was also painfully aware of Disha's precise beauty and of her own missing heritage.

She could have for instance, inherited two colossal eyes from Amma, at whose birth the name Kamalakshi was contemplated in tribute to the lotus-eyed tot, or the flawless full-cream skin that stretched goldly from tip to toe so that Mangala was almost called Suvarna, or even the crimps in her creased length of hair that no daughter could organise—

considering that she had two—in deference to the name classmates had favoured her with, Sukesini. Apparently, Amma had bequeathed her what she did *not* herself possess, since Sumangala simply meant happily married and Drupa, like her mother, was hardly wed.

'Has this girl swallowed a giraffe?' Daadiji asked when a post-pubescent Drupa began to invest heavily in height. 'Au, ab ruk ja,' she'd thump her granddaughter on her head. It was no secret that she favoured brevity in the female form on the grounds that short girls got short men *and* tall men for husbands.

While under her Janpath T-shirts, Disha sported trendy crescent moons talented enough to perk up like a pair of eyebrows, Drupa's chest went in for the Big Bang theory. This pointed largeness, with its inherent ability to indicate directions without verbal effort, also sank her shoulder not unlike a grocer's scale with secret weights under it, lending a lopsided droop to the breast and hip aligned with it. The puzzle of it was that the body had not come to terms regarding its relation to gravity; sometimes her entire left side sagged, and sometimes the right side shuffled out a door.

Secretly, this was the reason attributed to Brighty Singh's consuming passion, if the booze content in his bloodstream was discounted; one could barely make out the inborn tilt when she jigged behind the bridegroom's horse, a roomy venue owing to the animal's unpredictable anus—what bass drums can do to equine intestines!

It was also why guests had found her cute at five years of age when she pretended to be a kettle with one arm akimbo as handle and another at shoulder as spout. She'd come in at an asymmetrical angle—as if steaming tea was already aflow—that Disha didn't dare imitate.

'She looks good for her age,' a relative commented after Drupa had been exiled to the kitchen to get tea and namkeen.

Raising her sharp nose, a nose so sharp that one ran the risk of being impaled on it, the relative had laughed. 'So many divorces now, Guddiji, just keep reading the matrimonial columns.'

Good for her age! Unknowingly, Drupa had stepped into Deepfreeze. Ageing was anti-social, hence the tiptoeing around it, the under-eye creams. Inconvenienced by having to live life forward. Not backward, which would delete a year annually on every birthday—or would that be deathday?—to take life back, back till you were in a pram, then finally in the warmth of a womb only to detonate painlessly and silently into two unidentical halves that waited in their respective wings, disguised as nothingness, for future parents to be assailed by lust.

Of course, Drupa was aware of the specialness of her smile, though smiles were a moody thing at best. Had seen the lifting of spirits of all those who faced the smile, was aware of the forced or unforced elasticity in the nerve-endings as they criss-crossed across her cheeks and chin. Hell, her salvation lay in this smile. In her ability to affect bonhomie, to fake cheer.

'You can take Drupa to the water,' they said, after they had cried all over her and drained her to the bone with their woes, 'but you can't sink that smile.'

Unspoken was the comparison to the lush folds crouching at the bottom of Disha's face waiting to leap tiger-like, transforming her tameness into a vicious jungle, tempting men to taste her danger. It was a mouth that could collapse on itself, making for a blunt profile, but stood up gamely to frontal scrutiny. In the war of mouths, Drupa beat Disha only by a whisker. In all else, her sister was at the finishing line while Drupa snoozed, the hairy hare.

'A smile that dances into dreams,' her mushy father had drooled.

But even a smile that danced into dreams, Drupa knew, couldn't save her from culminating in crow's feet and wrinkles at the end.

Drupa had pals, but Disha had the proposals. The family had just begun to discreetly foam at Drupa's awkward gait at the gurudwara, at her inflexible matha-thek there that caught the eye of no prospective mother-in-law, at her thorough unfitness at the stakes when *this* happened; a demonstration that internal organs were in working condition, that she was fit, thank you. A uterine drill, so to speak. A trial run just when they had hoped in all politeness that, physically speaking, Drupa would learn to romance herself.

She returned home from hospital like a subjugated soldier, the mortally wounded PoW bleeding into bed-sheets who could never speak with pride of his patriotism. She clung to her porous purity in a predominantly doll-pink bedroom and dreamt incongruously of growing a moustache instead of child. She had so wanted to take after Papaji in every way!

Guddi Mausi paused at her needlework to shake head; not only had the curvature of her younger stepdaughter's spine hit a new low, the scenery she jabbed into the jute at hand was no *National Geographic* cover.

She shouldn't even be thinking this, but if it had been the other sister with womb woes, emotional stretchmarks there'd be none. God knew, she herself was no stranger to the perils of delayed mating.

Such a tragedy, wasn't it? Guddi asked herself rhetorically again and again in the solitude of widowhood and a general absence of ears in the vicinity except the victim's and those would never do.

The wall turned see-through at the window where a patina of sneeze-fresh mucous glisteningly misted the outside world and beckoned the eucalyptus-balmed inmates. Drupa's dry eye travelled decisively down the wallpaper where little girls in tu-tus twirled on their Bombay Dyeing toes until it slammed into the window and turned misty.

Compelled to inhabit the present since no one was prepared to do it for her, she never ducked players of noughts and crosses straight in her headachy path with either in a row; she just continued to stand and lose *smilingly*. As far as Drupa was concerned, there was a big No out there just waiting to get personal.

For some reason Guddi refrained from prying too deep into the grief that lurked in her younger stepdaughter's eyes, seeping out like rainwater from a filled pot and implanting cold horror in all those who faced that face, obscenely sad under its clownish smile. Better by far to get on with banalities, to take at face value and return with interest the muted bonhomie she gave verbal vent to. To that end, Guddi warbled a tuneless ditty and mused.

'I need a pearl facial,' Guddi declared restlessly, throwing the needlework facedown, pointy needle and all, least concerned about sundry bums that may sit on it and unintentionally embroider themselves. Crises drove her to the effete act of embroidery that graced no wall; even a rearrangement of fringe on forehead or bulldozing blackheads off nose was guaranteed to calm her dyspepsia.

The embroidery was easily explained. The first time Kedar suggested it, she had spewed, 'I am no Mangala.'

That was probably the only similarity she shared with his first wife: they each thought the other a laughable feminine stereotype. Guddi thought Mangala a dull housewife preoccupied with detergents and cobweb-detonation, while Mangala took Guddi for a commercial slut on the verge of taking over a chain of brothels.

After Kedar furnished a marital equivalent of a sworn affidavit to the effect that Mangala had never executed needlepoint except at gunpoint, Guddi happily picked it up and jabbed cloth and thumb alike.

'I'll ask Dish,' she said, taking for granted Drupa's refusal for beautification, examining the bottom of her skin-coloured stockings for holes. Not that she could darn; she only brandished the needle as hobby, it was important that nothing useful ever came out of it.

'Anyway,' Guddi Mausi went on, 'I want to talk to her. I want to tell her that zipped is more appealing, like a...post box. No one drops a letter into one with an unhinged door, swinging open wantonly. Not if they want the letter to go anywhere. This sho-sha crowd of hers!'

Laboriously, she got to her feet, the back of the Bonsai kurti she wore gathered into the bosom of her bum—most of her clothes hid in the crack of her ass when she sat, refusing to come out of hiding, waiting to be pulled out by hand. Guddi Mausi's personal touch was addictive, but she wasn't mean with it.

Off she went now, to play saviour to her other errant stepdaughter, to rescue her from the clutches of the Sho-Sha Monster lurking in Delhi's under-belly.

Drupa returned the wave, glad to bask solitarily in the winter sun stuttering at her window, striping her skin in lattice, content to watch her shadow shrink on the wall opposite till it condensed to nil in the latest edition of cold, foggy weather. Not that executive-class weather signalled an automatic revamp of despair, she sniffed self-deprecatingly, but for now, the only silver lining in her life was right here under her nose in a strip of snot.

Drupa groped for her glasses. Time to turn away from a wimp sun smudging up the sky, which could be trusted to warm no one, evaporate nothing, not even a tear or two. Time to feed herself. Food was her only companion. Constant. Though survivor's guilt did smite her in these encounters with food.

Unwrapping feet from their woollen shrouds, she wriggled toes. Some bare-naked feet managed to be tasteful, like they were the tip of an enormous erotic iceberg trick; twitch ankle and a whole unclothed body may slide into view. Not hers though. Never hers.

8

RECLINING ON THE PARLOUR'S CHAISE DISHA WAS WRIGGLING toes, too, in a basin of jasmine-scented water as she flipped magazines with a game look on her face, letting the sole male hands in the premises pamper her with a pedicure.

'Aah,' she occasionally moaned in encouragement, moaning widely acknowledged as her core competence. Thematically difficult to differentiate, moans, Disha knew, were separable only by application and to this end lost no chance to rehearse and add to her feminine reserves.

Ruminating on inner twangs was her sibling's territory and Disha seldom trespassed, inviting as she did oodles of informality in a remote-controlled way like that girl in fairness cream ads whose life was always saved by the timely advice of a friend, having perfected what Dave called an 'either-way' air.

'Look, she's got that face again,' he'd cry, clicking with his ever-present camera. 'Ready to join the convent *and* get married, whatever comes first.'

Perennially mid-crisis, at the edge of this or that precipice, about to turn irrevocably left or right, she was ever ripe for either of the diametrically opposing destinations. This rather furnished acquaintances the opportunity to counsel, to guide, to play God. She mirrored other's moods in instantaneous imitation, rather like a well-polished plate catching the light, leaving her with mentors galore.

A regular at the local gym, she signed up for overpriced weight-loss programmes headed by ponderous celebrity dieticians. A gold facial or farmhouse party with Bollywood starlets were average features of her week. Violently turned on by herself, Disha was in constant danger of giving herself to somebody, *anybody,* for affirmation of arousal. Even the liftman, who carried her bodily to bed when she slumped over drunk after a night out, was aware of an impending social overlap.

'Bibiji sleepy,' he'd mumble, pocketing the tip Dave fished out of his pyjamas, both men disregarding the disconcerting timbre of moans issuing from bed, which rather disproved the blandness of Bibiji's dreams.

The family privately mourned her exhibitionism just as they publicly did Drupa's plainness and halting vocabulary. Disha was even unable to adopt the physical economy that Kathak advised, flamboyantly twirling round and round during the chakradars with pedestrian embellishments and infinitesimal pauses between twirls, obliging photographers but maddening her Guruji into faltering in his bol.

She had once spied Drupa's rendering of twirls and huskily delivered kavit in her room and immediately made a joke of it, imitating not the rapidity of her rotations and revolutions, but the untrained gracelessness of the abhinaya, the inability to elevate solo eyebrow in mudra. But, she was the one who travelled abroad to perform, called up by troupes galore to exotic destinations, made to stay in lovely seven-star ambience. Disha came back from these trips loaded with cosmetics and clothes and a most curious satiety deep-set in her eyes.

Dumping her daughters—Deborah and Dorothy—with the big, beefy sister and going disc-hopping or shopping, depending on whether it was night or day, were birthrights Disha claimed without a conscience.

'They couldn't believe I was married, let alone a mother,' she often bragged, quoting a roadside Romeo or budding gigolo. 'How else will he seduce?' Guddi Mausi expounded circumspectly, patting saffron wisps of hair into place, when Disha was out of earshot. 'You'll never find them telling a young virgin that you look like a young virgin. Bhai, because she is. Men tell you what they think you want to hear.'

What Disha wanted with men who pulled out their credit cards and cocks, in that order, Drupa couldn't begin to envisage, but thankfully babies cured even the most chronically braless, and one day in the future, she hoped, her sister would settle down to home, hearth and the terminal thinness already attained.

She also wondered at the plastic money her sister flashed, though Disha was afflicted with what Drupa diagnosed as 'Brief Paralysis of Elbow' whenever money had to be paid. Ever since she had joined house-surgency, payments were Drupa's department. Pin Disha down on this or that and she dissembled like a doll; actually, along the way Drupa had overtaken her at least in ageing, not least because one of them tampered with d.o.b truths. Dave kept aside a hefty budget for his mountaineering trips, for his authentic Parisian champagne and caviar, and it was not possible to raise a family, however nuclear, and still change the carpet bi-annually, Drupa was well aware.

There wasn't much where Dave came from either, at least not money-wise. Two generations of the D'Costa family were known for their partiality to revelries and a lopsided spending on exorbitant guitars or first editions of ancient British bestsellers rather than the solidity of an overhead roof, preferring to carry on said revelries under a rented roof till dying day. They did not mind being accused of penury, but not being called a good sport would have cut them to the quick.

Three generations ago the D'Costa family did not exist, there was just a Portuguese soldier and a poor fisherwoman and their poignantly sordid love story that resulted in three blondes, one redhead and eye-colours inexplicable.

In December his family had kindly descended on the newly married couple and Drupa had been deployed once again to deflect any untowardness, taking into account Disha's mercurial disposition. Not for nothing was she nicknamed 'Bay of Bengal'; the depressions thicker and faster than her epithet.

On Christmas Eve his mother married herself in the seething kiln of the kitchen, baking rock-hard cakes that Drupa quickly soaked into solvent puddings, and fixing a minute manger with dried grass that advanced itchily up Drupa's nose and rendered it so roseate that she sang *Rudolph the red-nosed reindeer* with an autobiographical air.

Ma D'Costa sat shivering through the midnight mass as frazzled as Mary in labour. Her mission in life was to come calling for emotional debts and a live relay of all her sacrifices therefore crucial. To that end she toiled toward the toughest menial job in the domestic arena.

'It is a miracle Dave brushes his own teeth,' Guddi Mausi quipped. On Christmas morning she had disappeared on a long walk to Deer Park, clapping her ass behind her, partaking of a thela-driven breakfast en route, fearing the taut toasts back home.

His mother, claiming no intellectual pretensions, would shoot meaningless queries during Dave's anecdotes or the children's chatter. Cultivated or natural, she had the expression of someone with more urgent matters on mind as she slowly nodded before dashing off to some errand mid-speech.

'Like she forgot to flush,' Kedar had sniped behind her back.

'The real beauty of our family, my mother's sister, is in Boston.' Dave's frequent reference to his NRI aunt was a valiant effort to prove his Anglo-Saxon origins, a fact or fiction rarely contested by the Ahluwalias, the over-lap of Indo-Portuguese and Anglo-Indian identities seldom intruding into their thought processes except as a profusion of hyphenated words they had to unjumble inside the privacy of their heads.

Dave D'Costa's extravagance was high up on the mountains, mainly in Garhwal Himalayas, where he went with monosyllabic Sherpas and a backpack. Of course, he and his wife did not see eye to eye on this though invitations to scenic getaways were made and accepted on the honeymoon pillow before Disha impressed upon him the need to stay put while travelling, namely in a car, preferably deluxe.

The only time they seemed to reach an understanding was when she complained of nausea during the early months of her third pregnancy that he could equate to oxygen-deleted delirium on snowy peaks and they had stared at each other with sickly empathy.

Disha wriggled her toes voluptuously out of the warm, scented water and laconically blew bubbles with pale pink gum. Guddi Mausi looked deep into her own eyes in the mirror. 'You've left two blackheads on my nose.'

'That hair, not blackheads,' defended the young Manipuri girl behind her.

The parlour was purportedly pure 24-carat Chinese, but Guddi Mausi had taken each girl there to task, quizzed them about China and established beyond doubt their north-eastern roots, geographically quite a distance from any province in

China. There was a special rebate here for the Ahluwalia women, bushy-haired everywhere unfortunately for the 'Face of China' parlour owners, in apology for the Chinese con-job. Not that they were the first or last beauty parlour to don the Chinese mask in Lajpat Nagar, or even entire Delhi, new and old put together.

Disha was listening to the hairdresser with widened eyes as if the other was saying something wonderful. She always did that even if she was only being told there was something between her teeth.

'Bounce is out,' Disha protested, waving an emaciated arm. 'Can't I have Japanese bonding done? I look like Jennifer Aniston, na, so I need hair like hers.'

'Mmmmph!' charged in the parlour owner possessively, pausing only to extract a mouthful of hairpins. 'You need bangs on your temples.'

'Will I have to blow-dry all the time?' Disha wheedled plaintively.

A stout woman bent her head forward, revealing a neck-deficient back, her head attached straight to shoulders sans formalities of the flesh, advising, 'Just brush your hair like this.'

Then noticing the absence of an upturned mane, each strand of which was chastised severely with dampened henna, she emitted a weak beep of realisation, her resemblance to a cow that crapped on its own cranium so complete that it momentarily calmed the hair-hysteric mob before her.

Eventually, as she always did, keeping in mind the forthcoming tipping ceremony, the owner gushed, 'Such beautiful hair and skin. All the marks gone, no?' She turned to a thoroughly bored looking woman getting her nails done and in no position to break into a sprint. 'Always, always I seen baby here with goo on face, such good care she taken of self. And then to go have chickenpox on wedding day, it make me cry then and there. Shisha baby, remember how I cry that day?'

Disha, who broke into cold sweat even now at the memory of the heartless popping of miniature water balloons on her countenance as countdown to her wedding and who wasn't even Shisha baby to begin with, nodded. All her life, *all her life* she had patiently ground sandalwood twigs into paste in own gold mortar-pestle, applied apricot and other engrained scrubs and herbs, cleansed, toned, creamed and pampered her skin till it purred, only to have Drupa glow by default on the most important day of her life. Miss Drupa, who never sprinkled talcum powder even on the huge ugly brown vaccination scar tattooed into her left arm like a life-size sun she carried with her at all times.

'But by honeymoon time, baby back to normal, beautiful self,' concluded owner, mentally snapping shut the 'Wedding-Pox' file she had on current customer and opening the 'Retard-Child' one on Ms Manicure. 'Baba tying own shoe-laces at bus-stop I see with own eyes…'

By the time Disha graced the throne, everyone in the parlour had exhausted their entire quota of views on her locks, so that at the end she imagined herself to be in decisive hands. Debates and discussions, especially those that pertained to her, she took for granted. And when the scissors began to function, she said in her timid voice with its misleading question-marked uphill ends, 'A bit there, do you think?' And the scissors indulgently clipped a bit there.

Guddi Mausi glanced uneasily at the parlour girls. No one dared to catch her eye, fearing imperious summons for the performance of some menial act, enabling her to state hoarsely in a stage whisper, 'I am worried about *her*. Do you think she is depressed-vipressed?'

A film tune rent the air and Disha dived into her bag for her cell-phone. 'Jaanu...yes Jaanu. Of course.'

Guddi Mausi frowned. The Chinese food she had eaten the previous night had only intensified her dyspepsia and she rebuked the man at her toes. 'Those cracks have to go,' she said with the air of a nuke-strategist. 'Do it ekdum disco.'

The two women then turned themselves over to the unbearable warmth of imported bleach creams, their stinging eyes mollycoddled under rose-water cotton wads, going limp in limb and spine, submitting to the chemical magic of fairness.

Later they adored themselves in the mirror; it was like a wand had been waved along their bodies. But fiscal savvy had them shunt their features into a customary scowl in the centre of their face. Shifting dupatta around cleavage and t-shirt above belly, the two women inspected for fugitive unbleached patches, deliberately stifling any delight.

'Did you examine the expiry date on the bleach?' Guddi Mausi asked severely as prologue to the bill presentation ceremony whereupon she gasped and squawked like a dying parrot, albeit an albino one at the moment. 'Fleecing us. Calling yourself Chinese.'

Disha and the proprietress air-kissed like they were sniffing for earwax, 'B'bye, Darling.'

Guddi pushed open the stylish fibreglass door, twitching a cylindrical ass with a protracted fart. 'Now *that* was Chinese!' she gaily called out before disappearing from sight, a tress-teased Disha in tow.

The parlour owner, who had to keep her own stock high among employees, unveiled a bright orange head with a flourish and a snort. 'Saali! If there are no real Chinese parlours here, there are no real Chinese restaurants either.'

When Drupa first contemplated aborting the quasi-life inside her, she had felt no kinship for the foetus, had no inkling about the pain that would follow either way, of the sense of loss no matter what. And like with menstrual cramps, she attempted to roll with the ache. Guddi Mausi's constant interference regarding culinary and literary nourishment she stonewalled doggedly, focused only on equating the growth to a tumour or cancer, something that had to be plucked out and smashed to smithereens, something to be stubbed out with a toe. Perhaps, deduced Drupa, perhaps motherhood was hereditary; if you haven't a maternal example, you can't follow it.

'How are you?'

Drupa started. At the door stood an XXL salwar-suit, bursting with Guddi. The sun had long since sunk without a trace, plunging the furniture into shadowy hulks. 'You are back.'

'I don't have to wait there,' she shrugged, modest about small victories, trying not to wince at Drupa's hairy hands visible over the coverlet. 'You should've come with us instead of sitting around here...can I switch on this lamp? Okay, okay, no. You know Disha! He dragged me all over CP inner circle. Full of sales it is! I bought a shawl. Pashmina, they said, but I have my doubts. Disha was in a hurry or...why she wears no underwear, bhai? The poor, braless things on her chest, doing uthak-baithak! Chodo, tell me, how do I look?'

'Very...clean.'

Guddi Mausi gave a pleased smile. 'You should bleach, too. I tell you, unlucky things you are. At least both my parents were dark. Your mother was fair, Southie but fair. But both of you had to take after him not the gori Madraasan! Chalo...'

Drupa affected sleep, careful to keep her mouth slightly open; pug-ugly, she knew, was the key to natural. You could always sue pretty, but ugly was left well and true alone.

She heard Guddi place something newly purchased on the bed, a jar of herbal moisturiser perhaps. Tears made the best moisturiser, Drupa wanted to blurt out, but that would mean pretending to awaken. Against her will, a hand crept to her belly's underside. It was the cold that made her miss her mother, she wised up when it was warmer.

Guddi Mausi's footsteps were retreating.

'Do you think her feet are whiter too?' Drupa quizzed the skull, smuggled back home.

The skull presided majestically on a silk-covered cushion and, amazingly enough, winked.

9

$\mathcal{W}$HEN DRUPA'S FATHER PASSED AWAY THE PREVIOUS WINTER, Guddi Mausi had been steamrollered by grief. 'My best friend gone,' she had said in a flat alarming voice, the lowest pitch it ever plumbed. 'She has left me forever,' she added.

To begin with, it had been a year of funerals; months and weeks choc-a-bloc with deaths big and small. Politicians, business bigwigs, film stars, scientists and astronauts anxious to feature in obits fell willy-nilly by the wayside, obliging corpses one and all. But those had been faraway, black and white newsprint deaths, deaths in which they wrapped stale fish and soiled napkins.

'I may be dying,' Kedar, whose kidneys had opted for VRS, told her mildly during the pre-dialysis, post-deliberation days.

'Don't you dare,' she had cackled, peering into PC, sorting out junk in her mailbox, irate at the confused cyber-salesperson selling her cellulite on cleavage and cock at one go. 'Can't you see my hair is growing out? I can't go anywhere looking like this.'

As a second wife or stepmother, she hadn't meekly conformed to social patterning, so it came as no surprise when she refused to be clothed in white as widow. But the reason for it mildly shocked those who had thought her closeness to the deceased partly responsible for the decision. 'He/she lives on through me,' they thought she'd say with an otherworldly cough.

What she did say was, 'White doesn't suit me. May be if I was fairer...' leaving the listener with no choice but to protest faintly, 'Oh, come on, you aren't that dark.'

It was wonky Feng-Shui that did him in, she was convinced. Guddi practised it hotch-potch and ascribed all lucky events to their TV being in the west or toilets in the east. The death of her husband, she claimed, was culpable homicide by the wind-chime; the even number of its bells the metaphorical weapon.

'It could even be that we bought the Laughing Buddha for ourselves. I *told* Disha to gift it!'

One of the earliest Delhi memories the girls had was of her driving like a banshee to all the schools for Drupa's and Disha's admissions. Kedar had dimly recognised the necessity to educate them, but went soft-focus on details, leaving Guddi with no choice but to take matters in her own hands. Several schools had waved them away, 'Abhi admissions nahi hai. Close ho gaya.'

Until they approached the very last one on their list. The chowkidar barred them with demented determination, waving furiously for their car to turn its nose away from his precious gate. Guddi Mausi leaned out, 'Yeh Bhalla saab ki gaadi hai.' And the chowkidar melted into the cool damp air around him, the gates opened magically, and Guddi marched up to the principal's office where the nameplate read: *Mrs Bhalla.*

The girls developed a muttering of their own when they sensed the approach of her aggression. 'Betal, Betal, Betal...' Badi would hum under her breath, staring fixedly into space.

When the hapless victim began to stutter and stammer, Choti would join in tonelessly, 'Vikram, Vikram, Vikram!'

Gudiya must have resembled a cute doll as newborn to warrant such a label at the naming ceremony. Now some fifty years later, she was all puffed up as if too much air had been pumped into her, with plump hands and feet, manicured and pedicured, respectively, like the polished paws of a stuffed toy.

Gudiya had started life wrapped in the folds of an old maidservant's saree who hummed:

> *'Kaali re, kaali re, tu to kaali-kaali re.*
> *Gora sa ek bhaiyya ma ab lane wali re.'*

Though maternal loins did not spring forth the male fruit thus forecast, and Gudiya reigned supreme by default in the hue hierarchy, the racist lullaby adequately alarmed her into an almost umbilical attachment to umbrellas, muslin dupattas, face packs and milk-cream, anything that screened her from the wicked, wicked sun. Winter, with its dim wattage, was her season and even when all tugged at their charpoys to chase sunlit patches, she clung to interiors.

'Jaggery,' her father, a diamond merchant of some repute, called out when he returned in the evenings. 'Where's my little piece of jaggery?'

Gud, he said, you are my gud. But he was only using the raw material of her name to carve out an endearment, or perhaps that's how her name had come about, a ridiculous one for a woman who'd surely grow to adulthood and desi-ghee obesity.

When she was smaller, he'd say, 'Show us your jaggery nose, jaggery bum...' and so on but the dichotomy of a diamond trader dealing in grocery endearments hit her by and by.

Only her mother's strong and silent uterus contributed to her adolescent sanity; there was no heir in this particular branch of the family and Gudiya knew if a charcoal-coloured boy plopped into their unused crib, the jaggery crown would pass on. That was another guilt that ate her up, though going by her physical parameters it was difficult to imagine anything eating *her*, that may be she had ill-willed a brother away; a nice lily-faced, lily-livered little thing that would have ensured the family name's longevity by fusing concerned sperm to a pedigreed ovum somewhere.

Though Guddi Mausi's version of her early widowhood was liberally laced with celluloid stardust, the one her step-daughters preferred was their father's sighing—'on the first night Gudiya accidentally rolled over him, poor thing!'—which was comical in an antiseptic way compared to their Daadiji's, 'she was too greedy', imbuing needless nymphomanical nuances.

Barely fourteen, Gudiya had inaugurated her wedlock innings with a twenty-year-old zamindar. There was ample wealth and landed property, and if he wasn't exactly educated, well, our Guddi wasn't too pretty either.

Guddi publicly admitted to a palpitating heart in the vicinity of her fiancé on wedding dais, the first time she was allowed to venture near him, girls being on shorter premarital leashes those days.

There was some dissent from the groom at the wedding itself, which was vaguely dismissed as dissatisfaction with dowry but had actually been sincere shock at the bride's well-defined form, nicely lit up by the holy fire gurgling merrily between them. Since that was their first meeting he understandably reeled, but her relatives assured him of her golden heart, ruby lips and diamonds galore from father's kitty and he recovered.

'She kind of grows...on you,' they assured him, shoving him back onto the floral stage where a pundit yawned through Sanskrit shlokas.

At fourteen, Gudiya was not meant to biologically aggravate matters on the bridal bed. At best it was assumed she'd howl a stifled howl into her zari-bordered dupatta as the groom stifled himself in her, rather like a cigarette-stub met an ashtray.

She had been sitting there, on the flower-bedecked bed, trying to compose herself and pose femininely as advised by veteran brides in her family, when a little boy crept into the room.

'Bhabhi,' he said shyly. 'I brought you this.'

He handed her a glass of milk and Guddi, famished by the tedium of attending a wedding even if it was her own, grabbed it and downed it in a jiffy. The bhang went straight to her head and giddied grey cells into a fluffy vortex. She thrashed about the bed like a beached whale, her red sharara shifting over in blood-red waves, and mistook her brand new husband, who had been physically forced to join her, for a slippery pillow. And right there on the rose-petalled wedding bed, she pummelled him under her for comfort, reining in his seismic struggles with superhuman strength and snores.

In the morning she woke up, feeling something poke her middle and to her horror fished out from under her the smothered head of a beloved. It transpired that the groom's side had not let on an important fact about his health: he had a heart that beat, but barely. Now the important fact about his health was he had a heart that beat no more. It took the crisp whisper of many an RBI note to hush up that particular scandal and Jaggery baby was back with doting dad in no time.

It wasn't until much later, and when she was much larger, that she encountered Kedar Ahluwalia, a semi-relative, at a family gathering. They necked in parks, introduced each other as 'cousins' and celebrated the inherent incongruity of their association, married as he was to some obscure woman from the deep-throated South. The sweeping gloom that had been his involuntary domain was gradually burnished into a mild-eyed, attractive brooding; the union blunted the sharp teeth of his loneliness and took the edge off her social disgrace. If witnesses harped on the obscenity of a man hurriedly signing a wedding register in court with two daughters in attendance, marrying what seemed like fifteen brides rolled into one, they eventually veered around to her lack of 'encumbrances', the fact of her 'innocent widowhood' and the morality of marriages in general.

Gudiya had Mars practically squatting in her wedding houses, astrologers had warned when she was between marriages. She'd sit before them, legs folded sideways, oozing flesh from every fold, burping after eating too much too fast, and showing an immoderate amount of interest in her love life.

'You have to find someone with an identical Mars position,' the astrologers counselled.

But when Guddi lit on Kedar drinking lassi in her naani's house, Mr Mars meekly whimpered and slunk away from her chart without a forwarding address.

Kedar put down his glass and witnessed the large, flesh-dappled woman before him in Cinemascope vision, with hair streaming wetly like wind-combed waves, a wondering smile in anticipatory welcome of his whispered wit on a mouth wide enough to wedge a harmonica in sideways. Contrary to appearances and expectations, Guddi was at heart a Yash Chopra heroine and Kedar wasn't averse to the chiffons and lace she privately favoured.

He had gaped then, unmindful of the lassi droplets dripping from his moustache into his open mouth, and fallen thoroughly in love. Though this may seem to be one of those mad, impulsive moments, he had been careful to choose a mate this time who shared his linguistic and regional history. They spoke the same idioms and matched their earthy senses of humour. Mangala, his lawful wife then, had cultivated an inflexible blankness in eye and tone by and by, never getting what'he intended to say, letting him believe that love was a thoracic nuisance and lay in dialectic defeat. This time round love would not jump inside belly like gas.

If Guddi hadn't happened, Mangala and he would have gone on forever, he told her earnestly. His so-called love marriage had become a safe place as graveyards were safe for the dead. It was a place where he was no one; a dead tree was upright until a storm forked it out of the way, he declared with passable passion.

He followed Guddi in a hormonal haze when with coy, backward glances the miscast siren waddled back into the vast kitchen of her home and there in the acrid fumes of brinjals being burnt for the evening's barta, Kedar commenced his second round of courtship with coughs and watery eyes.

This time round he craved involvement, a hearty meeting of lives, less poesy, more motion to accommodate a long due blending at its core, someone to pierce the bluff exterior he projected by default, someone with a healthy bank-balance at her disposal to boot his daydreaming bills. Guddi compassed his career of sad ditties, which eventually steered to moderate success, and in most page-three photographs there he was smiling, second from left.

Kedar died a satisfied man, all were agreed upon that. And if his wife's refusal to wear white disconcerted his mother and sisters, his own eternal silence on the matter was guaranteed. There were some, of course, who cast aspersions on the purity of Kedar's motives, though they were quick to defend them, too.

'The influx of girls frightening him. Madraasan just wash her hands off them. Phoned one day, March first week, the day after the Chandni Chowk traders' ruckus, said they your girls, now only you know about them,' a relative declared with the authority of a freeloader who had hunkered down in the front room during a phone call, eavesdropping.

'I tell you!' exclaimed listener, to goad him into further insight.

'See, finally it boils down to money, neat and simple. Love, when it cost nothing, flies out of first open window. With a price tag, it wag tail, pay bills and Guddi loaded with the stuff. They tuck diamonds into after-dinner paans in her house! Once lights off, all cats same in the darkness, what thin cats, what fat cats.'

'Kedar's father was a rotter, too. Was house-son-in-law, ate off wife's family like a pet in a kennel and died a mosquito drunk on too much blood.'

'Like father like son, lucky vampires.'

Opinions on his intentions may be under a cloud, but Kedar's expression in death suggested that he had suited himself in many respects; his lax lips under the crispy moustache testified to this truth. While immediate family members sat about maintaining a dignified grief, occasionally referring to matters totally unrelated, thus mystifying those who had come ready to shed copious tears in condolence, the corpse alone managed a contented smirk, pulling off own death with rare elegance. It was as if he was a guest at his own funeral, so polite and solicitous was his retirement.

It was not one of those wide-eyed, oh-my-God-deaths men approaching fifty died, one hand spilling ink on a hasty will. More like putting up his feet in a favourite armchair and going to sleep in a splash of sunshine with the day's newspaper for awning.

Drupa and Disha bathed Kedar's body in rosewater and combed out his grey hair in the weak winter sun. A crinkled silk turban they then wrapped around his head, the tip of their tongues protruding a bit in their effort to get it right. 'My butterflies,' Kedar used to call them, when they tied his turban for him as little girls, and they so wanted to get it right for the final time.

'Kal meine usse haaloo ki, aaj uski daath ho gayi!' loudly lamented a neighbour, eyes darting from Disha's bite-sized breasts to Drupa's matronly mammary with gymnastic agility, his voice riding over Kedar's one-time hit—*Preet Ki Boli*—blaring incongruously from the stereo.

Relatives balked visibly at the organ donation plan.

'But Papaji signed the papers himself,' Drupa muttered, conscious of the accusing stares directed at her owing to her career credentials, tugging at the transparent Lucknowi kurta she wore. 'His body is to go straight to the medical college.'

And when the men came collecting, scooping out eyes into little ice-caskets, leaving sockets bereft of any semblance of sight, Guddi bent to press down the lids back on the black holes of emptiness, so that Kedar could continue to greet his guests hospitably, inoffensively.

Twenty years before he smiled civilly in his bier, Kedar had directed Mangala, the mother of his children, 'Go dream your air-coloured dreams!'

'At least I have dreams!' she had said.

She had his daughters, too, but Kedar understood the implied malice; that he wasn't even man enough to dream. That was the best gift Mangala gave him, daring him to dream.

His vision unfolded in a domestic, unassuming manner and took over his daily life; he had a new wife who never strayed from his side, he had his daughters back with him for good, their entire identities carved from his own background with nary a squeak from the ululating Aiyyayo blood. Mincing Kathak mudras replaced the wishy-washy Mohiniyattam, their dreams were dreamt in Hindi MA and not colloquial Malayalam.

Mangala's mother wrote once, to revoke the ban on custody.

'*Kedar-son, I am growing old*,' she inscribed in an obvious bid to secure his sympathy, stifling news about the rabid cancer dancing riotously into her blood.

'*We have met just one time and inauspicious it was, still I beg your reason. Mangala stupid girl; you know, I know. She did wrong, I am first to agree. But you are like my son only, won't you listen to this old woman? There is only one school here, where Badi and then Choti gone to. Now Mangala go there all day. She waiting, waiting for children to come out. Not her own, mind you, they are with you, but she gone little mad. Not in a bad way, only little. It go away by the girls coming back.*

'*It break the heart of old woman like me, with no husband, to have total strangers bring Mangala back from school, after all the children gone home and school gates closed. I know you are nice man and do the right thing. Like my son only you are, no?*'

Kedar sneered, 'The old bag, calling herself an old woman three times in a row. I am no idiot…Mangala waiting at schools! The…*thief*. This mother of hers, she never blessed the marriage and personally choreographed the divorce, now she lagaos makkhan just for own selfish ends.'

By then Kedar had hit his career peak, was imagining himself sitting snug on the crest forever and suspecting everyone of ulterior motives and vested interests. His ghazal '*Preet Ki Boli*' was declared a super-hit, the cassette carried Choti's faked whimper on the cover, and Sunday supplements carried his interviews in colour.

He was riding a high then, but kindness, he had decided, was going to be a belated move. It was his intention to relent after the old woman 'is begging some more,' as he drolly related to a group of friends, 'just so she knows I am no paav ki joothi!'

But she never wrote again.

Thus he revenged himself on his erstwhile wife, by obliterating every tiny speck of her life and ways, of her traditions and teachings and thereby doing away with any remote control she may have held. He could think of no better goal in life than to oust the tiniest trace of her from the gene pool of his daughters before him, to be their creator and not procreator, by putting in a fingernail and drawing a line right down the middle of their blood. Clearly, going by his final grin, he had fleshed out most of his dreams before demise.

To the men who manhandled him into a stretcher in the ambulance he may have been just another corpse, but to those who bid him farewell fondly at the foot of his stretcher, jostling for precious standing space at the white ambulance doors, he conveyed a smugness that was majestic in its moderation.

10

'SEX IS TOO STINKY. NO MORE FOR ME, THANK YOU,' BADI HAD scoffed loftily from the delivery bed. Little Deborah lay in an antiseptic regulation crib, licking and sucking air in smacking, audible gulps waiting politely for her mother to lactate. Dave was high up on some mountainous peak out of telephonic range and therefore unaware of the latest 'good news'.

'Hey, Sister,' Disha caught at a passing nurse's elbow. 'I'm having labour pains all over again. Am I dying?'

The nurse detached herself anatomically, mumbling something about post-partum uterine contractions and fate.

'Get me an injection or something,' Badi demanded emotionally. 'I can't take pain.'

Guddi Mausi laid aside the papers—matrimonial ads and obituaries were all she read—and snorted. 'People are putting photos now...'

Disha's keening cry cut her short. But her suffering, like Guddi's literary pursuits, was thankfully a thing of the moment. Badi's indigenous form of anaesthesia after the hospital sojourn, unfortunately, involved more sex.

The late night foreign films with subtitles on the black and white TV set, which had so fascinated them upon their arrival in Delhi, had given Disha and Drupa a fair idea of the birds and the bees. When Guddi had pointed out the dubious nature of the late-night celluloid fare, Kedar had silently alluded to the other half of their bloodline. 'In the south,' he'd say at such occasions, eager to let people know his daughters watched English and Spanish films and not the 70 mm hysterical Hindi productions, 'they are all born movie critics.'

And at the dead of the night, Drupa allowed Disha to practice her cinematically-inspired ardency. For a long time, Disha passionately inserted her whole nose into Drupa's mouth, having got the smooch profiles all wrong. It was only when she finally kissed a member of the opposite sex that she retired her nose and sister from the proceedings.

In the public aftermath of the loss of her hymen at the age of fifteen, Papaji had dragged Badi into the drawing room, having discovered her in the guest bedroom with an adolescent guest of the opposite sex at what he considered decidedly anti-social hours. Badi's lover, two years her senior, sobbed softly into a cushion, earning concerned looks from Guddi Mausi who worried the embroidered cover may run colours under the onslaught of such wholesale snot.

'Have you...? Has he...?' Papaji asked, unable to bring himself to finish the horrific query.

Disha, about to nod, took her cue from Guddi Mausi, who was shaking her head intermittently. Purity, apparently, lent itself to little white lies.

'No, Papaji,' Drupa stated tremulously before Disha could. And they all stared at her, perturbed, fearing another sidetracking attack of asthma.

None except Drupa witnessed the veiled irritation in her sister's eye.

Kedar's shoulders sagged and he stumbled onto a sofa. 'I am doing my best,' he muttered into his hands. 'I make mistakes. It's only human, na?'

Guddi gave him a glass of water in his hour of ceremonial paternity.

'I love her, Uncleji. Please, I want to marry her.' The avowal from the hitherto wailing lover of hers bewildered Badi the most.

Sensing her disbelief, he turned urgently to her, 'I only have two more years in college, then Daddy will set me up in business...'

'Are you mad?' she burst out, baffling her suitor. 'That was just sex, you dummy, sex. Have you never slept with someone before?'

Papaji's hand animated a scythe through air, landing resoundingly on her cheek.

Slap.

'You...*Mangala*!'

Disha turned to him with a feral snarl. 'You don't love me now, is that it? You never loved me, so lucky me, nothing to miss.'

'This boy, he means nothing,' she declared, savagely gobbling up the boy's flinch. 'You, you meant everything, but do you even see me? Did you ever ask for me in all those years?' She snapped her fingers as if they were cymbals clashing, hurtling up a verbal crescendo. 'Not once. It was always Choti, *"give me Choti, she is small, she looks like me"*. Unfortunately, you got saddled with both of us. Today I am not a virgin and it is all because of you. I have to look for love *somewhere*.'

Papaji clutched dramatically at the left side of his chest and Guddi Mausi glanced uneasily at Drupa. 'Your clock starts now,' she seemed to say. So Drupa thought it prudent to suffer an asthma attack. All of them, she thought in hindsight, had been playing their parts rather well.

Despite Badi's scoff, her premarital and then extramarital escapades became Choti's business when the former involved latter in her lies and liaisons in stellar roles. The first time she cried on her shoulders, Choti took the man and the matter very, very seriously, feeling intensely foolish when the matter reallocated itself to another man.

At Hanuman Mandir, amidst the hullabaloo of henna-hawkers two days before her nuptials, Drupa had condoled, 'No more affairs, you know that, na?

'My tits were touched for the first time inside that theatre,' Disha sighed nostalgically, pointing at Regal's grimy, paan-stained walls. 'And I felt nothing. Can you believe it? I thought I was gay.'

Drupa attempted to prod past the incredulity, 'The worst thing that can happen to a marriage is turning it into a triangle.'

Her facial pores swathed in sunscreen despite the cold, Disha sniffed her disagreement, 'This is not the design I wanted.'

'Henna once applied, cannot be removed,' the woman before them pronounced fatalistically, waving her dye-stained hands at them. Dissatisfied customers, jammed horns and legless beggars were routine here.

'They think they are bloody artists. Who can't do this? Mix henna with water, stroke, stroke, stroke!' Then she changed tracks, as she was apt to do when she smelt man. A youth chewed gum impassively by, his aged relative squealing at the coldness of henna plopping into her palm.

'Pants look stitched at Mohan Singh Place,' dismissed Drupa hastily. 'Imagine tailors measuring his crotch with a tape!'

A solemn little boy came by to squeeze lime syrup into the greenery on her palms, bunched up like contusions, and Badi perked up. 'I want it red, like I've just killed someone,' she said, denting the boy's solemnity somewhat.

The hands were blood red on the auspicious day and very much in view as the bride insisted on pulling down most decorously over face the white net-veil, which also hid the hideous boils. They had appeared out of nowhere two nights ago and she had initially attributed them to inferior facials and creams and spent considerable time popping what she presumed were pimples, only they turned out to be a sturdy strain of chicken pox. The long, lean length of her thigh, paraded via a thoughtful slit in the skirt, bore the eruptions with medicated equanimity while the tightest corset in the East squeezed her breath, elongating her waist to snapping consistency.

For a long while, until her first daughter came along, not a peep was heard from Badi's hormones and Choti took for granted a hibernation of the heart, like the receding rat-a-tat of a pensioner's cane.

'Thank god for plastic money,' Badi would swear as she rearranged large potted plants that stood still in the air-conditioned coolness, without all that silly swaying about that happens in the freely available suburban lower middle-class breeze.

Then the affairs began, graduating from seedy motels with their roach-infested beds to nippy encounters against bathroom walls during parties with designer dudes who thanked her politely and zoomed back to their own planets and dudettes.

Gradually, Drupa noticed an escalation in the quality of her sister's lifestyle; more than Disha's breasts were upwardly mobile. Her daughters were pulled out of their middle-class convents and admitted into schools with top-notch fees and air-conditioned corridors. She was always calling Drupa for advice from luxurious locales with people in the background calling her 'Sweetheart' in Spanish or Irish accents, both put-on and real, with the muted splash of an ice cube into cocktail or a nude body into pool.

The confrontation was a week into Kedar's demise, when Disha's mobile was with Drupa and Drupa's with Disha in the usual muddle-headedness following a familial tragedy. Though Disha had nothing interesting to report except a commercially sponsored SMS, Drupa's shellshocked look bugged the life out of her.

'Where and how?' was all Drupa managed to croak, her ears ringing with the acrobatic arrangements mooted in her unsuspecting ears all day long. Just before she entered the operation room, and was about to switch it off, a stranger buzzed her to gauge the distance travelled by her tits, disturbing the line of her scalpel.

'How do you think?' Disha shrugged while Drupa fought visions of her sister shouting 'sex le lo, sex. Taaja, garam sex' on railway platforms. 'The men are easy to find if you are not too picky.'

'Surely you don't need the money.'

Disha threw her an incredulous look. 'I have no intention of living like a beggar.'

'And why foreigners?'

She put out her palms. 'Exchange rate. Pound sterling to a rupee.'

'And then there's Dave.'

'And then there's Dave,' she agreed. 'And then there's the night ahead. Loneliness smells. You should know, you reek of it all the time.' She shivered delicately. 'I will smell, too, of camphor, of mothballs, of carefully preserved hand-embroidered dupattas buried deep in unused trousseau trunks if not for my...foreigner friends.'

This then was the spice that the white men came looking for in this century. Exotic, oriental, post-Raj, brown-skinned sex exported in dhows of Kathak and Kamasutra. Drupa worked the hinges of her jaw and closed them at last with great effort though her strings-attached spine sloped some more; the spice trade had moved on since she last checked!

'And you may not believe this,' Disha declared, though Drupa felt she had no trouble when it came to beliefs anymore. 'I *enjoy* my job. I enjoy pleasuring with my body. It becomes an instrument of beauty, of sublime grace, charming the Brit snakes out of their zippers...'

'Spare me the poetry. What it is is an instrument with an expiry date,' interrupted Drupa.

A savage curse rode the air as Disha's doe-eyed dreaminess gave way to fury. 'Will you stop picking up my words and checking under them, you...you *congenital virgin*?'

Left with no choice but to be covertly sanctimonius, the Congenital Virgin thought it best to stick close and not alienate sole sibling. Late into wee hours, the sorority went back and forth over every commercial transaction and extramarital possibility. Perhaps Drupa was even mildly entertained, but when the 'affairs' ended, their innards splattered all over her like the puddle-splashes of a thoughtless DTC bus, because Disha could never get the cardinal carnal rule right, that of wiping the heart clean of blood like the edge of a butcher's knife.

Her marriage, like most Indian marriages, had turned into a divorce. They were together only because they were not together and a better separation could not be decreed even by a divorce court.

The last time she called up in a panic, Drupa grappled with déjà vu.

'I woke up with a bad taste in my mouth.'

'Don't we all?' yawned Drupa with less sympathy, more sleep. 'Just brush your teeth.' And let me go back to dream my hairy, brown-skinned dreams.

'I think Dave knows.'

And why wouldn't he when wife wanted blood, gore and broken soda bottles at sunset and to this end dropped hints like lint all over the relationship-rug. Nothing less than verbalised vandalism with a topping of slashed wrists would satisfy her beloved sister.

Disha was overwrought over the latest tycoon in her life, the one with a rabid ex-wife and myriad children in myriad boarding schools to maintain. 'You know why I love him?'

Oooh, that's a tough one, Badi, now let me guess. He has a cock and balls? Bingo!

'Youhavetodecide,' she spoke on autopilot, having said it all before. 'Maritalblissorsexualthrills.Noonecanhelpyoudecide,youknow.Thinkofyourtwoinnocentdaugters,' etc etc.

Disha gulped audibly, 'I missed a period.'

Her younger sibling sat up, dislodging warm bed-covers. 'What?'

'Think of *three* innocent daughters.'

Of course, she went on to have a son. He was eleven months old now, born with a gravity he seldom broke with wind or toothless cackle and was basking in the unbearable radiance of his own glowing fairness when his aunt stole his thunder by missing a period herself.

Actually, Drupa had fallen in love.

Camouflaging with candour her agony over fat breasts, fat cheeks, fat everything, Drupa waddled—the desi duck of her own nightmares—through medical college, debating if the government shouldn't pronounce burkhas as the national costume, a nice black opaqueness to lock into its shroud shocking deformities like her. Academic brilliance eluded her, too, exploding myths about Plain Janes making it to the top; her brain didn't get it, this hirsute bone-deep ugliness that all could see and spurn.

An addiction to books, as if the words, in their large bold print, could fly up the nose and through her eyes, fill mind, and transform her forever, had her bend over in the medical college library. Having blown the dust off a tired looking book, she was keeled over thus, with no thought in mind except activating her nostrils and treating them to the powdery feel of antique papyrus despite the antihistamines that lay in wait, when another nose, almost Himalayan in its aquiline arrogance, thrust into the back of her disarmed neck and nuzzled intimately, accompanied by a muffled, 'So you waited after all.'

Strangely, she had. Her abhorrence for physical intimacy evaporated on the spot, in that sunny familiarity of a stranger's nose and, grotesque with disuse, out lurched the drunken secret of her smile. She considered herself a mature woman of…reasonable age, beyond cardio callisthenics until then, but when he plucked his nose away, she began to intensely miss the olfactory organ. Indeed, the tip of that nose was burnt and branded into her skin, making her ache for those pre-nose moments when the neck had unconsciously arched like Shakuntala for an amnesiac boyfriend.

Getting off on a crooked facial cartilage dried up any common sense and saliva she could lay claim to, still, applying some emergency spit-gloss to dry lips, she managed her end of the scramble for apologies, of embarrassment, of unnerved, unbrained adoration.

'I thought it was someone else…' he stammered, leaving her vaguely dissatisfied that she was not *someone else*, that she possessed an impostor neck of all things, that along with inadequate limbs and organs, this stem that wired torso to brain was no unique piece either. He had that kind of glance, the kind that rendered her conscious about unlived-in hips.

For long nights she had lain in bed, tormented.

'Whose neck had mine been posturing as?' she had asked the silent skull by the bedside. Whom had she mimicked with her bent stance? Who was she for that brief instant, ass cupping an alien crotch? And what if the real owner of the edible neck turned up?

The skull on her sideboard had neither a ready response nor a neck of its own. Still she blew it a kiss before switching off the lights.

'Meri bauni kara do,' she had been tempted to plead with begging-bowl eyes like those of the mobile hawkers at Sarojini Market, for she so ached to be inaugurated. But life continued to kick her gently upstairs. Writing exams, gaining degrees, applying for specialisation, getting second choice for MD; she had all the side-effects of ageing and none of the perks.

A parched era later, curled up in her own limbs and musty virginity, she literally ran into him once again as she took a corner too fast. She thought he rose before her, unfolding like a superb vision in Technicolour. Only later did she realise that it had been her who actually fell to the ground and not him who levitated; she had gone *down*, not him *up*.

'I am an intern here,' she informed him, when he had scraped himself off her windshield mammaries, breathless with her readymade belief in miracles and their application to her, little knowing that nine out of ten times this love that everybody broadcast was an inside job. All she could coherently cull was that Providence, bounding up to her with rotten offerings between its teeth until now, was suddenly wagging tail, having flushed out this tall, polysyllabic man especially for her. So she bent over and patted Providence on its back, for what else could she do?

He didn't remember her, he confessed, flexing knees slowly, having no doubt nuzzled countless necks, his nose taking nine naked necks from behind for all she knew, in the interim between their two run-ins.

Sucking at cigarettes with the innocent greed of a newborn at a teat, he was young and charming and carried his youth, charm and nicotine with him wherever he went, though hospital placards were nauseatingly sentimental against smokers.

'I am not going to die,' he assured after she had glanced unseeingly through his file, still inhaling the air he exhaled, intoxicated by it if truth be told. 'I am what you'd call an eternal patient.'

Depressed by the inheritance of muscular dystrophy, zipping on his bike, feeling the breeze fasten fingers in his hair, pumped up with a lifetime of late nights and bitter latte, he had not feared the road as it frothed up at him in painless razing, met the tar long and hard, bumping against it for a distance, attached as rider to bike till a wall brought the bloody journey to an end, separated his sinews from the rear wheels, muscle from pillion, hopes from heart.

So handsome, with a handsomeness transcending even halitosis, that Drupa hadn't dared to dream of him even on a particularly dry day, and now here he was at her medical mercy, an off-the-peg pal she could try on in the trial room.

'Mine is a long-term illness,' he had grinned boyishly, in no hurry to recuperate and dissolve into the night.

He wasn't lying, she found out in her cursory conversations with the doctor who attended him. Muscular dystrophy had struck unusually late—courtesy an athletic past that explained those appetiser ankles—but was now establishing base, re-doing bodily interiors, well on its way to parking itself within his physical parameters.

'It freaked me out,' he admitted. His elder brother had been in a wheelchair at the age of eight and consigned to crematorium by early teenage, but they hadn't traced it then to anything appallingly hereditary. Now the cellular connection was made and it had freaked him out, as he said so trendily. Rewind to Harley Davidson, rewind further to incessant boozing, rewind further still to the frustration he swore no one would understand. And then fast-forward to the Florence Nightingale trapped in Drupa Ahluwalia.

With painful physiotherapy and mineral reloads, his reticent bones mended half-way and there was a tremble of a hope that he'd go back to his abandoned lifestyle, replete with virile all-night coitus and all-day booze sessions that would straightaway dispense with Drupa and her droopy plait on a droopy ass.

Only the non-glamour of a pouch attached to intestines for all to see while he relieved himself any given moment— courtesy the abdominal dent sustained in accident—and the treacherous advance of his genetic dysfunction kept their platonic friendship going.

Not only did they naturally bump into each other in the out-patient ward when he dropped in for physiotherapy, but she took to visiting him in his PG digs at irregular hours, telling herself in all nobility that his depression did not keep a clock, after all. There was a growing lethargy in his physical life and it made bland even the violence of a sunset, turning his conscious hours into heavy viscosity of deceptive longevity. Besides, that slowness growing into his future was solvent with the slowness growing out of her past. This then was where they met with mutual consent.

Unable to meet the empty eyes of the skull presiding over her mantelpiece, she fled daily. Announcing, 'I am your chauffeur,' she'd land at his door in her rut-phut Zen, wishing he was less soulmatish.

He yearned for the breeze to finger-comb his hair, so she swapped her father's elderly car for a third-hand, roofless jeep with ample insurance hassles and drove him to the crowds he claimed to miss.

'My Sheelavati,' he called her and she had felt pleased until she found out that the mythological character had been famous for transporting a paralytic husband to hookers!

To the exotic flour offerings at Parathewaali gali, to the milling tourists at Janpath, to the Baha'i temple, to the dry Martinis at Djinns, hissing sizzlers at TGF's, ice cream peaking from waffle-cones at India Gate. She took him wherever his dying heart desired and, lit by the barbecue coals at Karim's, she huddled away from the swarming horde and sheekh kebabs to bask in his glow for, however flickery, he was her Sun God. Even with his voltage at its lowest, she had to shield her eye when looking his way.

'I love you,' he'd wink, sugarcane juice running icky-sticky down his tasty chin, contrasting his greeting of each day like it was his last against the tedium she doled out to every never-ending moment in her life.

'I love you, too,' she'd say gaily, knowing better than to take personally his gaiety, running in a theatre near her. The vendor inserted the cane under the crusher, once, twice, thrice and then with ginger and lime until the flattened debris he threw away attracted neither cows nor flies. That, Drupa soothsaid, is how I am going to be when he's done with me.

'You are my angel.' That was what he said when he was stuck for small talk.

Sexless, he thought her sexless. Yep, that made sense: angels had harps, not genitals. Her smile, he had told her, was money in the bank. And she remembered his cursory scan of her face that first time, his eyes travelling down the rugged terrain of her face—two astigmatic eyes, the toe-in-a-tight-shoe nose—to snag at the horizontal hollow of her smile. As if her smile was intended not as smile but strategy. Smile, the saviour of her doomed face's soul! Alas, her smile wasn't an official spokesperson, so that it went on lying and posturing while she carried another face inside.

When he ominously brooded or lost himself in the absorption of a sunset or her smile, rendering the latter a gunpoint rendition, then her smile and eyes felt like they belonged to two different faces.

'Thoughts wander into the back alley,' she warned hopelessly, gluttonous for attention.

'Then they must go with a gin bottle in their hand.'

They snorted in companionable silence and she felt a degree of relief in silently observing. No longer was she inclined to fill up long-winding silences with chatter. All her talkativeness had been a defense mechanism, a way to clog up potholes in her own special way. Papaji rarely spoke at first. But she overdid it, she thought, with a flash of remembered weariness. The responsibility of verbally recording every moment, every experience had then settled upon her with the alarming firmness of sheer habit. One of the things life taught you early was the worthlessness of words.

'I was a terrible daughter.' To sound cool around him and to override the everlasting shame of her untouchability, she sometimes borrowed Badi's biodata. 'I once tried to bed a boy just to get back at Papaji.'

'Sex is never what it seems,' he returned. 'Erogenous zones have humdrum histories and rebellion is an economically viable aphrodisiac.'

'I should sleep with my sunglasses on,' she said more truthfully, bypassing his dubious wisdom. The sun always hurt her eyes, even when curtains were drawn and the stars came out on night duty.

'I should sleep with a whore. I hate to say please.'

Sitting cross-legged on the carpet, she beat it, expecting it to magically fly. How can paid amour interest, she wondered; a man should dance nude in a packed hall because he was aching for her and not because he was broke or his balls itchy.

'Please don't avenge my incontinence by going all wifey on me,' he charged impossibly when she arranged his books or medical papers, or even bed-sheets. He snapped his fingers, the ones the crippling disease was yet to walk down. 'That's why marriages don't work. Wife takes over from mother until takeover and ageing combine to present men with a creature less wife, more mother and oh the horror of taking mothers to bed!'

'You're married,' she realised flatly, thirty-two teeth guillotining a tongue in tandem inside the privacy of her mouth.

He nodded, eyeing the pallor under her tightly scraped hair. Then studiedly casual, 'I'm meeting her tonight. Come along?'

She wouldn't have accompanied him if he hadn't pulled out his tube and disconnected the pee-bag, bothering the medico in her. That's what she told herself when she went in for a bikini wax and perm in preparation for meeting his wife; the other woman. And just like that, on a mid-winter morning whim, her Amrit Chakna came undone.

'Hands up,' said the parlour girl before blanching at the dense mane in Drupa's armpits. 'Looks like you haven't shaved since you parted with your afterbirth.'

Her customer glumly shook her head and then yelled as strips began ripping the undergrowth.

'How you wanting the hair, miss?' asked another parlour girl, dangling a loose pair of scissors in her hands. 'Badly needs cutting. Split-ends, dandruff, grey hair, sab kuch hei.' Look no further, she meant, if you were cataloguing hair maladies.

Drupa found that she couldn't stand the slow, slow sinister hiss of the scissors up her tresses as they climbed inexorably to snip, the silent suspense as they parted to mutilate and maim her hair. 'No,' she backtracked hoarsely. 'I mean, no cut.'

'Then?' asked the girl, bored. 'It is so lifeless... What about a perm? You wanting perm like this?' She showed Drupa an array of celebrities with curly-haired profiles on posters. What Drupa had in mind came from no bottle, but from snapshots buried deep in a seashell in her head, where jet black waves tumbled down Amma's shoulders. The smell of chemicals hit Drupa's nose before it did her hair, but gasping for a breath or two was preferable to abandoning hirsute principles of a lifetime in a jiffy.

He had stared at her nonplussed when she arrived at his door, aching and hurting in every waxed, pumice-scrubbed, *naked* pore. 'You look... different,' he said.

'My wife? We are like two peas in a pod,' he told her en route to the club and she imagined them shake out a pod-shaped bed.

The woman had, Drupa discovered, a fuck-me freshness about her. But it was like biting into an unripe mango, the outer skin an attractive yellow while the inside steadfastly held on to a sly sourness. Also, it helps to clash with the decor, Drupa decided, watching her sitting whitely on the white leather sofa like she'd ooze toothpaste from mouth if pressed in the middle, dangling feet capped in black leather shoes that corpses customarily wore to coffins.

Their frosted glasses kissed—clink!—the fruity rinds snorkeling down lazily.

'She's a doc,' he introduced her and Drupa immediately focused on looking distinguished, as if her newly acquired curls was a frivolous wig that concealed a stethoscope and printouts of the Hippocratic Oath.

The wife—they were still to be formally divorced—smiled fully then for the first time, establishing easily the superiority of straight white teeth. Drupa's drink was something boring and non-alcoholic, pale yellow swirl of pineapple pulp with a soda rapidly going flat. A paper umbrella perched by the rim was turning soggy.

'How are you?' she was asking him, her voice dipping with false concern.

He cocked an eyebrow but Drupa could see he was touched. If she really cared, you sucker, she'd be with you no matter what. She'd know you live four grimy flights up a stained suburb and paddle along the window ledge summoning nerve enough to jump, sidetracked only by the march of black ants or the pealing phone selling insurance you don't need.

Mellowed by wine and the sight of young girls in short skirts, he whispered something into his wife's ear and Drupa felt powerless to fight history. They had so much to remember jointly—honeymoon, in-laws, divorce lawyers—these two, him and his wife.

'That reminds me,' supplied the bitch loudly with a carefree *coiling* laugh, 'of the time we called that number.'

Drupa assumed her brightest expression; yes, yes, that woman with two pillows on her person, those indigenous, homemade USPs. 'Yeah, he told me about it,' she said, peeking discreetly at the other's chest where sat two unmoving half-shells, not on talking terms with each other. At home I am sure they float down free like all good breasts do or come, let's notify Newton, thought Drupa mutinously.

'The rates of calling such numbers!' expostulated a friend.

'Worth their weight in gold,' said another with an exaggerated leer.

'Gold's another word for it,' someone quipped.

The bitch displayed yet more teeth, yet more perfection. 'She said I'm bathing and there is water all over me, remember?'

He remembered all right going by his rougish grin. 'I told her to lean back with legs apart and towel herself real slow.'

'You gynaec,' Drupa poked him with a playful finger, hastily manufacturing a chuckle. So many chores one can get done on the side, she couldn't help thinking; chop veggies while slurping over phone. Age no bar, bad breath no bar. Ah, the sweet anonymity of phone sex!

Glasses cheerfully clinked in the club's brightly lit terrace. Drupa stood up, momentarily queasy, fingering her pager. Then sat down again. She didn't want anyone to suspect haemorrhoids, merely a touch of madness.

They talked shop about mutual acquaintances and missed weddings, her black shoe breathing down his brown slip-ons, the colour contrast barely discernible in the rapidly falling dusk. Drupa noticed absent-mindedly the other woman's lovely drunk accent, her pillowy pout reminiscent of anal fissures in medical journals. Everything was so somnolently pleasant. The ice cream sofa, atop which she sat like a sun-dried cherry that said, lick me, lick me, softie follows. The ice-cubes sighing as they melted, the murmur of amiable banter swirling around…

'Do you agree?' he asked.

Drupa blinked.

'You look so lost,' he commented and she tried to hastily compose her features into a destination.

'We plan to go on to the disc.' Where there would be no soft sofa for this aged spine of hers and no terra firma for his imbalances.

'You can go on home if you like. Somebody will drop me,' he began kindly but she was too smart for all of them despite red-rimmed eyes from nocturnal disturbances of the professional kind.

'Count me in,' she called out, stroking her hair, subtly trying to extricate fingers from the snarls at her scalp without making it appear a tug of war.

At the disc, Drupa fervently hoped she wouldn't catch her sibling flaunting her pointless thinness, attracting tourists with her 'Welcome to India' tits in backless, mirror-work cholis from Rajasthan.

Here elbows and fingers pointed randomly while stereos said 'dancedancedance' in all seriousness. Here she got to watch them cry for madder music and gin refills and laugh their visceral laughs, rumbling up straight from god knew where, and alliterate non-rhyming hips on the dance floor, self-consciously casting off inhibitions.

No, she didn't dance, she demurred. Not unless alcohol shimmied up her arteries, loosening limbs and tongue. Then she had been known to boogie unto doorstep like a dizzy top way past its string or bedtime. Dance for her was the advent of the anti-clumsy, when her feet twisted and wrists curved of their own accord, because in consultation with her lucid self, they only stumbled and staggered, pointing out in all solemnity her salient and not too dormant ungainliness in strategically placed mirrors.

They danced together, of course, the bitch and him, but only eventually. First he danced with the three other females—the behanjis—in the group, all of whom had the collectively preoccupied air of waiting for the pressure cooker to go off before they could season the dal. Then he turned a purposeful turn, bowed playfully to her, paying homage to her primate giggles, and hand in hand they walked to the floor. She had the kind of walk habitual saree wearers have when they opt for dresses or trousers, a sort of ill-fitting southern movement, hips careening out of control, Drupa noticed.

At last the two peacefully jiggled hips at each other. She was smiling, swaying her bottom serenely. His crew-cut head looked vulnerably bald opposite hers, from which man-made curls spouted like bubbles big and small.

'Please,' prayed Drupa, used to praying for her own lumbering self, 'please don't let him trip and fall.' He couldn't bear that, not in front of this woman. This woman who had once told him that it was only when one stopped dancing with a corpse did one realise who had led the dance. This woman who had the right to say these things to him.

Eventually, Drupa had had more beer than her bladder could bear. Her new companion and she indulged in a waltz of their own as he deftly moved to his right when she stepped toward the door to her left. The bulge on the side of his head, she was convinced, was budding brain tumour.

'I have to pee,' she told him finally and frankly.

'That's exactly what I said,' he opened his mint-freshened mouth to say, instantly transporting Drupa to Alpine heights. 'I have to see. With my own eyes, that too. Show it to me, I told them, then I will believe you. Proof, bhai.'

She shuffled feet, trying to find a pose that would make her bladder see sense. There were not many chinks in his monologue, no pause where she could interject delicately the topic of her call. He would continue with the story of his life even if she piddled right there at his feet, though she was sure no one would notice damp patches on the carpet in this dim a light.

But prudently she decided against hydrating his hind limbs, mainly because he could return the compliment and adopt higher angles while doing so. She pressed her lower limbs together lest seepage occurred. Was enough being a wallflower, no aspirations to be leaky wallflower to boot. Did not move at all, in fact, just stared fixedly at him, keeping mind over matter, however liquid, as electrified by commonplace thoughts and sentiments, this man was his own monument to mediocrity.

Later, warbling farewells outside in the cool night air, the bitch leaned against a cab, lips pursed together, merrily going mwaah-mwaah in the general direction of his cheek, the right one since the left one faced Drupa, tempting her to mwaah-mwaah it from this side just to redress the imbalance. She then turned inexplicably to the anti-micturation moron still by Drupa's side and mwaah-mwaahed his medulla oblongata as well.

'Take care,' she whispered to him.

Drupa frowned; didn't Crocin use to say that?

'What did you think of her?'

'Who?' Drupa peered vaguely at the woman who was reading the news on the TV even at that time of the night. She tried not to have an opinion on public figures. Especially these TV women of all women in the world, returning again and again to tell her the same stuff like they really cared that she didn't miss a thing.

'You know, my...wife.'

Drupa could feel her nostrils twitch, like she needed a spare breathing apparatus, viscous mucous encrusting their innards. Was it heartbreak or her tit on fire? She looked down, no smoke. Say the word and I'll hit you, said the voice in her head. She said it and it hit her. Wife he had said and it wasn't her. Funny how you felt exactly like a wife and weren't exactly a wife.

With his back to her he bent to blow on the low stool for imaginary dust before sitting lightly on it to remove shoes.

Each shoe would then be encased in a plastic film and off they'd go to sleep tight in their snug little shoeboxes. Then it was the turn of the trousers to be shaken free of crumples. He secured the crease before hanging it in the cupboard. All the while his shirt-tails would hang aimlessly down his thighs, awaiting further orders. She knew the rituals so well.

'Yes, her,' he prompted when she had said nothing.

She looked at him then and admittedly he was busy with his little compulsory acts, the convulsive twitch and tatter of hygiene that he followed up so meticulously.

A peculiar dryness invaded her mouth; the coolest springs of the world wouldn't have done then. 'She is sweet,' she sought to dismiss.

'Suck her tits and they flow with milk,' he agreed, leaning against the wall for support.

Drupa disappeared into the adjoining bathroom. After a life-saving pee, she lingered over cream and comb. Foot propped on the closet, laved her entire leg with a 'satin-finish' face lotion. Much smoother. Examined thighs for stray hair; she had highly fertile follicles, a Sikh legacy. Before the waxing spatula was wiped dry, an army of hair rushed out to replenish the lost battalion, Disha always complained.

Turning, Drupa toppled over a lotion long past its expiry date for he loved to collect these pretty looking beakers but seldom remembered to use them. The putrid smell of green apples instantly rent the air.

Went back in and lay down. Now it was his turn in the bathroom. She knew exactly what he did; she could time him from the platonic past they shared. Splash water on face. Dry with towel in anti-wrinkle upward strokes. Brush teeth. Replace brush in holder. Pee; swipe; flush.

He had barely slid into bed when her legs clamped him from both sides, stapling him down, stuffing breasts down his throat like so much old sock, gagging him, and kissed him till root canals buzzed, every sagging inch of her craving attention. She felt him stir, then cooperate.

They were kissing because that was something to do with lips; that was the point where his speak-before-you-leap vocabulary met her deep dead-end quietude. The entire body machinery that had to be activated for verbal communication was just as handy for this. Hello, they were saying, *hello*. It was okay, she soothed his slack lips, to blubber while you smooched.

The corners of his lips were salad-leaf crunchy, contrary to what she had imagined, and initially seemed content to pray silently against hers in a meditation of mouths, but then sparking seemingly disconnected seismic tremors in elsewhere terrains, tracing and slipping into nooks and crannies of nerve-endings with accommodating elasticity and turning two pairs of decent human lips, of all things, to chewy lava.

'You are stunning,' he whispered, forming the words with heartbreaking honesty, smelling of fruit past its prime.

And she did not argue with that honesty, how much ever she may have wanted to contest fundamental facts. For how did the truth matter here? The very union between them she had in mind was based on the acceptance of the other's version. If he began to see her as she saw herself, where would lust be? Stun was in the beholder's eye.

She vibrated agreement. 'Bon Appetit.'

For a while they lay in bed, their eyes going nowhere but deep into each other's, then his slipped to the azure veins that ran helter-skelter down her untanned portions.

The mouth-watering fragrance of freshly uncovered flesh soon seeped into air and in mutual worship began their pilgrimage. A bra surrendered its tumescent inhabitants, legs wrapped, hands delved, noses slanted, tongues duelled, and everything spiritual that could be reached within the conjunction between two bodies was eventually attained.

Next stop nirvana, she thought, stretching against him, luxuriating in the physical security provided by his body's blockage, his tongue a live fish caught in her mouth, drool dewier than fresh botanical extracts. May be this was one's true purpose in life; to please and be pleased in the physical realm, all the highbrow posturing merely an affectation, a prelude to the holocaust of pleasure building up from the moment of birth, to the unloading of an inbuilt backpack of bliss that one day, bam, just blew up as violent as a vocation and just as inviolate. Their past, even as they spoke, was being rewritten into a run-up to this, and it rid them of some of the sadness associated with loneliness up until then. Touch morphed into touch, melting into a melange of whispers and damp kisses.

'Aren't you scared or aren't you fertile?' he enquired, hands steering a careful path through the bouquet of static curls atop her head.

'Every little thing has scared me all my life. I guess I've run out of fear.'

She showered without latching the door. The warm water sluiced over her, dripping curls in downward spirals, washing away any inveterate virginity. In the vaporous mirror she failed to locate her face or limbs, but there were just meters of skin shot with dreamy silk, like Amma's used to be.

'I suppose we must talk now,' he said with a tinge of tragic inevitability when she returned, his palm rubbing her nipple to make the genie reappear.

She didn't see why silence couldn't be kept golden for a while longer. A silence that sensed its place within parlance, punctuated and demarcated verbal arenas with subtle nuances.

Positioned thoughtfully among words was the pause she sought. This room, it said, decisively, nodding its head, smacking its lips. This room and these two people. Perfect, perfect, just perfect.

At dawn, she fled.

The next day he had broken every breakable thing in the house, cradling his bloodied fist, batting an eyelid when she walked in. She welcomed his rage, took it as an indication of personalised treatment, because then she could begin to unload her own satchel of liniment. There were bruises on her body, too, like fingerprints in a lump of dough, but they were honeymoon hickeys and to be borne undercover.

'How do you expect me to play house-house? I have no control over my bowels, my bladder. A nappy peeking at the hip is not half as exciting as a thong's edge. I talk to people while relieving publicly into a container...you know what it does to my social life? You *should* know, it got me stuck with you in the first place. Now, to go have wet-dreams over you!'

She held out a glass, so he could aerate throat and soul.

'Daily my control slips. I walk like I'm juggling multiple testicles. I am a vegetable, my muscles are dying inside me everyday. A fucking coffin, that's me, carrying my dead hands, my dead feet. And do I die, oh no.'

'Open your eyes, you cannibal,' he bid in a different pitch before despairing, 'There's nothing in there. Who can hide in those?'

She knew that he'd unleash a leisurely tendril of smoke into her mouth in farewell, would whisper something fond in her ear, his tongue wetly swiping the sensitive undersides of her lobe. 'I never meant to betray you,' he'd say with that same heartbreaking sincerity. For she knew he would be sincere when he said sorry. Everyone was while saying words they had to say and to cope with that pressure, she felt herself unequal.

'You are my tough little Sardarni, aren't you?' he chucked lightly under her chin.

'Actually, my mother...' But he had turned away so she asked instead, 'Should we eat?' It did no good to address queries only to the soul. The body was deceptively casual about things, but Drupa's guess regarding its merger with soul had her reaching out for badly sliced bread and melted margarine that pooled unappealingly in its own wrapper. Barbed wire was closing around her careless loving. Quickly she shut eyes, trying to inhale the scent of a song playing in the background— was it her father's famous market-driven lament?—still she saw him. Illness had honed his six-foot frame to aesthetic proportions; at times his perfection caught brutally at her throat, dried her spit. However, his words were what she wore like bullets in her heart, that inserted the catch down the chute of her throat.

Just breathe, she ordered herself, *just snatch at any air going spare and suck it in in fistfuls.* Up the nose and down the nose...the trick was to keep breathing.

He whacked the tablecloth with a playful fist. 'There is lot of love out there.'

Yeah, no dearth of people on this planet. Watching disturbed dust motes hitchhike on a sunbeam—it had been summer then, a summer long gone—she smiled, but all the while she smiled she scrutinized him carefully, his face, hands lying over the table, for signs that he lied, and of course she remembered not to inhale. Dust in snout addled incoming oxygen.

Nice, I am nice, she reminded herself. It was a curse, this cheerfulness she had cultivated along the way to compensate for being an eyesore, leaving genuine gloom clueless about tissues. Pink-nosed and high-strung, it ferreted about now, reversing into vacant breast-lots and filling up the last empty drop. She took off her glasses, holding up her eyes in a tired squint and to the man slumped before her, her eyes seemed denuded somehow, like barely hatched things yet to grow the covering of hair or fur.

'The Web's a whimsical pigeon,' he said, nevertheless handing her a card with his e-mail punched on it.

I am being packed off, she thought, contemplating the swollen waste-bag on his stand, flashing a smile to divert him, a sunny-side up smile.

'What's fucking funny?' he rasped. If there was an absurdity going about his condition, he wanted to know it, too. That gave him a handle on the whole thing, an edge over others to whom it could just as easily have happened, this genetic mishap.

Though something dark and furry with blackened teeth was pulling her howling down the nearest sewer, she hung on to that fresh-frozen smile and met bravely the goodbye in his eye. 'I was thinking packing bags has a different connotation for you.'

His smile was remote. 'And look at you, no bags to pack.'

11

ʕDʔRUPA'S RETURN FROM HOSPITAL WAS NEITHER CRYSTALLISED orally nor tangibly shored up as history, indeed could later barely be recalled since Dave chose that period to disappear in the hills. Disha saw him last when she dropped him off impatiently to board a bus to Hardwar.

There were five of them in the group, two Germans who spoke guttural English and two Britons who went patronisingly 'pardon?' at everyone's speech except their own. Dave's latent conceit in the ease with which he picked up foreign accents—at the call centre his demand that John in Wyoming pay his bills 'right away' was an inspiration and not just for John—was justified when he decoded their rumbling speech and facilitated all-round communication. He had anchored a mountaineering show on TV once, just told Disha how he would have loved to do it, and next thing he knew he was on air. Phone calls followed with everyone praising the way he spoke. It had been hard work to get all the foreign names right, calls to embassies at unearthly hours and taping the right pronunciations, but worth it in the end.

'But you never say my maiden name or, for that matter, my family name right,' his wife had puzzled. 'You say Meledeath or Mle-daath... And Ahluwalia is Aaloo-wallah as in spud sales!'

Like he deciphered consonants and worked vowels into them for the sheer pleasure of it! Dave shrugged in the icy breeze. The Chaukhamba massif, majestic in its shroud of clouds, stood bang before him. It was sunset and as sunsets went, it was simply breathtaking, and coming on the heels of the sight of Lake Nandikund, this burgled the breath all right. Such trekking moments made it all worthwhile—the climb, the uncertainty, monosyllabic porters...

The chaste brahm-kamals were abloom on the virgin-white snow just for him, he thought fancifully. How he longed to bring Disha along, to share this splendour! Of late...of late they shared little.

An earlier attempt at this high-altitude trek through the Madhyameshwar ranges in July he had had to abandon because of the weatherman's dire predictions. Now the hinterland in October, with its dew-dappled riverbed, rope-trolley above Madhyamaheswar-Ganga since the bridge had disintegrated in the 1998 landslide, overcame his geographical grudges. This tiny strip of land that he temporarily called his own did away with petty patriotic prejudices, his sense of belonging shifting axis.

What the hell, thought Dave, peeling off woollen cap and running frost-bitten fingers through his matted hair, Disha and the kids had no such transcendental qualms, yearned no transfusion of blood or roots. Birth in a static spot helped, pointing as it did to a stationary death; he couldn't uproot his family and transplant it in alien soil. Here he was on superior ground, his complexion, his accent, were worthy of a salaam. But there who knew? What had Gonsalves said? Something about a strawberry seller in a Manchester street giving him the rotting ones, saying the fresher ones were not for *him*, conveying contempt for the same skin that fetched Gonsalves a peach-and-cream bride via matrimonial ads on home turf.

Reaching out to pluck a pristine lotus, Dave decreed grandly, 'If she doesn't come to the brahm-kamal, then the brahm-kamal shall go to her.'

His reflections granted him a reprieve and he wallowed in the unaccustomed pleasure of it when the German shouted up with great urgency, 'Verzatvyssel?'

A second later Dave had decoded it to 'where is that whistle' and dived into his backpack for that small part of the pressure-cooker that added to its whole. He smiled; standing on peaks brought on vertigo and an attack of asinine philosophy.

They pitched their tents nearer Chaukumbha.

'This is the roof of the world,' he listed in his best tour-guide imitation, pointing at the visible peak before getting horizontal with a thriller, and the curvy blonde in it had just got shot, in the leg or ass, or wherever her brains were situated at that precise moment, when he felt his stomach give in.

'You sensitive, man,' grunted the sleepy Scot next to him.

Outside, Dave unbuckled his belt, picking and placing his boots on the crunchy snow with the careful imbalance of sleep and frost. At first he took the voices for that of the German inhabitants of the other tent, then his exhausted ears tuned in their data—Hindi, spoken in an unrecognisable dialect.

'Chal, Saale, teri tho,' said one and Dave nearly crapped in his polyester Marks and Spencer twenty percent off pants from GK. Then mistaking him for a 'gora', they instructed, 'You calling friend, all friend, and coming, you and all friend. Understanding?'

Their guns eased understanding. It was during the unscheduled trek down the rugged side of the Nandikund that Dave's bowels decided to do an on-the-spot transmission of what his wits had already executed.

Back in the capital, the militants' request for funds was sieved through many channels, too many for Disha to get a grasp of the real situation. Were they Kashmiri Jihadees or Khalistani kin? One daily said this, another daily said that and eveningers went so far as to call it a publicity stunt by an adventure firm since no group came forward to take responsibility. The terse note, made up of alphabets cut out of newsprint, only asked for money, this much, on this day, at this spot. The police dismissed it as amateur greed, while the Central government was busy defending itself in the Parliament. Disha, distracted enough to stop shaking her groin at strange men on dance floors, did not really believe in widowhood, not for herself, nah.

It was amazing, summarised Drupa, how people adapted to non-beliefs. Wives and girlfriends of the missing men formed a little band and appealed to the government, likely militant outfits and the Almighty, but these appeals failed to flush out the hidden men or further economic epistles.

The band played a sad little concert in church premises in the mistaken belief that this was a populist platform; very few people turned up for the concert following the mass, where mainly hymns and bhajans were sung. An old lady who snoozed in the pew now snoozed through the snazzy songs, head resting on own bosom that doubled as desk.

Then suddenly a decomposed body surfaced in a rhodendron jungle and the waiting turned ugly. It was one of the Germans, presumably done in by the loss of one dictionary, German to Hindi. The state machinery for a while toyed with the idea of declaring it the Indian's body so that at least the tourism sector was left untrammelled, but the concerned spouse took one look at the piecemealed body and sobbed uncontrollably whereas Disha stonily spouted, 'The shoe doesn't fit.' She had arrived at the spot with one of Dave's discarded sneakers.

'Choti, I am doomed,' she cried, not realising that her newfound vulnerability was turning on more men than she had ever hoped for; she was suddenly so *touchable*. Eyes that penetrated, stripped, gang raped, the menacing multi-men lounging on sidewalks, she no longer noticed them, not even when their shadows fell on her. Biology began to vacate her brain along with birds and the bees and French letters were reassuringly foreign literature once again.

Ma D'Costa cut a trip to the capital, tirelessly keeping house, baking inedible cakes and with simulated cheer stirred rice wine, all the while reminscensing over her displaced son's childhood until Disha was inclined to banish her too to an exile. Drupa guided Dave's mom to Nizamuddin railway station and bade her farewell, listening with an interested visage the last of the tales.

'My Dave used to climb all the windows. All day long, climb, climb, climb. I knew then that would be the end of him. The good Lord taketh what the good Lord giveth.'

At the station, when the Guwahati Express tooketh what the Guwahati Express gaveth two weeks ago, Drupa heaved a sigh of relief. A congregation during a crisis was not the best path to peace despite the crowd's view to the contrary.

The maid's husband, fairly Catholic when it came to spirits, refused the rice wine she left behind. It was while they poured it down the toilet that its best use suggested itself, that of disinfectant. Copiously they washed basins and bathrooms with it, the abundance of its acid content washing surf-white in its wake.

After some cerebral tinkering, Guddi Mausi chose to put the house on the market. 'No need to live in South Delhi. Let's find a cosy flat in Faridabad or Gurgaon. Vaishali is a comfy place I've heard.'

That was Plan B: to sell the house and draw a fiscal piechart between them so that Disha could get constructive with her share. Plan A, of course, was to drag Dave by the ear and whack him hard for vanishing like that and putting them through this Stygian darkness. And he would say, 'Sorry,' in that loaned accent of his and they'd sip Goan Feni and call it French champagne once again.

'Ghost?' Guddi echoed.

In her drawing room, the good broker, nicknamed Mr Ten Percent like all good brokers, had just apprised her of the diving value of realty in general and her own domicile in particular owing to its tenancy of the inhuman; in short, a spectre.

'Come on, a ghost!' said Guddi playfully, poking Mr Ten Percent in the chest and jumping a bit when his chest began to ring.

He dived into his shirt's pocket and extracted a cell phone. Luckily, he was a man of few words despite the cell-card schemes flooding the mart, or else the caller was spouse and men who had much to say to their wives lived very secretive lives if they existed.

'Behanji,' babbled he, when Guddi Mausi harassed him in a way reminiscent of a poem on Jhansi ki Rani that he learnt in school, something about popping baby into armoured backseat and going into battle without a backward look. 'The ghost puffs and pants there,' he said, pointing at Guddi's posterior.

This rather shook his future client till she realised that it was the room under her rear-end rather than the rear-end itself that was implied. 'You mean the junk room.' Disha's exit had elevated the 'gym' to 'junk room', its main ingredient an exercise bike that no one sat on, let alone pedalled.

'The...ghost runs up and down the stairs and then creaks open the door, sits on the bike. This the servants say, not me.' He coughed apologetically but with adequate affection for the apparition that had brought down rates, his dye-dappled moustache quivering under his nose; a very small bottle of dye, for he left the hair on his head a dirty grey. 'And it,' here he pointed once again at Guddi's crotch, 'cycles in the dead of night.'

Guddi, who at her fattest couldn't be induced to get on to the thing, was impressed. 'You mean, something that people rarely clamber on to when living, this ghost leaps on to after, mind you, the stairs and push-ups and death? And what do people hear, anklet bells or rubber-soled trainers?'

A mite peeved at the insult to the ghoul, he accused in his turn, 'I heard, Behanji, that your husband's body was not cremated.'

'Body?' she started as if Kedar had just gone to the Mother Dairy booth around the corner for two litres of full-cream milk, then collected herself. 'Yeah, yeah, body. We donated it to science. He was a very forward-thinking man.'

'I know that, you know that, but people, they say things. You better perform a havan,' he blurted out, turning agitatedly to his left and wishing he hadn't, since there sat the entire Ahluwalia clan staring frankly at him from the confines of a 5 by 8 photograph frame. 'Nobody will buy it off you otherwise, this haunted house.'

'Why? Let him live here. He is a peaceful man.'

'Was, Behanji, was.' He was frankly puzzled over the slow bliss invading her obesity. As if the Centre had just declared a posthumous Padamsree for her husband!

Guddi decided to go with the flow and perform the exorcism, to ride over the rumours no doubt spread by some disgruntled servant or gossipy neighbour and also to convince future buyers the departing direction of the phantom footprints. She went to invite her mother-in-law for formality's sake, knowing full well Maji's inability to attend.

Maji lay motionless. A malmal kurta covered her torso, but legs were left bare to dry out the pus from a festering bedsore, the cold breeze invited to act like a blood-sucking leech. Guddi witnessed for the first time, courtesy the current immodesty of attire, a gargantuan tattoo on Maji's calf; an inky figure, a goddess perhaps, dating from her Hindu past.

Despite the sputtering warmth of the angeethi, Guddi shivered. 'Kedar di atma sukoon mangda.'

No flicker of response smote the lined face. Kedar had been an only son and she a gushing mother, never really getting over the glamour of his gender, and his death was becoming the death of her. Her daughter, denied ghee, milk sweets and any pampering while growing up on the sole grounds of being born girl, was now in charge of her deteriorating body, and revenge, however justified, made for an ugly spectacle.

'Who will look after me once she is gone,' the daughter lamented by rote, in training for the forthcoming funeral.

The occupant of bed let out a disconcerting groan.

'A nerve is crimped along the spine. I've asked Biji to get her granddaughter as soon as she wakes up. One kick from a newborn baby on her back and she'll be fit.'

'Why don't you call a doctor?' Guddi asked faintly.

'Arrey, Sanju Bhaiyya was here and he actually charged! Can you believe? After all we did for his starving family in those days. Maji used to send pure ghee dabbas to their home during exam times. And today he won't check her pulse because of her empty purse.'

Guddi fantasised fleetingly of being bodily trapped thus in the care of her two stepdaughters and couldn't control a shudder. 'Vaahe Guru,' she prayed, 'give me sudden death. A blow to my head, cardiac arrest, car accident, anything that will take me straight to you in one stroke without middlemen. Please, please, don't punish me with natural death.'

Guddi got the Guru Granth Sahib, decided to skip *Akhand Paat* and stuck to *Khulla Paat* as partial readings were more to the point, swayed to the Shabad, fried sooji halwa in pure ghee and hoped like hell that the house was hereby purified, disinfected, whatever. Relatives, puzzled at a ceremony neither housewarming nor any anniversary, duly kissed the holy book with their foreheads and were glad to be part of a ritual so religious. The neighbours, on their part, discreetly balked at the absence of an eye-watering havan and pretended the Shabad that melodiously rent the air was *Gayatri mantra* in reverse, and if they did not get crimson threads to tie on their wrists, they tentatively tasted the prasad, which at least tasted reassuringly Hindu.

Eventually, the house went for one crore rupees, spectre and all. Guddi spent a whole day ostensibly cleansing the interiors, but in reality bidding every Kedar-less corner of the premises an emotional goodbye. The Gurgaon apartment's pig sty imitation soon took the edge off her grief.

'It is the damn superstition that prosperity in a new place depends on how messy you leave your previous tenancy,' she muttered, wielding the broom like a witch readying for takeoff.

'Judging by this, he is a millionaire wherever he is!' Drupa quipped, moving into Disha's flat in sorority haze.

Guddi, who had not bothered to load things she did not want into the truck, was surprised when later that month a little van mutely dropped off the exercise bike at her Gurgaon residence. The new owner did not want it either. By and by, she stopped hanging her clothes on it to dry and began to pedal in the evenings.

The pedalling came to a standstill when Badi brought over her offspring—all three of them—one fine day, roundly cursing Choti.

'She just threw my maid out. Can you believe that? As if life isn't difficult enough as it is. Now who will look after them? Her MTP Majesty?' sneered Badi, adjusting a Cellophane bra strap.

'The maid,' said Choti with gritted teeth, 'was a bitch. Look at Dorothy, always wetting her bed because of the bitch.'

'The bitch, as you call her, took up only one thousand rupees of my meagre allowance per month and looked after my kids much more and for much longer than you ever can even if you begin babysitting this very nano-second. Why do you think I let her live after she burnt the seat off my mauve pants with the iron box? One shuts one's eye to slave eccentricities just so one can get by,' Badi explained with pretend patience.

Drupa waved down the belligerent drivel. Guddi Mausi, whose primal priority was to ensure neighbours' empathy to her general state of bereavement so that they intermittently ran her errands, hushed them both by alluding to late husband

and sobbing loudly, a politically—if not contextually—right move. 'Cuteheart, my cuteheart.' She then pounced on Daler with exaggerated affection, holding his wriggly body against her chest and his will.

Riding over Guddi Mausi's cacophonous ode to widowhood and her half-hearted coochie-cooing, Badi riled against her irritatingly silent sister, 'Did it ever occur to you that children exaggerate?'

Drupa prompted mildly, 'And why would they do that, Badi?'

Shrugging, Disha walked away with the walk she learnt at a ramp somewhere; placing each bony knee diagonally before the other knee as if to trip self.

The voice in Drupa's head was icy, 'Your yardstick is dated.'

The next day Dorothy, dragging a naked Barbie by its tumbling golden hair, joined her aunt on the terrace. Daler, with systematic and gender-specific precociousness, disrobed dolls as soon as they were unwrapped, providing his sisters with the single largest collection of Lactating and Streetwalker Barbies.

Aunt and niece stared down desultorily around the new neighborhood, at the wet washing flapping in the wind, at the one-for-sorrow mynah that alighted on the electric lines, causing them to crane necks in search of its mate just so it could turn into two-for-joy. Barbie dangled by her golden mane before hurtling down in one determined suicidal leap.

'That must've hurt,' Drupa remarked.

'It is plastic.' The child divided her high pigtail into two equal parts and tugged them apart to secure the lace band, craning neck away from Drupa.

'Auntie,' she eventually lisped in the pseudo-Yankee way taught punctiliously by her parents. 'Could you tell mama it was all a lie? She wants to bring Ayah back.'

Drupa looked at the little face tilting up anxiously. There were words of comfort, of caution that automatically sprang to her lips, words she swallowed unsaid, tasting bile instead. She nodded, the easiest option by far.

Unable to sleep that night at Badi's rented flat she had seen the child surreptitiously tiptoe down the corridor early dawn, bed-sheet trailing after her.

'What are you doing?' she intercepted the stuffing of the sheet under a pile of other dirty sheets.

Dorothy started, her usual six-year-old's composure nowhere in sight. 'I had a dream that I was sitting on the pot, please Auntie I promise I won't do it again. Just don't tell Ayah.' Moving her legs tight together, she added. 'She said this time she would burn me right there.'

'As if!' Drupa dropped to her knees beside the child. 'That is just empty talk. Ayah says all kinds of things just to frighten you.'

Then it was upon the child to convince a disbelieving adult. 'She say…she say I need a stick up my su-su…then I will stop wetting the bed and making so much extra work for her.'

'Does Mommy know?'

'Please,' yowled the child. 'Ayah will kill both of us.'

Drupa confronted the maid when the children were in school.

'This Dorothy-baby and Debbie-baby, both like their mommy, wearing small-small dress and making big-big talk. How you can believe them, memsaab? Chee, what a dirty thing to say. Shows the character.'

'I don't care if she is lying. This is her house, not yours. Pack up and leave right now.'

'Just because your niece talks about nicely filling up her pants with sticks and what not, why must I be kicked out? Like mother, like daughter, and me suffering in the middle.

All kinds of men coming and going here, am I opening mouth? I keep silent and this is how you pay me back for my loyalty.'

Drupa suffered the vile tongue, keeping in mind the health of her own vocal chords, though the other's decibel levels weakened her resolve considerably and she was on the verge of picking up a kitchen knife and stabbing Ayah to brutal death when the latter dabbed eye and deemed it prudent to depart.

Badi's brood now wandered about in Guddi's teeny flat, donating their time and expertise to create and then maintain a shambles in the interiors, while their mother went about overtly articulate and fuschia-lipped like TV serial heroines, serving piping hot opinions on any subject under the sun.

'Look, he can't be dead,' declared Disha. She was a permanent fixture at her own home these days, an absent spouse took the fun out of infidelity, she was the first to admit. 'And if he is, where is the money?'

When next summoned to identify a corpse, she went wild with recognition. 'This is him,' she swore, though the postmortem put the age of the deceased in the region of sixty years. 'I know his...fingers.'

For good measure she added finger-related sentimental claptrap; how she had slid wedding ring down that finger once upon a time, how the finger had walked her first-born, how that very same finger had wiped her tear when she dropped him off that fateful day at the ISBT. By the end of her digital ditty, not a single eye was left dry in the morgue and she got her certificate and her money. The insurance people were in a hurry to kiss goodbye to the little hundred-rupee bundles, as this death was a national event going by the deep frowns on the foreheads of well-groomed newsreaders and they did not want the government to come out with egg on the face in this, not when they sprinkled the government's iodised salt on their own eggs. They had so wanted their sector to be kept to themselves a bit longer, not to be deregulated and thrown to the MNC wolves.

Disha battled the fear of Dave one day shoving his face under her satin quilt, *alive*. That was the content of her latest nightmare, wreaking havoc with her financial plans and what sex-life she could still muster.

Then she met Babaji through an aunt in Boston whose darshan had her incoherent with awe. 'He can tell you where naughty Davender is hiding in two minutes,' Aunt had vouched, assigning screens and Sikhism to him in one overseas stroke.

Disha's first meeting with Babaji almost never happened and Guddi Mausi rued her preoccupation with new flat and its varicose plumbing for the mishap.

'I am not going. *I am not going!*'

'Oh, do go or Dolly will keep calling and we will have to make up lies. Best just go and finish it off. Tell her I saw Babaji, Babaji saw me, our eyes met across a crowded room, end of story.'

'The car is at Shamu's garage anyway.'

But in the end, Guddi dropped her off as she had to go to Central Delhi to Gurudwara Bangla Sahib to collect langar food with her own hands, and pick up sundry pipes and washers.

At the temple, she locked up the car, with Apache Indian and AC switched on full blast for Disha's brats trapped inside, covered her head sedately with a polka-dotted dupatta in hot pink and walked in for worship.

Upon return, the leaky tap had slowly and steadily flooded entire kitchen and water lapped timidly at Guddi Mausi's en-socked feet, enraging her. After the children had been put up in desiccated spots, from where they proceeded to drop bits of langar food and advise her continuously, she managed to separate the soaked from the dry, muffle the tap's monotonous flow, convince the plumber's nephew to come himself before his uncle switched on mobile and could be located in the first place.

Radio Mirchi was switched off with a savage yank, the children were put to bed; it was a foggy night with stars nil and Guddi worried about Badi making the return trip all alone when the call came.

'I will sleep here. Babaji wants me to since it is an all-night jagaran.'

'The Babaji, she just wants a glamorous assistant,' Guddi Mausi roared, but could do little short of going all the way back and dragging stepdaughter by hair. But in a couple of days, it was crystal-clear that Badi had found a new diversion. The body shop closed down—Disha no longer hawked genitalia—but the soul opened a self-service counter.

Guddi went there personally to shoot some sense into her if necessary. 'We need to pray,' Mausi agreed grimly when Disha displayed unusual piety with constant references to Vaahe Guru, 'but we have responsibilities... You have children and I am too old to look after them. I am not their mother. I am not even *your* mother!'

Disha blew out her cheeks. 'Take their trust fund, I've nominated you guardian anyway, and put them in boarding schools.'

Gudiya gave up then. God knew she'd tried her best; no one could fault her on that front. When the motherless children, as she thought of them, were thrown at her, the first thing she did was rush Kedar for a vasectomy.

'They are the only children I will have,' she forfeited, knowing full well the self-defeating exercise in sacrifice it was going to be. As a mother she was only an impediment. With her, the girls were safe, but they were no one, least of all daughters. Strangely, despite the sincere fillip she provided her last husband with, it was Mangala who inspired the commercial success he enjoyed in his lifetime. It was Mangala whom he berated through those lyrics in a kind of celebration and contrition of whatever their union consisted of. Guddi had taken him that far, a long way, walked companionably arm in arm, shooed loiterers off his path, but she couldn't take him past that last bump ahead, that of transcendental talent, where he could travel into the chaotic Chakrvyuh but could come out armed only with truth. Until then he had a bagful of ballads—skittish ditties that stirred only die-hard drunkards—and suddenly he had the hit he craved. *Preet ki Boli* went into melodic history and Mangala was lyrically exonerated.

That evening blood pressure rode high along Guddi's cheekbones. The crows cawed up a cacophony, a leper hit the child pulling his hand-cart with an undone slipper from his own sore foot, cars turned left and right without indicator lights, drivers cursed; life went on but inside her the veins were overworked. Her temples throbbed and shook with blood; the Baby's Ass at the bottom of her chin wobbled.

Guddi clicked her mobile furiously. The party at Manish's farmhouse to bring in the new year, well that would be her re-entry into life. Apparently, Mr Mars was back, but she was damned if he was the only man left for her to dance with. Guddi snapped her fingers and, just like that, arranged for a resurrection.

12

DRUPA CLAMPED HER GAZE ON THE SUNLIT SMOG KINDLING dolled up flowers in Connaught Place. Rays splashed onto the pavement and walls, drugging those who dare roll eyes, catching ascendent eyeballs on the raw, thwarted here and there by stubborn sunglasses. Here in CP there were only two seasons, the season of sales and the season of no sales, and going by the gigantic waves of populace sweeping up and down laden with packages, it was now the former.

The minimum temperature was up, thank god. Nice day, in short, if you own the sun, Drupa thought, reinserting fingernail into mouth. Though visually unappealing and potentially smelly, it was the equivalent of a cigarette and what's spent on saliva was saved on ash. She sucked deeply; thank god, hearts were portable, if somewhat accident-prone.

Now why couldn't she have been born Badi? Why, when it came right down to it, couldn't she become her sister for one night? Forget one entire night, what about starting somewhere less ambitious, like right now for instance, in the middle of a nippy afternoon? Dish wouldn't moon over some unattainable member of the opposite sex or brood over rust hues let loose in unsuspecting pre-February hours. No, she would just have sex. Nice and simple.

But they didn't even *look* like sisters to begin with. Disha bared such a disciplined dental arrangement while she had inherited the southern gummy pout of extended mandibles in womb conspiracies one couldn't sue. (It was only when they smiled that Drupa could crow, but grinning non-stop was just as unaesthetic as the distended frown in repose.) They didn't do the usual sisterly things either, girlie things that other sisters did, like pick nailpaints or clothes off each other. Disha seldom wore the same thing twice, but the discards failed to fit Drupa, who needed eight times that material to go around *her* globe, though she strictly believed that what mannequins wore were only samples of the real thing!

'I like the way new clothes smell. I can wear them twice may be without getting my scent into them. Then…' Disha trailed off. Then the dress or man began to reek of her and that would never do.

Ah, a café, Drupa noted. Not one of those pretentious la-di-dah ones where ordering coffee dislocated your tongue, but a small, dainty one with teetering unpainted chairs and coffee in a teapot. All around her were people staring into cups or eyes, daydreaming, falling in love. There was a time that did not happen, the blistering of skin in the presence of happiness. Making her want to dive into self and scratch from inside.

The waiter threw up an eyebrow.

'Poison,' she ordered with a purportedly mystical smile, feeling her hind-limbs go latex. He'd look cute in a diamond-studded G-string with a rose clenched redly between his teeth!

He shrugged. There was such delicious detachment in the gesture that she wanted to suck the gum clean out of his mouth, take away that free, free grin. Trap his tongue with hers. Ravish the grimy independence out of him. A new man may undo the done, overwrite with italic font.

'I am all alone,' she lisped, crinkling eyes, shaking ponytail in 'I-am-so-cute-and-helpless' crinkle and shake witnessed in revolting times on revolting girls.

'Cappuccino?' he asked, pushing the printed menu toward her and she changed over reluctantly from coy to literate, giving up her one-noon-stand reverie. Though in her fantasies men nibbled hotly at her earlobe, whispering gruffly, 'Stick up your skirt, it's a rape', she knew she'd grow another view spread-eagled against a seedy lamppost. Most women had lubrication problems if they didn't know the man, her patients testified.

'This says cream extra. Do you mean to say, the milk is otherwise toned?'

He nodded exaggeratedly in slow motion, like he was ICU in-charge and she a potential corpse; if she'd just pop it, he could lock up and go home. No white knights here, the meter on their horses were all run out and the dry-cleaning bill for rusty armours seen to be believed.

'Just for the record, I wasn't born a middle-aged hag with dull eyes,' she rasped but he had gone, her rasp groping uncertainly at his rapidly receding back.

She watched the words waver, mouth to ear, then dissolve like wind in water, just as all the words ever spoken before. Promises and vows, rebuttals and rejections; where did all the alphabetical arrangements go when they died? But then he, her lover, had not used up many verbal combinations either, bed being that rare place where they rode roughshod over words and their sensibleness in the scheme of things. What did she want anyway? Play bed-bed happily ever after, chase him down for every orgasm owed? A pity her heart wasn't labelled 'this side up' like her body.

Her hands enfolded the cup, sipping from it, blistering tongue to which apt lexicon never came canoeing. Should've dialled Disha for him; now that would have left Drupa as dubiously wholesome as before. Sex sieved from love was hindsight served in foresight.

Maudlin *and* muddled! She laughed and two nymphets at the next table looked up and laughed too, making Drupa glad for all the other hearts, whole or halved, beating near and far, making hers one of many, many, many. Stepping out, she looped the cardigan around her shoulders.

'How,' she asked herself, walking out into the open. 'How could something as definite as a baby shape inside me when we weren't making love, when we were making nothing, a big, vigorous nothing.'

She had no idea how long she walked, inner circle of CP to outer circle and back, but she was aware of a desire, by and by, to stop. Exhaustion slackened her insides and made her feet sluggish; the evening, when she wasn't looking, had turned meat-cleaver cold.

Three ghosts jumped rope in the lane where she spied the fire, leaping, licking, kickboxing the air higher and higher, flames in the savage cavern performing a bestial bop, beckoning delicate dancing hands with every moan of the wind. There it was in a large abandoned plot of land and people were wandering away from the fire, having flung in their menial offerings of jaggery and peanuts.

Drupa inched closer, fascinated by the bonfire's warmth, the molten turquoise at its heart, rooting for a riotous mingling of flesh and soul even as the corn popped. Her feet pedalled air wildly as she sprawled on the ground and bruised knee, her nose grinding into the dry dust, mouth in rubble.

Sobs dried so close to the heat, tears licked up like raindrops before they formed, branded where they rolled in a sleight of flickering hand. She cooed to those flames, burnishing them with jerky breaths, copying the conflagration, matching tongue to darting tongue, writhing as the wind trembled in her veins; *this dance is mine.*

'Please,' she pleaded, arms kindling, eyelashes scorched to cinders, her whole being combustible straw as she heeded the fire's hiss.

It had been a dank day in January when Mangala kidnapped them.

The girls had been crossing out every needless date in their haste to out-foot into the month of March, the month Papaji had promised they could wing back to Amma's lap. Their practise of patience was commendable and the surprise therefore the greater when Amma came to them instead.

She just appeared at their school gate one fine day when the bell had rung, grinning wildly, her face different from what they remembered, yet the same underneath that difference.

'Come, come,' she said, shepherding them into an autorickshaw and they had fallen upon her like demented pups, telling her entire stories at once, swinging like human pendants from her neck, her hands firm around their thin waists, as if those endless days and nights of loneliness had never existed.

In place of the old homestead, she took them to a remote hotel. 'We will stay here,' she said and they happily agreed, reassured to be integral parts of her adventure.

'Amma, why do you look so changed?'

'Worrying does that to a face,' she laughed and they were reassured for the sand dunes in her voice were still there, little folds of softness their feet could sink into.

The whole night she cuddled them, fed them stale food she had cooked and carried all the way in a train from Kerala. In the morning they gorged on ice cream, for cunningly the girls realised they had the power to move mothers if not whole mountains.

By next nightfall they were fretting. Amma babbled non-stop of a future that did not take into account present discomfort, extempore diarrhoea and tonsils that acted up. The drone of Mangala's voice, which had instantly lulled the girls to sleep the previous night, took on the edge of petulance to their untrained ears.

Barely had they shut their eyes at midnight after answering Amma's questions, repeated endlessly like she did not really hear their replies, when all the lights came on at once and people barged in threateningly, lifted a cowering Mangala away from the cot, barking at her, waving handcuffs under her nose and quoting FIRs filed against her. Later, of course, there was the court injunction; she was not to come within such and such radius of the girls and she'd haunt schools, any schools anywhere, keeping a vigil, waiting for her daughters to emerge from them. But for then she only had to cringe and beg and prove she had not fed them poison.

Papaji scooped the sleepy girls to his sides. 'Everything is going to be okay now. I am here,' he soothed, bending down to kiss the tops of their heads.

'Kedar,' Mangala screamed in protest when a policeman prodded her roughly at the back, but with a slight nod to the policeman, he continued to cuddle his daughters. Her hair was matted, eyes wild. No, he did not recognise her. The Mangala he remembered was always washed and strong, bouncing back for the next salvo with teeth bared. Not this whimpering creature with matter in the eye.

'Kedaaar,' she screamed again when they yanked her by her hair, speaking like a small child, 'Make them stop, they are hurting me.'

'Amma,' Badi cried, alarmed out of her sleepiness. Papaji's palm crept down to Choti's mouth, covering it, so that she had to struggle for every breath with an uncooperative nose.

'Wait for me...' Amma babbled to them in Malayalam. 'Just wait like last time.'

Badi moved forward.

'Disha!' Kedar's strident call held her back. 'Take her away, this woman is mad, can't you see?' he shouted to the policemen. 'Can't you see she is frightening my children? Hurry up.'

'Chal, teri tho,' a man harshly bade, dragging her out into the corridor, but her nails still scraped the doorway, holding fast.

A broken plea, 'I have some money, see?'

Then an inhuman cry rent the air, making sense of the indistinct thuds before and after. Drupa and Disha had heard the turnip sacks thrown by the farmhands in Daadiji's home fall with the same muffled thud.

'Wipe her mouth,' a voice advised outside. 'Or they'll make a big thing out of the blood.'

A uniformed man came back, looked randomly about for a rag, homed in on the thorthu Mangala had wrapped the homemade sweetmeats in. He held the napkin up in the light, suspicious of the rancid coconut oil stains, was sniffing it gingerly when his superior bellowed for him to hurry.

'Sir,' he responded, rushing out with the rag.

They heard mutterings, then the footsteps receded, a careless dragging of two inert feet in their midst and a docile calm, however unnatural, began to emanate from the corridor. Kedar took his arms away from the girls' shoulders.

'You never have to see her again,' he vowed, picking up their schoolbags and water bottles, shepherding them out into the corridor after an all-clear from the hotel staff.

The girls nodded wordlessly, walking behind him in dazed silence, not daring to look back into the darkened corridor into which their mother had been returned like a genie back into its bottle. For long they imagined her to still be there somewhere, getting better, biding her time, chatting up passers-by, cooking them minor feasts. This time when she appeared at their school, they'd be more prepared, *they* would take her somewhere; cunningly they quizzed Vicky bhaiyya on hideaways and wrote them down in code in their notebooks so no one could guess their whereabouts when they disappeared. If only she came back like she promised!

Therefore, it was a while before Amma's muted scream from that night winged back to them. Then, like a ghost denied exit, it stayed with them.

Drupa blinked into the dying fire. Lori meant climatic change. It was the air calling out, 'next please', to an unseasonal season. Time to unpack that naphthalene ball from her summer suitcase, she reflected, and head home.

'Rise and shine,' she called out gaily to the skull at home. 'It's party time!'

Part III

SOUTH–NORTHERN MONSOONS

13

POOR EYESIGHT HAMPERED MANGALA NAMBOODIRI'S floral offerings to God; most carnations fell on the newly tiled floor instead of the idolatry feet they were aimed at. God knew, she always expected to fumble less while occupying *his* territory. The temple, though recently done up to its teeth, was familiar ground compared to her home, Meledeth Illam, which crumbled and groaned at every stroke, giving out strange rheumatic twangs, dripping unashamedly during monsoons.

The temple renovations had displeased devotees, not the least because their piggybanks had been raided. Each had to donate twenty bricks and some chosen ones were called in to repay divine favours with solid spadework. For a long while no one went public about recent miracles for fear of celestial reclaims.

If a wife declared the magical vanishing of her beloved son's fever, the husband hastily attributed the phenomenon to pills and prescriptions. 'Don't go disturbing the poojari with your jabbering or he will ask for your kidney!'

It was as if even God was busy waiting with bated breath for his abode to be readied, so sparing were people with their prayers. The new quarters assigned to Divinity were not straightaway praised, a caution was adopted to sustain a semblance of the hitherto reluctance.

'His real accommodation is in our heart,' Keshavan piously opined to the women in his family, a wife and four sisters, and one mad brother, chained to a post in the verandah by ankle with the chain extending all the way to the outhouse lavatory in what was a practical length.

It was his duty as the mobile sibling to report back happenings in the outside world, and Keshavan took this duty seriously. 'How do glazed tiles fit into a place of worship? Prayer is a matter of the soul and not marble slabs.'

His elder brother snorted, seemingly in sympathy to the sentiment just expressed, but given the fact that of late all he did was snort or grunt by way of articulation, this ought not to have spurred further speech.

'If you are fond of pappadoms, don't salt your gruel, that's all I say,' Keshavan summed up obscurely, chiefly because it was self-spun wisdom and needed a trial run notwithstanding contextual platforms.

His half-hearted ire kept the women away from the temple for three whole days. Then one day he came back unexpectedly early and found a sacred mutiny on his hands. Each woman held a coconut, foreheads gleaming militantly with sandalwood, spiritual starch stiffening their gold-bordered sarees, prepared to pray or kill, causing Keshavan to chuckle weakly and accompany them on their pilgrimage.

'The coconuts will break better on an altar than my head,' he joked.

As one of her florets wobbled precariously at the shiny new idol's ankle, Mangala worked a spurt of sputum up her throat.

'Aargh,' she gurgled. A younger sister held her by the hand and took her to the courtyard where Mangala spat out a smooth arc in the air with the ease of practice.

You could show her any spot in the world and she would spit with Olympian accuracy or take your money back, her sisters wagered behind her back, the safest place to be when the spitting was in process.

The triplets began the parikrama, walking excitedly around the temple, trampling the hems of their half-sarees underfoot, chattering excitedly amongst themselves about every minute detail of the renovated interiors, their youth enabling them to circumvent the elderly route to acceptance.

'It is all so spotless, like Chettiyar's house.' Chettiyar's son was married to a nurse who worked in Dubai and sent entire salaries so that the resultant architecture was the talk of the town. Being invited there was high on every suburban socialite's priority list and suddenly pappadom-making, which was what the Chettiyars ceaselessly performed by the roadside, became an art form like origami or Mohiniyattam that everyone wanted to learn.

'It is all so moving,' sighed another sister, who unblinkingly monitored the cable network.

'I feel like just curling up there,' declared the third, pointing at the mandapam.

The other two hooted. 'You are missing Amma's tummy.'

'Where is Chechi?' she frowned, changing the subject.

'Leaning against a gold-plated pillar. How much she prays!'

'Easier to pray now that everything is so pretty-pretty,' they all agreed, watching Kanaka and Keshavan hover possessively over the polished deities.

At home before lights were switched on Kanaka went through the house whispering, 'Deepam, deepam...', skipping lightly over the supine figure of her brother-in-law in the verandah as he was known to trip her up with sporadic irreverence. Cunningly, he'd lie unmoving, supine and fat like a sun-drunk crocodile, then wham, his leg snaked out and Kanaka fell, lamp and teeth clattering down with her.

She'd shriek loudly to flush her hero, Keshavan, out from home interiors while Ettan would curl his leg back in and grin. Since it was her painstaking research and groundwork that put the final signature on his insanity, his possible sanity was an unintentional secret between them, a conspiracy that brought them unwillingly closer on the floor thus, eye to eye, thrice a month at least. Once in a while he'd look at her and something about his eyes gouged, gave pause; she could swear the sinister smile was whole in sense but apart from voicing her hatred for him she kept such doubts completely to herself.

'Poor thing,' Keshavan would mutter. 'Used to scour the seas like a pirate. Now a patient!'

And Kanaka would sniff some more, remembering the hard time when the patient's faeces beaded the verandah like so much coral here and there. It had taken all her cunning to checkmate that!

'Let's put him away in a...place for such people. It will cost a lot of money, which means your sisters will have to stay spinsters all their lives, but we will suffer that,' she said with a self-sacrificing sniff, as the triplet sisters-in-law let out a howling protest.

Those were the pre-modernised temple days, so one could freely thank divine intervention for Ettan's subsequent toilet training. Clank, clank, he'd go, rattling the chain purposely loud on his way to the outhouse toilet now that the leash had been unfurled to reach there, and when Kanaka said it interfered with her slumber, he pretended to be her, holding up the chain.

'This is my necklace. Look everybody, I am dancing under this huge gold necklace around my neck. Ooooh, it is strangling me, this mountain of a maala. Save me,' he screamed piteously.

Upon this Kanaka preferred to lose sleep rather than provoke so powerful a foe. His loss of memory, or mind as she preferred to term it, had been gradual. It had been there in the way he woke up that first time he returned home like nothing had happened; his eyes stayed vacant until mid-morning and then the vacancy occupied his eyes longer until soon the alertness had been all but ousted except at the most unexpected moments. Nonetheless, it was disorienting to have him greet her formally, like an elder brother-in-law should, to await the sneaking of some recollection into his eyes, some recollection that revealed their estrangement, some memento in memorium that exposed her before those eyes emptied out again.

She had once heard him chant behind his wall, 'Water jug to the right, clock in the centre...' and she knew he was marking them, committing them like photographs to his mental album, but she revelled when he opened their bedroom door once, mumbling, 'I thought this was the bathroom,' leaving Keshavan unsure about voyeurism. Piously, Kanaka prepared for bed fully dressed, pallu tucked tight into waist, just in case...

She took them away, the clock and the jug, or switched their places so that he'd wake up in acute alarm, staring wide-eyed at the grimy walls around him, hands and heart trembling like bones in a dog's jaw, eyes darting to locate familiar objects, eyes full of a nameless fear of the unknown. And she'd stand there soliticiously, lips moving in prayer, knowing full well his mounting panic at her presence, the banging at the centre of his chest.

She did not know what she abhorred more, the calm of his vacant eyes or the flurry of his faint rememberings. It had been a curious thing to witness, the slipping of his present away from him.

'Such a pity,' she often decried to vegetable vendors or immediate neighbours who dropped in on the pretext of plucking curry-leaves to take a peek at Madman, hoping he'd expose himself like it was rumoured and they could run away shrieking, their modesty outraged. 'A pity that Ettan could not handle his wife's demise, that he had to give up his lucrative job and rot thus. Still, it goes to show there's someone up there.' This hint of malevolence she slipped in with a sigh. If only, she insinuated, if only he had not been so lucky to begin with.

The hand snapping tender curry-leaves would still to observe a two-minute silence in requiem for the afore-lived luxury and rue the Madman's tenacious hold on his loincloth.

Sometimes they felt it their neighbourly task to sneak up with inflated plastic bags that went 'pop', causing him to emit disoriented screams, wreaking much humour in their wake. It happened more and more now that his lucidity dwindled and he no longer growled at them.

Of Keshavan, who got up to scrutinize with every vestige of compassion, Madman had once enquired, 'Why are you standing? Am I singing the national anthem…or is it wind? Bloody thing, won't let you sit, eh?'

The crew had been courteous about the onset of their Captain's dementia, handing him ground duties but his grave reprimand—'sa-ni-da'—to an absconding sailor and answering of coffee cup instead of phone, had them pack their optimism and him home with all emoluments, most akin to a state funeral this side of death.

Keshavan's eyes had snapped with a canine alertness at his brother's return. The pension he had taken as a lumpsum and, according to Kanaka's wishes, invested in some land off

Chaavakaad. It wasn't his fault that the government had decided to broaden the highway and wanted land for a shopping complex. A bunch of them was affected, having to sell off their property in haste.

The air grew heavy with the promise of rain; wafting it along on the jasmine combs stuffed into long feminine tresses, in fresh and rancid coconut oil that ran down the strands; on the pulsating soil they stirred up under their rubber-soled sandals and bare feet, even in the yeasty turn of starch in the cotton folds draped around them. The heaviness had begun to ferment, coiling languorously down the streets until the sidewalks were as sour as the houses, pushing people out and out, seeking spaces where the promise of rain had already been kept.

The triplets waylaid those swarming the temple's foyer, hurriedly unloading their arsenal of small talk like three Cinderellas with a stopwatch, hailing those who would have scurried by, detaining them with quick-bite incidents, snacky gossip and short-winded rhetoric.

'Coming to the temple?'

'Going so soon?'

'So warm…it may rain tonight.'

Presently their thrill at the outing fused with fret.

'Ettan will be waiting for his tea. Why won't Kanaka Chechi hurry up?' a triplet said.

'You mean you haven't given him tea yet?'

The other two shook their heads.

Soon they let up a mild wail, growing in pitch until Keshavan found them just before they hit the highest note.

'You know Mangala,' he tried to calm them down. 'Gets glued to the paintings on the wall, she's staring at the Kans-

Krishna encounter right now. Did you all see it, its framed in Meena enamel, worth seeing but not for this long. Kanaka is still trying to coax her into returning.'

'She forgot...' hiccupped his younger sister, 'she forgot to give him tea.'

'That's okay,' dismissed Kanaka, walking up to them. 'Lunatics don't know tea-time from nap-time.'

'Where is Chechi?' asked Keshavan.

'Still there,' scowled Kanaka. She came here ardently seeking offspring, anything to lay some claim to the future, though doctors had told her to adopt or meditate, anything but come eat their heads on this. 'I think we should just leave her here...' Owing to the involuntary swallowing of a mosquito, who met her outgoing yawn halfway, Kanaka maintained a suddenly prim silence, discreetly spitting to the left and right to dislodge the purely non-vegetarian morsel from throat before she inadvertently digested it.

Keshavan smiled at her in approval, assuming the silence a propriety measure and not the accidental carnivorous consumption it actually was.

The evening drums began to thump, pulsating through the temple's acres and interiors, the throb spatulating Kanaka's brow and blood so that she craned neck this way and that, seeking a pair of eyes she was convinced watched her in masculine appreciation, an appreciation rightfully accrued to her.

Her last visit to her mother's house had coincided with her elder sister's, the one who bred non-stop. There were twelve children of different shapes and sizes with varying quotas of snot in their nostrils—'one child gets a cold, then everyone does,' her sister had said—taunting her by their very existence, by their unintentional tenacity in boarding a womb, travelling the course and alighting at said destination on said hour.

When Kanaka held a nephew by the tailbone as he spewed curdled milk, her sister had come running. 'Are you pouring him down the basin?'

She did not know how to hold a baby or to have one for that matter! It simply maddened her, this deafening silence of her empty-shelled womb that roared an unending oceanic echo in the ears.

She had visited every god-man referred to her, performed each puja, each ritual they prescribed. They stared above her head, exhorting hovering spirits to vacate her soul, her womb. She suffered their curses, purportedly addressed to the evil spirits, and their marauding hands, squeezing her all over her body to nab the culprit ghoul, the fat globs of saliva they spat at her while communicating contempt to the spectre she housed.

'A relative has performed a goododhuram,' a pundit pronounced, prescribing that she march naked at midnight to the said venue and dig with spade at a particular point. And when Kanaka did the needful, she actually encountered a mud pot buried there with lime and green chillies!

'He must have put it there himself,' Keshavan realised a year into her womb's muteness.

She had accorded him a bitter look, remembering the undignified pilgrimage, utterly exposed, with desperate hope in heart, a lit lamp burning up her palm with its vagrant wick, when her insomniac brother-in-law had visually recorded her humiliating exit and re-entry into the house.

Madman had clicked his tongue at her in exaggerated sympathy, 'It is my brother's fault; not manly enough to stand up to you, not manly enough to make you a mother! You've emasculated him, Kanaka, struck at the whole ardha-narishwar equation. He has to play woman to the man in you. You can't grudge him what you drove him to, can you?'

She did. She couldn't have asked for a better husband she knew and yet she chafed in torpor. For the Catholic butcher who went whistling past their house, his hairy chest displayed in the hot sun, steel crucifix glinting; for the courier man who came looking for some address in the neighbourhood and spoke solely in English, accepting the glass of water from her serious as a commitment. Oh, how she had wanted to take him into her room upstairs and fashion a dainty baby there and then!

Strange men all around her, on the streets, at the temple, in magazines and TV serials, they all ignited her with an anonymous passion, burning her witchingly at its stake, inviting her to an orgy of tenderness only to tease her with their crucial absence. Restlessly, she'd lower lashes and look penetratingly at her toenails or snake out a hand with its trembly fingers to pull agitatedly at pallu, her teeth worrying the bottom lip incessantly.

There was this man she had met at a wedding. He had stared through heavily hooded eyelids and she had flushed, hotly tugging her brother's baby into her lap, cuddling him, kissing him and when she looked up, the man smiled knowingly.

Kanaka's bosom heaved and breath forked, the nadaswaram grated in her ears till she could sit calmly no more. But nothing came out of her restlessness; it was like a rat that nibbled at the hem of her soul.

Later, she hunted furiously for him in the wedding albums. There was no sight of him, but there she was, looking searchingly at the camera, in her lap holding a petrified baby.

14

MANGALA STRETCHED IN THE DIM-LIT ENVIRONS AND HEARD the conch blow. She felt the same urgency she felt long ago when the pressure cooker's whistle blew.

'How many, how many?' she'd run in, panting.

'Not how many whistles, Mangala, acting so illiterate. It is how long you keeping that thing on fire.' Her mother whose peak cooking years did not include a cooker or mixie knew these things almost mystically. 'And don't wipe hands with saree's edge like that. You know the girls come and blow nose into it.'

Earlier, when Mangala had written from JNU, gushing over Kedar, Amma had warned, 'Men never marry woman he take to cinema.'

Mangala tried to explain in a fifty-paise inland the matter of his wit. At all-night tea sessions at JNU dhabas, he had enthralled her with his premarital awareness of ground realities in politics and pedestrian issues, with his mellifluous humming and dexterous shaayari in supposedly chaste Urdu.

She had just squatted with a Sikkimese friend, bitten into a jamun. Her teeth tingled and she put out a purple tongue; their eyes had met then. She looked away and he came to her with a glass of water, a sweetener straight from his sweet-talking tongue.

Later, when she wrote about her impending nuptials to Amma, she shot back in a telegram, 'Fire, water mix?'

'Doesn't want to pay wedding expenses, the cow,' Kedar interpreted to his own mother.

They married in an Arya Samaj Mandir with classmates for witnesses and garlands, two of each. Kedar's family kept away out of respect for Mangala's.

'Will look damn odd, if they are there and they are not,' Kedar had explained tenderly, speaking of his own people and her people, respectively. Privately he had warned his mother, 'Best stay out of it, then nobody will question the shoestring budget. You've seen how people fall mouth first into butter-chicken vats.'

'Yes,' shuddered his mother, 'They starve for months before a wedding. Oh my son, take my blessings at least!'

Like two orphans, Kedar and Mangala clutched hands and repeated bravely any jumbo-mumbo the pundit cared to spout, circling each other's necks with garlands they had made out of flowers with their own hands the previous night.

'These are funeral flowers,' the pundit pointed impassively at the marigold and they almost burst into tears at the poignancy of their own ignorance regarding the joint adventure that lay ahead.

Married, breath ricocheting like wind in oboes, they returned to their respective hostels and applied for married student rooms. She wrote carefully in her diary that night, 'I do not feel any different.'

As if marriage was an external application! How naive she was, she thought now, trying to dislodge a sister's arm on her shoulder, the one guiding her back home gently through the night.

'Look at those stars,' Mangala told her sister, who clutched her elbow. 'They are not as close as they look. Millions and millions of miles away from us and millions and millions of miles away from each other. They only look so close.' Her knowing smile disappeared as she stumbled.

'Hold her tight,' Keshavan directed. 'You know how potty she is.'

'Blood tells,' murmured Kanaka with a click of teeth.

Kedar had also clicked his teeth long ago at the profusion of coconut-based curries and vegetable concoctions before him with frank distaste. 'You are no wife.' And later, regardless of uterine contractions, 'You are no mother.'

His own mother had tried to take charge with disastrous results.

'Beti,' she had told Mangala at their first meeting, 'I will not call you bahu, you are my beti. I now have one more beti, ah, God's been benevolent to me.' A big production was made out of folding back the saree draped over Mangala's head. 'Now let's see your face.' As if she had been flashing her ass instead.

Later she phoned and Mangala disconnected saying wrong number. Kedar's mother sulked until he intervened and gleaned the real reason: 'She thought you asked for some Betty.'

'Beti,' said his mother with gritted teeth. 'I said beti.' That was the last time she called her by anything but name. 'Mangala nice name,' she said, not wanting to eat crow. 'I'll call you Mangala from now.'

'Yes, Maji.' Since she called guests, strangers and the servant-girl 'beta/beti', Mangala wasn't particularly offended at the altered nomenclature.

'Beta,' her mother-in-law would serenade the maid sweetly when someone had walked in and Beta would promptly bring the drinking water on cue. She had been trained to serve tap water to guests, just like she was advised in advance to add ginger shavings to tea for certain people, like the lawyer who handled Kedar's late father's paperwork or an aunt who occasionally played marriage broker for the family.

Mangala was also witness to Beta boiling her own rice, some cheap variety from the market, the money for which was deleted from her measly allowance, and the lack of non-vegetarian fare, a daily luxury at Kedar's place, in her crack-riddled plate. Back home, Mangala remembered personally serving princely fare to even drivers who brought visiting relatives. In fact, her own mother ate only after the domestic help. When she mentioned this, Kedar mumbled something about Marxism not having infected the northern masses yet, making Marx sound like a mosquito formally charged only with malaria and dengue as yet.

At his request she stopped marinating her hair in coconut oil, the freshly churned oil her mother conveyed with anyone travelling down in Jayanti Janata, because night after night it broke her heart when he turned away from her, holding his nose, but it would have broken her mother's heart if she asked her to stop sending the oil.

On Sundays he'd open out his turban, apply mustard oil to his waist-length hair, and when she sat later on his lap, their sun-dried hair kissed tip to crackly tip, the union seemed worthwhile.

Such halos soon went into hiding when swords were unsheathed. An attack of the grins stopped interfering with their disputes, tit for tats turned increasingly childish until he began to throw History at her. Then she read up furiously and fanatically on her own regional past and they came out with daggers from dawn to dusk, fighting a clandestine clannish, provincial war, which they garbed in the petty differences of the day. Food was the arena where their artillery found arti-culation, where they could cloak the burbling foolishness with oesophageal essays.

His dismissal of ruling ministers, well-rehearsed jokes, the applause and resultant temporary high that fired his imagination then to a thousand null dreams; nothing touched Mangala in the right way later, she was too close to the bone and could strike at the void now. She cynically observed him watch out for chinks in conversations where he could swing in with the panaché of a trapeze artist with his punchline or couplets, timing being everything, and guiltily enjoyed the running out of the batteries in his garish-looking radio. Glued to his ear was this tiny transistor, the source of commercially soulful ballads that Kedar took to heart, tongue and eyes. Humming along, he would shed a tear or two, usurping a sensitivity his spouse suspected with good cause, making incongruous the comparitive unsentimentality he brought to her table, her bed, her very life.

The satisfied burps he suppressed while licking spoon clean after rajma-chawal at somebody's place exasperated, especially when he patronisingly spouted, 'Go ahead, eat with your hands. Sukvinder won't mind,' as if she had applied and headquarters had sanctioned.

'Free at last,' she'd affect ecstasy, waving her fingers high in emancipation. 'My fingers are out of jail.' And she took to eating their thickest makki ki rotis with knives to get back at him and his spoon.

'Like baby's stools,' she'd pronounce after scrutinising his favourite kadi, kadi that his mother thoughtfully served in a white china dish to offset its bright yellow-hood. 'And this cowdung,' she deglamourised sarson da saag, 'we get free globs of this at the canteen all the time.'

It was all she could do to wrestle down her gorge when Kedar extended bowl for extra fluid at the gol-gappa cart or slurped down chaats drowning in a sea of pungent mint, instructing majestically, 'Less sugary, more scorching, bhaiyya,' then wave a hand near his mouth as if to extinguish flames.

'We don't eat out on the streets,' she explained when he tired of solo feasting.

She began to send his long khaadi kurtas to the dhobi, no longer taking sensual pleasure in blowing suds off them or starching them or ironing them or even folding them with bare hands.

Then the babies came along—she gave up her PhD plan with the second one, so that they had to move out of JNU hostel. Maji had warned grimly at the news, 'ab lete mat rehna,' as if Mangala intended to turn her confinement into one long weekend.

He chose the first baby's name; exhausted and recovering from general anaesthesia in C-section aftermath, Mangala nodded her head at 'Disha'. She had been glad just to get out of the ordeal alive. Then the second naming ceremony too he tried to take over but this time she was prepared and combated with 'Drupa'.

'We are naming babies, not writing poems,' he mocked her penchant for alliteration, but let her win the round as, contrary to popular opinion, a second girl instead of boring him had flattered him, though his mother clutched his elbow sympathetically at the hospital, mumbling about the need to be brave.

In casual chats with Mangala in the hospital after the second delivery, Maji had rued the baby's genitals.

'But we knew I was having a girl,' Mangala replied, as every changing aspect of her personality had been put under the microscope and declared 'girl carrier'; from the way she held her hips to the menu she favoured.

'That,' her mother-in-law shrugged, 'was to ward off the evil eye. We all say, give us a girl dark as coal. No one means it. In my own house I survived only because I was the eldest girl and my complexion could be seen at once. All said and done, bahu, only one girl per family was allowed in those days.'

'But we have no choice! It is not the food we eat or the prayers we say that determine the baby's sex.'

Maji threw her a shrewd look. 'In my days, the second girl didn't exist. Honeyed cotton wads stuffed in the mouth saw to that.'

After a pause, Mangala swallowed and said, 'That's why your sons look outside for girls to marry.'

Kedar brushed it aside as he always did his mother's dubious wisdom, 'She is a woman of her times. You can't change her mindset overnight. But you…!'

His exasperation sprang from her attempts to create gold paste by grinding her gold chain on a stone for the purpose of the baby's first meal. 'Are you mad?' he asked.

'This is what we do back home.' She was firm.

'*This* is home,' he reminded for the umpteenth time.

Ground in the inexorable machinery of motherhood, Mangala was not inclined to repair the rupture in her marriage, but unabashedly indulged in its intrinsic warfare so that she whispered in sleep-deprived whispers, 'Thakazhi.'

'Amrita Pritam,' he'd retort.

'Satyan.'

'Sahni, Balraj.'

She'd rouse herself up to recite laboriously, 'Manasa maine varu.'

'Aa laut ke aaja mere meet…' he'd retaliate.

Neither worried that the sonnets were originally mating calls.

Décor suffered, too, so that the residential radius resembled nothing either aspired for. If he wanted resham-wood, she yearned for self-deprecating cane; the compromise jumbled her bookcase with his rocking chair, both side by side not on talking terms. Nails were hastily embedded into walls for sundry sunsets and scenery to be dangled upon, then they'd debate and alter locations of said sunsets and scenery until the entire house looked decorated with nails. Much of their time was spent adjusting to the scrambled interiors and grudging the time thus frittered.

It had all started with his admonishment, 'Let's not do it typically South.' And his wife, who got her take on 'typical' completely from spouse, merged her newfound prejudice with furnishing tastes.

'So sparse they keep their rooms,' he feared, so she went and filled it up with bargain bric-a-brac from the streets, hoping he'd applaud her Punjabi aesthetics while he, to his credit, initially kept a tight rein on any critical faculties at this accumulation of junk.

Ultimately, upbringing was dragged into every possible clash. For instance, when his sister dropped off a son at their house, saying casually as she departed for her monthly Central Market shopping, 'He may get a bit cranky. Poor fellow, he's got chicken-pox,' she was not to know how much their bilateral talks suffered.

Mangala rotated swiftly on her heels to glare at Kedar. 'How can she?' she burst finally when he showed no signs of comprehension. 'This spreads, it is infectious. How typically Punj, that's all I have to say. As long as your job is done, why worry about the others, eh?'

Kedar was putting their firstborn to sleep, walking up and down to calm her colic. Occasionally he'd raise his eyebrows at Mangala and she'd put a finger to lips in hush and encouragingly mime the act of sleep though the seriously wide-eyed state of said baby was evident to her from the rear.

The small boy had innocently replied to all questions put before him. Yes, he went down to play every evening. Yes, he went to school. No, he had not taken the country into confidence regarding the watery boils. Mommy had said he would turn into a chicken if he told anyone.

'This is Delhi,' she lamented and she was thinking not just of the anti-social stunt pulled by sister-in-law, but the colourful birds captive in their cages near Lal Qila. 'Here,' said the hawkers, 'here are the rarest of birds, really unique.' What was unique was their handpainted plumes; the dyes ran out at first rinse.

Mangala, doe-eyed grateful for this opportunity to play martyr, overrode all of Kedar's embarrassed apologies. 'When our daughters die of the pox, then you will wake up,' she declared dramatically.

Wake up to what, Kedar was careful not to ask, but his reprieve came in her mother's multiplication.

'Mangamaa,' wrote her mother, 'there are two types of marriages. One where husband rules and other where he doesn't. The trick is to have second type when he thinks it the first. My heart is crying when you complain. Not good. You doing something wrong, very wrong. You are not making him believing he is king.

'Kunjumon's son-in-law, the Army boy, going to Ludhiana via Delhi. I am readying two litres of oil though coconuts growing smaller day by day. Put nicely on heads of girls. This is the time to blacken hair and make it grow.'

Post-script was the shocker, 'How can I say what I am wanting to say. Your daughters, they are having one more aunt or uncle. Yes, I am with baby. I thought bleeding stop with ageing, but doctor say I am mother again, sixth month finish she say. Your Appa stop talking to me.'

'Isn't she a bit old for all this?' Kedar asked and she knew his considerate bewilderment was put on, for it was established in the course of subsequent conversation that Kerala was filled with rabbits fancy-dressed as people.

'That's why they wear mundus. Very convenient for breeding! When the movies are about sex, what else can you expect?' he asked with pseudo-sympathy.

'Just because you went to see a smutty movie and it was in Malayalam, don't presume my parents spend all their time copulating in a hutch. Not all our movies are subtitled "Thunder Thighs",' she fumed. 'And you need money to see movies, smutty or otherwise, of which you make none.'

When her father passed away she took offence at his casual call to someone, 'Sasura mar gaya,' though he straight-facedly insisted he had been referring to the colony's cat and not her late father.

'And your brother,' he added self-righteously, 'gone for a bath!'

Keshavan was in Rameswaram for a holy dip and her Merchant naval brother was mid-sea, both therefore incommunicado.

She had left the babies with him and travelled South alone to attend the funeral. Kedar was punctilious in his refusal to accompany her. 'It won't be right. Maji says it is inauspicious to meet your father-in-law for the first time this way.'

As her father's flesh sizzled up in flames and her brand new baby sisters bawled into the smoke, Mangala strained eyes and rationalised in the aftermath of the disappearance of this first physical barrier—in the form of her father—between her and mortality.

He had told her once, 'In the old days when daughters married, fathers read their funeral rites and the girl took on a new name. Marriage is rebirth, you become part of that family, that blood. Your children will take that line forward. You shape their destiny, it is like taking an oath.'

Mangala squared her shoulders. Nuclear families had no pathway to paradise mapped out, no aunt, no uncle to bear the brunt of familial frustrations or fatigue, naked membranes glistened everywhere like exposed electrical wires and bliss was first come, first served. What would make a mother happy, Mangala tried to envision, surely not a henpecked son or a dutiful daughter swallowed up by fertility or in-laws. This mother, that mother, mine, his, maternal expectations connected on the map dot to dot just so. While her mother lay supine following childbirth and the Ayurvedic aftermath of hot-herb baths and bitter iron kashayams, she wiped away her tears with new determination and marched into a Christian home in the night, asking for non-vegetarian recipes. Marital com-promise had clearly been on her mind then.

But when she returned to in-law land after a month armed with relevant recipes and a bagful of koda-puli, the pitch-black tamarind to complement fish, her elder daughter was speaking fluent Punjabi.

'Malayalam is not their lingo,' Kedar said slowly, breaking up each word as if speaking to a retard. 'Malayalam is not their dress.'

And Mangala at last packed away the off-white long skirts, the ones she had sat patiently with a tailor pal and got stitched, and lovingly embroidered. Kedar's mother sent across what she called suits, salwar-kameezes for the girls with dupattas made of silk, so that when they wore them, these flew up from their little shoulders like Bonsai banners of belonging.

There had been a suit for Mangala, too, during the early days when they had made painful efforts to bridge the gap: a rainbow-coloured fabric from some textile sale with a chikan dupatta, though she didn't dare quiz her mother-in-law on her own lack of sarees. Except for other people's wedding receptions, Maji eschewed sarees in favour of suits, and her blouses were testimony to this disdain with their loose shirt-sleeves, hasty necklines and ill-fitting anti-gravity darts pointing emptily to what looked like a pair of amputations on upper torso, very unlike Mangala's loving chest-drapes that settled on her like second skin. No tailor in Delhi could stitch this. In fact, Mangala had junked, despite being broke, two blouses she had optimistically ordered at a Karol Bagh tailor-shop. 'Stitch up the bottom part and they are like sacks,' she had reprimanded. No self-respecting Malayalee woman would be caught dead in a baggy blouse!

'It is all in the arm-hole,' she had tried to explain at the Karol Bagh shop. 'They fit like a glove but in such clever cross-cuts that you can move your hand in any direction.' She demonstrated by pointing to the shop's roof and then sideways at a boy who freelanced hemline-removals with a sharpened nail, and then at the floor. 'See, you can rotate your arm any which way.'

'Mangala,' Maji had sweet-talked, happy in her suited world, unaware that her bosom had just never met the right blouse. 'My family tailor will stitch the salwar-suit for you,' letting Mangala imagine a bent-backed geriatric seamstress who spun the wheel in candle-light only for the Ahluwalia women, sewing 'until death do us part' in minute letters into the backs of their collars with a hair-thin needle instead of the busy Sardarji who astutely pretended to bow to bargains while keeping his profit in the black and clients happy.

They made a big ritual out of it, hurriedly soaking their stock of rajma in water, squeezing lime into milk, curdling it into cottage cheese and simmering milk till it thickened like damp cardboard for dessert. But the feast would have been incomplete without Mangala's ultimate humiliation.

'Aha,' her mother-in-law greeted, holding her by hand and drawing her in.

Mangala tried not to flinch at the fluorescent outfit lying in wait for her, smiled as she thanked and disappeared into the bedroom to try it on.

When she came out, they stopped speaking, staring hard at her so that she looked down at herself to confirm she wasn't nude. She didn't know that their delay in exclaiming stemmed from their struggle to fit her into a frame, one where matching glass bangles would ride up her wrist and the two oiled strands of hair that she coiled up behind her ears would untie and merge into a knot at the bottom of her skull.

'Now you are one of us,' they said as if a secret circumcision had just enabled her to join their cult. As if they had never told her disparagingly, 'We never let our girls wander out of hometown to study or work,' and she hadn't replied, 'No, you just get them married to sweepers in the US instead.' As if they hadn't prodded Munnu to do his Madrasi mimicry and she hadn't puzzled over the punchline since his put-on accent only overwrote her usual accent.

Mangala smiled tentatively, unmoving.

'Come, sit with me,' her mother-in-law cooed, as in company she rather tended to coo.

'I…I can't. There is no string, ji.'

They all laughed and laughed harder when a week later, to please them, she wore it once again, this time with elastic at the waist. Ha ha, they went, imagine elastic, like a small child's chaddi!

Ha, haji, returned Mangala, the doll dangling on their car's dashboard. 'Here,' she shifted utensils, rajma almost spilling from the dish.

Rajamma, as Mangala thought of rajma in her haste to personalise the inanimate in her antipathy path, had sat voluptuously in her watery bath the whole night and was now all soft and dewy, but Rajamma was Rajamma and could never be the rajma of popular demand. So Rajamma, like Mangamma, sat like a bit of forgotten chutney in the curve of their Melamine plates though Kedar later lambasted her for not providing katoris.

'You gave them dal and you gave them raita, but no katoris!' he frowned, reminding her of his mother who had delicately broached the topic of utensils the first time they met. She had brought in the plastic dinner set very hush-hush at midnight, whispering, 'Tell everyone your mother sent these. Here mothers stock up their daughters' kitchens. Not steel, but silver.' *Tang-ta-dang*, one more black mark against Mangala's family.

'I too will sail into the trash-can like leftover Rajamma,' his wife lamented and he had marvelled at her well-developed taste for theatre.

Meanwhile, the chicken-poxed nephew recovered only to come to a hasty end under a skin-specialist's salve.

The sister had swanned in importantly, 'Name a good paediatrician for Tinks. He has these blackish spots here and there. First I thought they were chicken pox scars... I want them off before Dolly's engagement; the reception is in daytime. Do you know anyone? I mean personally. I hate going to second-rate strangers who don't know me.'

Mangala's suggestions were all shrugged off in favour of the 'costliest skin daaktar in all of Delhi'.

But the prescribed steroid-based cream had the skin off in strips and the boy soon in coma for the doctor had failed to warn about reactions and the mother had laved with a heavy hand in her hurry to join Dolly's reception.

That evening when Kedar came home, in continuance of their state-based struggle for supremacy and ignorant of the fatality, Mangala crowed, 'What does our five-star patient say?'

'Nothing.'

'The five-star mother?'

'Nothing.'

And he had locked himself up in another room, not giving her the privilege of sharing his grief or watching him weep—she was his rival, not companion—leaving her to learn the news of the boy's death from phone calls, her resultant repentance making no noticeable inroads into his mourning.

The following week, when he footed bills for most of the funeral aftermath, like the Chautha ceremony and putting up sundry relatives in hotels, their food bills etc, she had to contain her fury at the unnecessary expense. 'He was not *your* son,' were words that danced on the tip of her tongue, crept up her eyes and attitude, words held back only for the vaguest of reasons: tact. But Tact demanded a hearing sooner or later.

The money was from her savings account, breaking the fixed deposit that her eldest brother had initiated for emergency purposes. Erecting a backyard pandaal to make gaajar ka halwa was not emergency, she fumed.

Winters weren't conducive to physical bonding either, bringing out as they did his mercurial sense of hygiene and her deep-seated abhorrence of intimacy.

'The water for your bath is warm,' she'd yodel, delicately fishing out the rod-heater out of the bucket, and he'd play hide and seek. In retaliation she howled when he cuddled under the quilt, his hand homing in on a toasty breast, kneading till, partially identifying with dough, she came brutally awake under his ice-cold administrations. Then they'd begin to tug the quilt from each side like two fuck-locked dogs pelted by pebbles trying to separate. Their favourite non-Kamasutra congress was in the back-to-back position.

'We should've bought a double-quilt,' were words beating in their minds, but prudently never voiced. Buying a single-quilt had been an instance of their desire for unification even when unconscious, and they were loath to declare defeat in sleep.

They thought nothing of dragging their personal differences before mutual friends though; hers were single pursuing higher studies with single-minded determination, causing sour grapes to drop pell-mell against the walls of her chest, and his were unemployed, unemployable 'intellectuals' who honed their political passions against her indifference. Mangala would wait for an opportune moment to spring sarcasm on spouse.

'Mangala, take these empty glasses away,' he'd wave a hand.

'He sees a maid when he looks at me!' she'd mutter, whisking away the glasses.

'As long as I don't look at the maid and see a wife, I don't see your problem,' he'd quip, and in the ensuing laughter her apathy to his wit was seen as an endearing wifely trait.

Exasperated, to trick him out of his languor or genuinely curious, she'd ask him, 'What do you want?'

'World peace?' he'd shrug, offering her the mangled remains of an aaloo-chaat he'd acquired along the way. 'A new wife?'

Then there was the matter of funds, gaining relevance as the family expanded. Kedar got by on hints and promises, innuendos and pledges; so long as he didn't have to deliver, to express in deeds what he freely vowed with words, he was everybody's darling. Implications were what he was best at. But anticipation, perennial and intense, began to ebb, leaving in its wake dregs of bitterness and guilty greed for a better life. How, Mangala wondered, could two girls made entirely of song and sugar bind her to the material world and its worries so irrevocably. Debts and insurance, car loans, rent and advances, higher education and even faraway marriage ceremonies, they all loomed while the babies kicked up pretty ankles and blew bubbles that danced on the tips of their tongues.

'Can we eat air-coloured food?' she asked at last, frustrated by his inability to hold down a decent job, one for which her Indian Oil uncle had pulled strings only to have Kedar pooh-pooh the pay and walk out. Offers of employment abroad or even outside the city were anathema to him.

'I worry,' she burst out.

'It's easy for me to say don't worry, but I am a professional worrier myself and understand the importance of gnawing the lower lip. Look at me, I am a wreck,' was his sarcastic retort.

That night she ripped the quilt off him in a flash, tugged the graceful long curtains off the windows, setting him off on a round of allergic sneezes at the dust, cleared the table with a sweep of her hand so that a breakable ashtray landed on an uncarpeted spot on the floor and, well, broke.

'The Sultan of small talk! All you do is pluck at air for something to talk about in your Delhi Durbar.'

'Delhi, not Del*hhh*i,' he edited groggily. 'The *h* is silent.'

'Sidetrackings are all you can deal with,' she said wearily. 'When it comes to grains and pulses, you turn tail. We can't build a house on your dreams.'

'Your dreams,' he condensed in return, 'are air-coloured.'

'Have I been a bad wife?'

'No,' she answered herself since she was her own keen listener and never missed a word spoken by self. This marriage was her stage, her version of things. It was hers and hers alone, so warily Kedar said nothing.

'You use your silence, your indifference as a weapon,' she hissed, fragments of his face inside her nails. 'You are cruel.' Then she flew into the adjoining bathroom.

He cradled his bloodied skin.

'Dab some antiseptic cream,' she had suggested hesitantly from inside, voice echoing surreal from the glazed tiles. She occupied the bathroom floor for the night, stark naked, crying copious tears into her upped knees. He hadn't slept a wink either, fearing the blunt fruit knife against his neck.

And that had been that; she couldn't eat air-coloured food and he couldn't see her air-coloured dreams, so they parted ways. Next morning she got rail tickets booked via friends and he did not protest, just kept out of her way, hinting at his wholehearted support for the move.

At the station he chatted cursorily, watching out for the green flag. Mangala shifted the baby in her lap and wondered at the tedious journey ahead, if everything would be all right at the end of it. If everything would be all right ever again.

Black and white movies where intertwined couples sank from the screen, leaving the kettle to do all the hissing and acting had her believe in kettles as cupids. In the package basically. A cat's cradle of likes and wants was all she had gnarled up between her calluses now.

When Mangala looked up the wedding date in her diary, she discovered that the marigold she had pressed into it was still fresh. Funeral fresh.

15

'CHECHI,' SAID ONE OF HER SISTERS, LEADING MANGALA IN through the front door, 'Want to make Ettan's chai?' She spoke as if talking to a child about a treat, her voice lilting up at tail end.

Lifting her older sister's wrist, she asked, 'Mangala burn hand. Mangala naughty?'

The older woman nodded proudly.

'I put on TV for you?'

Another nod.

Later, after soft, over-cooked rice chased down a dry yam concoction along with curds, they all subsided before the TV, which snipped the need for conversation. Madman clanked his chains and leaned against the window, idly looking in.

The verandah walls sported sepia portraits. There were seven pictures: one of Mangala's parents with a boy each to their left and right, another just the children, Mangala and her two brothers, all smiling fixedly for the camera. The third was Mangala's wedding picture where Kedar, seated on a cushion in the studio, towered over her in a becomingly manly manner, the next two were the wedding pictures of the two brothers, brides grimly holding lips over malformed teeth like saucers over cups, and the sixth was a big picture of the patriarchal head of the family, late and much lamented in his time. The triplet daughters, late arrivals in the family, had tucked their own passport-sized snaps into three corners of the last frame, so that three identical faces stared small-ly and solemnly at the viewer from their father's shoulders and foot, forming a kind of internal crucifixion.

It was the seventh photograph, swaying gently from an upraised nail, which had all of them in one frame, festive but frazzled, the coconut held precariously between the newly married Keshavan and Kanaka like a newborn.

Inside the house, a woman in Kanjeevaram silk was cutting vegetables on TV, the glycerine-tears in her eyes held at bay by a thick forbidding line of kohl. I will cook, she said, moving her red, red lips delicately, but I won't eat till he feeds me with his own hand. 'Karvachauth,' she mouthed, activating Mangala by strongly reminding her of a long-forgotten day in her life when her mother-in-law had woken her up at an unearthly hour to stuff sargi down her lap and force ghee-soaked parathas down her throat, only to merrily starve her for the rest of the day.

'Quick, look if the moon is out,' she sprinted from the room, three sisters at her heels.

'She will look for moon, they for her,' Kanaka encapsulated, turning back with moist eyes to the TV.

Eventually everyone was in bed or mat when a footloose hen somewhere let out a loud cluck.

'It's a wolf,' said a voice in the darkness.

'A ghost.'

'To eat us.'

All three voices belonged to Mangala.

It was actually a taxi and Drupa, as she stood shivering lightly in the damp air outside, was haggling only out of habit. Three days and two nights on a southward spiralling train had her feel like she was born and brought up in a train. In Palghat, when the breeze blew its saline breath on her, she had felt aerated, imagining the measured amble of backwaters in the darkness, buckling her knees into two bits of jetsam. But at the unearthly hour that the Rajdhani reached Trichur, renamed Thrissur, she seemed to have stepped right into a hairy armpit. Drupa put up her palm, testing the air. Nothing. No rain, no welcome; just a skinny breeze going briskly about its business.

The taxi driver, with his BA certificate framed above the rear-view mirror, was dragging her luggage out. He had asked at the station, 'Accommodation?'

Tricky, this business of an address, of where everyone thinks you live, of where you let others think you live. As he drove off, pocketing the change she shelled out, taillights flashing, she was tempted to throw his query back, 'Accommodation?'

She cast an eye around for a boulder to relax artistically upon, but there was an age when sitting with legs split open at ground level was casually flirtatious without being a come-on, and she was well past it. Besides, that meant a synthetically straight spine or the bra said 'you sag, I sag', and withdrew support. Nothing stopped traffic faster than the sight of a woman squatting by the roadside, body neatly divided into so many saddlebags you reach for a calculator. No, she wouldn't sit around like a mightily sprouted bean with her lanky hair up in a high ponytail; she'd stride right in.

'It is okay,' she turned to the tumbledown mansion of her memories and addressed the skull in her suitcase with some trepidation. 'We are here.'

Touch-me-nots when toed went into hiding, but when no one watched, out they'd come, unfurl their petite petals like pretty lace petticoats to sift sunlight and dance anonymously in the breeze. They were the Plain-Jane peacocks of the jungle, curling greenly under the climeless sky, holding secret scents from seasons past, each leaf poised like a gazelle pinned by headlights. Passers-by worried them all the time since something about this plant called out for brutality. Snap, they catapulted with thumb and forefinger, vacuously rejoicing in the rapid retreat of leaves, losing all interest in the stripped spine thus presented to view.

'That how girls must be,' Ammooma used to recommend. 'Like the thotta-vaadi. Doing all the work when alone and shrink in shyness from outsiders.'

Drupa sat on her haunches, extending the tip of her finger very, very lightly toward a sun-turquoised touch-me-not. Bending, she sweet-talked, gentling, willing the capricious creeper to curve and cover that infinitesimal distance between skin and stamen so it wouldn't modestly scatter into self this time. She didn't dare breath, but the stalk bowed to eavesdrop on her exhalations instead, brushing with exquisite timidity against her skin; its silk rouching inward despite her hush.

Drupa missed the leaves, now playmate, now fugitive. Like Ammooma herself, gone into hiding, leaving all her gender-based homilies behind. How she had wallowed in that pre-pubescent no-man's land of childhood nebulousness before a bewildered boy burst in on her in the bathroom to ask why she peed with her ass.

'I do it standing,' he had reproved and bungee-jumped her bang into genital differences where peeing style wasn't the last of it.

Someone coughed.

She looked up. A triplet aunt was drawing an arabesque in the fine sand with her toe. 'Breakfast,' she said, her hands miming the act of eating.

Drupa smiled. Last night they had overridden her protests and served her overtly fermented curd and rice. An aunt had made rasam in a jiffy, with enough peppercorns to set an army afire. Politeness and a certain awkwardness had forced Drupa into gulping down the steaming tamarind brew.

After a breakfast of appams she wondered how to break the ice, especially since Mangala was keeping her distance after a quick nod of head and wrinkling of nose. 'Rains soon,' she had mumbled, which was what all strangers said to each other. Here everyone was gainfully employed as spokesperson for the Met department. Her mother's smile, Drupa noted, was still the showpiece on her facial shelf. Her Bengal-cotton sarees flapped everywhere as tattered curtains and kitchen rags.

No momentous monsoons marked her first day; only the old man stretched out diagonal in the verandah stirred and said, 'Five by five.'

When she looked at him quizzically, he pointed at his pen, holding up the fingers of a gnarled hand. 'Five feet by five feet.' Which meant Velyammavan slept diagonally across that floor, much like the poo-noolu used to lie across his chest.

Cheriyammavan nodded at her, pinching the loose skin of his forehead quoting and annotating as usual. He had collapsed inward, Drupa observed, with wrinkled puddles running down elbows and eyes; it was the same body of his youth, but somehow the spirit had congealed within, pooling superfluous skin like an empty bag over his withering. He had also donned the mantle of 'knowing' in an attempt to usurp Velyammavan's former domain of discoveries.

She noticed other changes, too, like the white ants on the aisle in Appoopan's moustache. Like the jade sidelock of the nadu-muttam that once curled about the house was now an impromptu gutter. She watched Cheriyammavan cast away his bidi stub into it. This was no bangle on the home's wrist, this was a spittoon, plain and simple.

Extremeties had made a caricature out of Kanakamami. She still spoke in clichés and weeded the good from the evil in one mighty verbal yank, but the self-imposed moralistic curfew had taken its toll.

The kitchen sills offered a beggarly feast. There were all the ingredients—spices, pulses, tamarind, dry red chillies— but the plastic containers were ancient and meltingly twisted in places where they had stood too close to the fire. Fresh vegetables from the backyard were plucked every morn, only they forced strange menu combinations; too many raw plantains meant a sambhaar with it, an aviyal with it and also a thoran with it.

It was at the primordial burst of mustard seeds that Drupa ran down the verandah to escape the coconut oil smoking in the frying pan and Mangala came out into the yard, looking curiously at the retching girl. 'Who?'

And Drupa apologised for her gut reaction to their staple oil.

When her mobile pinged, the triplets chirped agitatedly among themselves and Mangala arbitrarily commanded, 'Open the door.' But now it was in the triplets' hands; thirty fingers probed at the keys and sent syrupy SMSs to unsuspecting people.

A mild commotion in the verandah alerted her.

'His heart has stopped beating,' a triplet aunt informed her.

Velyammavan lay on the floor flanked by two women on both sides; Kanaka fully prepared to beat her chest in mourning and Mangala humming *Madurashtakam,* which praised the sweetness of talk, walk, eyes and breath, not in past-tense as dirge but sung with a vacant air, like a beggar-child rattling stone in a tin and singing in railway compartments.

Squatting with difficulty on the floor, which gave out a faint unwashed whiff, Drupa cradled her uncle's head in her lap, arresting mid-way Kanakamami's fist en route to breast, 'Of course he is breathing.'

'Always, always fooling,' Kanaka huffed, getting up.

'But he needs a doctor.'

'Every doctor in the district has been here,' Kanaka vouched brazenly.

'I have something to tell you,' began Drupa. 'I have an MBBS degree and if you all have no objection, I would like to treat uncle.'

There was a clamour all around her as Sambhaar Pieces took the lid off their collective burgeoning diseases, every ache and pain glorified in the exalted medical company.

Kanaka put up a palm, signifying an end to this sycophantic twitter. But before she could speak, Drupa patted her palm, the one up in the air. 'This is so stiff, seems like arthritis.'

Kanaka, flattered despite her misgivings, nodded reluctantly. 'See this,' she said, closing all fingers except one into a fist, raising the little finger up with a flourish one reserved for kindergarten teachers while indicating kidney status. 'I have an Ayurveda ointment for it.'

'May I see it?'

Kanaka hesitated at the threshold, malevolence mingling with dust motes in the air; she knew very well the defeat she would accord herself at obediently crossing over. As pauses go, it clocked about fifteen pulse-beats, but ended in the global scrap heap of all pauses in the end.

'Is Badi doctor, too?' a triplet aunt asked.

Drupa thought of her sister's hormonal path through the heavenly way and blinked a 'no'.

'Because Kanaka chechi could be your family patient then!'

Drupa stared down at Velyammavan. Dementia did not pare down its patients clean to the bone. It did not rootcanal them, render insensate or snip neatly from the satellite dish. Merely muddied mental waters so that memories pulsated like electrical currents in a series of startling sensations and they quivered or cackled, as dialogues and duties from the past reared non-contextual heads.

An ironmonger was summoned to sever the shackles so that the prone figure of Velyammavan could be transferred pronto into a comfortable bed inside.

'Our family famous for madness,' Keshavan told the ironmonger with a proud chuckle. 'Each generation saw at least three under lock and key. What to do if they attack people coming home like dog gunning for strangers on road?'

'He is your elder brother, isn't he, Namboodiri?' the ironmonger asked breezily.

Keshavan shrugged. 'Had to tie him up here. He forgot toilet-training.'

'Easier to climb the hill to worship Ayappan,' was the insolent mutter in response. 'After all, Ayappan never shits.'

Keshavan knew the type, the brother-less mother-fucking non-caste pieces of virtuosity who thronged the moral arena with imaginary good deeds for ammunition. He receded into the kitchen where Kanaka was carefully measuring out tea leaves into boiling water.

'For who?'

She pointed at the verandah. Keshavan blinked rapidly to indicate negation.

'Already made now,' she protested, miffed at losing a platform where femininity and hostess duties could be merged to her advantage. The ironmonger was a man in his prime and the way he purposefully hit the iron was biologically distracting.

But the ironmonger declined the tame beverage. 'Only fresh toddy for me,' he bared big, square teeth for her fascinated perusal.

When the saw stopped buzzing, ironmonger and Keshavan tried to help up the prone man, whose legs' strange twist due to erstwhile chain made the job tricky. Finally Kanaka joined in, huddling bonily under Madman's armpit so that he leaned against her like she was a walking stick.

The ironmonger panted a little. 'The position was cramped after all, he will not walk straight till he dies. The ankle bones must have set that way.' He looked fully into Kanaka's eyes, confusing her, cutting through her castaway heart. 'I remember two boys making a study of churches here, coming all the way from Calcutta by motorbike. When they come to my shop, the one at back got off to ask me for directions, but walked like still sitting on bike.' He imitated the walk, splaying legs in chronic Bharatnatyam pose, causing the patient to tilt his way alarmingly and clutch Kanaka convulsively. The move-ment caused her to turn and catch a suddenly sensible eye and stumble slightly. She never looked into those eyes if she could help it.

'Give me Keshu's box, hurry. He must be waiting at the school gate,' the Madman bade, stalling at the threshold.

'Memory gone,' Keshavan waved a palm upward in explanation to ironmonger and bent to shove his brother's dangling foot over the threshold. 'He used to bring me my lunch at school.'

'Don't forget the curd. You always forget his curd,' the patient exhorted, stumbling in. 'Keshu needs his curd or he won't eat.'

Thus did Madman move back into the house that was once his own.

'Do you think it is right?' Keshavan broached the subject when his wife showed no inclination to discuss threadbare this new domestic development.

She sniffed and, encouraged, he launched into the machinations of fate and his helplessness. 'It is all God's tricks. We can only do the tasks he assigns us, not question why,' he sighed.

His wife's continued silence disoriented him. 'Kanakan, say something,' he pleaded. 'It is not my fault this time, is it?'

'Why don't you drink toddy?' she burst out.

'I need all your medical records.'

Eagerly Kanaka brought them forth from hiding place, hearing Drupa mouth the long-ago medical jargon with something akin to enjoyment. The terms, scientific and unchangeable, splashed on her skin like cool droplets and she listened all over again to the visceral state of her pickled uterus, the dawdling motility of her husband's sperm, the tangled web woven by the fallopian tubes when first they practised to deceive.

Drupa cleared her throat. 'The problem obviously is with Cheriyammavan.'

'He cannot do anything in bed, for ten long years he making me virgin.' And Kanaka put her head down on the desk and sobbed, the rapid weft and weave of her protruding teeth reminding the other of the wedding day, when she had sobbed just this way.

'The only way out is artificial insemination or, of course, intercourse with someone else.'

Kanaka started; she wondered if the heat in her blood escaped in steam about her person. No, what would this chit of a girl know about passion; that sometimes a glance met can constitute an entire marriage. Doubtless some matrimonially plucked boy would grope under her petticoat one day and, wham, her stomach would swell. At this age desire dared not make a din, it made a noise only when eternity turned tail and the lap lay bald and unblessed.

'You can discuss it with him and decide. At your age you don't have the luxury of time on your hands. If this does not work, then IVF is an option. But considering the high expense of the procedure, I'd advise you to try it only once.'

'Yeah,' thought Kanaka with a quick dental jig as she swallowed. 'You wouldn't advise for a second try, you are Mangala's seed and wouldn't want to see your wealth dispersed.'

It was Keshavan's casual mooting that since his own sperm had seemingly gone into hibernation, it should be from a family member that caused others' eyes to dilate, rotate to the right, where the only other living male member of the family reclined horizontally, digging passionately at underfoot corn.

'Nobody else's baby I can accept as mine. His baby, my baby, all same.'

Kanakamami's expression revealed her diametrically opposite view, but diplomatically she kept her own counsel. She was ardently wishing she hadn't sought a consultant so close to the family, she should have found her own solution, after all there was nothing the matter with her, she wasn't the one with bungled insides!

'It is a highly delicate business,' Drupa was saying.

Kanaka closed her eyes and was instantly transported to a hayloft painted in deep sunshine, smiling as a faceless lover took his time playing with the surface of her skin...

'It is settled then,' concluded her husband, misunderstanding the smile, anxious to conclude the whole controversy;

his Kanaka wasn't a bride of twenty now. Time was of the essence.

'Time is of the essence,' he said, not noticing the flash-bulb sweep of his wife's eye or the bile that burped up her tongue at the reference to her years and their inexorable onward journey.

Kanaka hated mirrors. Age dribbled into youth, hardening arteries and lip-lines, drawing comical crow's feet at the end of eyes, puffing eyelids, plucking out lashes one by one till eyes were peeled to the pip in a gelatinous jumble, staining and corroding leftover teeth till they glinted like muddy, mutilated stumps and narrowed speech unknowingly to the era of past birthdays, boring those with puppy-young retinas and rhetoric. Still, the young strutted and bragged, not noticing the dimming of their swanky spotlights, uncaring that any two given seconds were lovers under the skin, fusing, merging, gangbanging till they brought you back from the washing-stone crumpled, creased, crinkled and completely *mortal*.

'You know, Kanaka,' he enfolded his wife in his arms in the bedroom, 'I was thinking. This is our last chance. Why spend on this syringe, clinic and all if we can do it here in our own house? You know, how far gone Ettan is, he won't know. It is adultery only technically,' he soothed her by habit. 'I just feel…you know Kanaka, I have no false manly insecurity or anything, but it may leak out from all those outside places. People laughing at me, I don't mind, but laughing at our son… Here, here it will be private, just between us, you, me and him. You are understanding, no?'

'Private,' she clarified, her chin beginning to wobble. There were old women she remembered despising in the extremity of her youth, old women she was now beginning to resemble.

16

THE SMALL IMPORTED TAPE-RECORDER WAS TAKEN OUT OF Velyammavan's sparse almirah, where he used to keep the treasures he brought them from foreign shores long ago, and dusted.

'It may never sing,' an aunt was apologetic.

Nevertheless, Drupa inserted the plug and switched on the tape-recorder. Instantly, a tinny voice flooded the room.

'It sings, it sings! What I told you?' the aunt declared joyously.

Drupa took out her father's tape. His recorded voice, temporarily rich with bass-enhancers and double-toned microphone filters, spread akin an awning in the room.

At the window, Mangala gauged the distance to her bed, took the required two shaky steps and collapsed on it in a baffled way while her husband of yore sonorously picked his way through a melodious minefield of unkept promises and pledges.

'Kaun kahe hai
preet ki boli
preet bhari hai,
preet bhari hai.

*Neer nahaye
jab nainan-va
kaun kahe hai
peer khari hai...'*

Mangala was dumbstruck. Her eyelashes fluttered down, to cork bedlam.

Save me from metaphors of squirmy butterflies pinned on a board, make the first move, his eyes had begged her during hostel Holi; don't, don't be the typical good girl my mother will be crazy about.

'Stop looking at me like that,' he had warned that first time they were alone, eyes glinting outlandishly through slits in the myriad cheap colours plastering down his spiky lashes.

'Like what?'

'Like you are doing now. I watch you all the time, you know. I want to tell you...'

'Stop it.' Mangala had modestly moved away, setting off a powdery halo that glinted in the cloudy sunshine.

'No, really, I must,' he insisted, sneezing.

'These plants are real?' she asked hurriedly, unconsciously caressing the leaves in an ungainly pot by the window.

He plucked a withered flower off its stem and presented it to her with a partially parrot-green hand.

'Please,' she moved away, putting out her own skin-coloured hands as if to ward him off; his own personal traffic police. 'You are drunk.'

'May be,' he had to agree.

'I think I should leave.'

'I love you.'

She shook her head. 'No one actually says that.'

'I am saying it. I adore you, am mad about you. I can die for you.'

'We only met yesterday.' But there had been that readiness to believe.

When he bent to kiss her, she moved away to the wide terrace outside his dormitory, squealing.

'This is too fast. It is...indecent,' she had sought to assert, but a pant spoilt the statement's sensible intent.

'It is beautiful.'

There was a cloying sweetness in the air that day; you could stick out your tongue and it would melt in the mouth like drops of lassi.

'Crazy.' But her lips fused with his obligingly, penultimately. No coy last-minute twist of head engineered, he was allowed entry into that warm mezzanine stillness, her lips elasticising on his in a snug rubber-band fit.

It began to rain. Great gusts of wind snatched fat drops from the sky, pouring a granulated paste from each other's scalps into mouths, past their tongues that tingled, clogging their throats so that they gasped apart at the lack of drainage.

'Please,' she began incoherently, breathing fast, the rain honing her nipples into shards. He placed a wet finger on her mouth so that unmeant words swirled with the water, not wanting to put her through the routine schedule; she lambast, he apologise.

'Please,' she said, turning toward the corridor, toward imagined safety, plucking at his hands. 'Let me go.'

A touch of lunacy and oncoming flu grabbed him by the throat and he ground into her mouth almost furiously for daring to negate the carnal import of the moment, drawing blood, inserting carbon paper between oral orifices so that passion copied passion in a kiss that blended pasts with what was to unfold as they tasted each other that first time.

Marrying the burnt pumpkin southern specialty she was yet to serve him with the fenugreek-daal of the roadside dhaaba he'd eat dispiritedly when she did the bunk, merged their belated margarine-rich wedding feast to the sour burp of an unconceived baby, channelled his mother's blackest, bitterest winter-proof chai into the jaggery tea served in a glass at her father's funeral.

Flavours broke over them in waves, washing and drenching in their wake, trailing a tantalising tang on taste buds, insinuating, tipping them off about the future. That kiss rendered them different people, people they dared not be until then, people they couldn't be unkissed and sober.

By the time her saree gathered in soft folds at her feet and she stood mute as a candle melted down to wax puddles around its wick, their breaths were mingling in a single cloud and he was turning her carefully into his embrace, his unwrapped gift.

'I can never let you go.' Kedar bent, the rains chasing the colours of Holi like multi-coloured worms wriggling down his face. *'Never.'*

That night when Choti investigated shuffling noises in the dark, she found her mother sitting on the floor with yards and yards of forgotten Bengal cotton sarees spilling out from the box under her bed.

Her nose buried in the soft folds, Amma was inhaling the scent of long-ago dreams.

Dasamma charged in as soon as she got the news of Choti's arrival. Drupa, tending to plants, noted the bits of bullion at her ears and the roll-gold bracelet wrapped around her wrist, obvious signs of prosperity.

'I was welcome here after you left, mole,' she began, refuting the persona non-grata status that may have lingered on in Drupa's memory. 'Your Ammooma's night-soil needed to be cleaned,' she said in coy reference to the older woman's effluents. 'And the painkiller injections only Janaky could give. She the only nurse in district, you know. How she cried, oh, how she cried.'

At Drupa's swift look, she elucidated, 'Not Janaky, your Ammooma. Couldn't walk in the end, mole. Bent double like plantain trunk in strong wind. Too many babies, that's what I told her. Off she ran to vaidyan and asked for herbs to stop baby but he mixed wrong and out came three instead of the one she may have had!' Dasamma paused. 'Still, she was kindest member of family. Her help I never forget. Plucked me right out of the pond, which had become my permanent address. She called for me, when they hived off her first breast. When the other breast came off, too, I came running despite the young hussy's frowns. Kept her company till she died; we Ezhavas know how to repay the debt of rice once eaten.'

Drupa nodded. *What's a lump like you doing in a nice breast like this?*

'Looked after you, too, when you ran around here, little and naked.' She viewed Drupa's back measuringly as the latter continued to untangle weeds in the courtyard. 'And now you and my Janaky are both working in hospital, side by side. Will anyone believe?' She bent to the left, like she was about to whisper to herself, and spat out some red juice.

A triplet aunt handed Dasamma a glass of black tea, which she proceeded to devour after intensive spitting and cleansing of mouth under the water-hose in Drupa's hand.

'Ask her about her elder daughter,' the aunt instructed Drupa in an undertone.

'What about your elder daughter? Rukmani, wasn't it?' quizzed Drupa in halting Malayalam, pushing back sweaty strands of her long, long, never-to-be-cut-in-this-lifetime hair from forehead, vaguely glad to be handed a conversational gambit on a platter like this.

Dasamma abruptly brought the glass down, wiping a hand across the tea and scarlet spit dribbling down her mouth. 'Rukmani? Baaah! Worked in fancy Ayurveda centre not far from here, only two hours by bus, where all foreigners coming for massage, giving her big, fat tips over and above monthly salary, but she go fall for someone like film heroine.'

Drupa delivered a humming sound in response, to keep her hand in, so the discussion would move along without much of her. Humidity rinsed the summer air, slicking it back with a gigantic hand like locks from a child's sweaty forehead.

'Now you say, so what.'

Drupa delivered another noncommittal hum.

'He make her pregnant, this foreigner, then he remember, what he had for dinner last night just like, that he not Hindu, that he not Indian. That he, in fact, chosen one to start own order of church with foreign grant where no one marry, not even to mothers of own children.'

Drupa sat back on her haunches and felt perspiration trickle down her back; a bashful monsoon had ensured all-round clamminess. 'She have the child then?'

'The child have her.' Dasamma spat again. 'Went to massage the white people one day without a word to me and jumped from the terrace there. Two bright girls I had, *two*. Will anyone believe?'

Drupa returned to the rose bush, pricking her finger, stroking bloodied dewdrops off the startled thorn.

The triplet aunts took over the tale gladly while Dasamma finished the rest of her tea with a resigned air.

After a heated row, during which Robert the foreigner alluded to the Almighty's mysterious ways and Dasamma's daughter pointed to the tangible bulge in her belly, he had crossed himself and stormed down the stairs and she had jumped off the terrace, the venue of the heated row. She sailed down with a faint whistling sound and landed on the bent back of Robert, who had just reached ground floor and was meticulously attending to an undone shoelace.

Both were rushed to the hospital right in time to be declared 'dead on arrival'. Though Dasamma swore her daughter's mouth moved while the certificate was being made out, the triplets dismissed it as dismantled overbite. About Robert no one had bothered to actually enquire. It was presumed the medical fraternity knew what it was about when it checked for signs of life and found none.

'Robert's body go straight to the altar of the church he planning,' the aunt concluded.

Dasamma sighed loudly, scratching rhythmically at her filarial foot. Cathedrals around cadavers, however romantic, were outside her comprehension. 'Fancy tombstones for murderers, that's what we have come down to.'

Another aunt continued, 'Rukmani made a midget corpse, legs having crunched back into her thighs on the impact with Robert and earth. You should've seen the body, like a child's body. My daughter not so short, Dasamma told the Ayurveda doctor who came for funeral juggling two wreaths. Your daughter give us bad name, he reply.'

Dasamma began to cry and Drupa remembered with a start her particular brand of mourning with its coating of merriment. 'Aa-ha…' she wailed, her face wearing deep happiness in sartorial mishap.

'Yeah, small corpse,' agreed the other two aunts, like they had gone for the funeral with a measuring tape. 'Hardly four feet.'

'Choti,' cried out Mangala with elderly imperiousness, cutting into dwarfism debates.

Drupa dropped the spade back into the soil and hastily went inside, wiping her hands on her dupatta.

'Must go out…where are Mangala's chappals?' she flapped her feet futilely under the bed. Drupa found them, slid them under her feet and drew the Kolhapuri toe-string gently between her toes.

'Let's go.' Mangala got up.

They cut up one rope into three equal pieces, one for each one of them and contemplated the hook; only two rooms had ceiling fans. The beams amidst the red tiles on the steepled side of the house suited them, so they climbed up to it now that Chechi and Ettan had left for the clinic and Choti had taken her mother for a walk.

They always rehearsed when left alone.

Wanting to meet their Maker with uncommon grace and synchronicity, with just the right soupçon of pleasant surprise, their dress rehearsals followed a well-planned script.

'*Ammey*,' called a nasal voice at the door just then.

'Forget it,' said a sister. 'A beggar.'

But another climbed down athletically, counted two fifty-paise coins, jangled them in her hand as she ran lightly down the steps to drop them into his tin.

'May you live long,' he blessed automatically though God knew one rupee was no goldmine; still, begging was what he did best and in this profession, he was learning, hyperbole was a prerequisite. Waving an overtly grateful stump, he exaggerated, 'A thousand years.'

'We do not have a thousand minutes between us,' they giggled after he limped away with his remaining leg, the voluptuous illicitness of their choice filtering into their collective conscience, giddying them with their own daring.

'Kanaka knows to wear her irritation well, couching it in seemly gasps, but I see formalities take up Keshavan-ettan's time.'

'The curious will crowd out the police and a scrawny man with pointy elbows from the press will go back to office to write a longwinded human-interest story. "Born Together, Dead Together".'

They squinted into newsprint of the future till the rebel aunt said, 'I know what! Let's just write the story ourselves. Sort of a suicide note for our would-be fans. They should know we stood together.'

'No, no standing, only hanging.'

'Perhaps they will click pictures of us...'

'You look dead enough in photographs.'

So the playful squabble commenced and they postponed yet again their rehearsal for The Suicide that would rock the world; being identical was a photo-op in itself, after all. The ropes went back to sleep in their innocuous baskets in the storeroom like coiled cobras, waiting for another day when life would really be unliveable and they could play snake-charmers.

In the busy mart, Mangala ran harum-scarum, like a wayward child at a fair, tugging at Drupa's restraining finger.

'Mangala need that...' and she'd be off again, staring this way and that. 'It is for... Here,' she said triumphantly, stopping at a papier-mâché stall, overflowing with colourful Kathakali masks. She cocked a head, lost in thought, remembering how she had woken with aching joints in the middle of a winter night, checked the quilt on the children, and laid back with a sigh of bliss, knowing she could close her eyes and go back to sleep, cuddling into the limp embrace of her husband. That moment, with her mind poised on the precipice of sleep, that moment was the only eternity she had ever tasted and her mind referred to it again and again.

Mother and daughter stared at every mask in detail, Mangala's nebulous strain currently in abeyance as she briskly fingered merchandise. Finally, they found him. Hidden behind two female masks was the face she sought, with black, long locks covering both ears and colours running out; that was the faulty one the shopkeeper had kept half-hidden, the one that sat under the leaking part of the roof, with myriad colours run out. She stared until Drupa, afraid the shopkeeper may hike prices, hastily made a bid.

'No, don't,' Mangala decreed tenderly when he rustled paper in preparation to pack it. 'Mangala carry.'

Drupa never failed to recognise her own voice under her mother's. At home, watching sugar dissolve in a glass of milk, she stitched her speech as separate as she could in her semblances of response.

'Can you open this?' Mangala handed her a rotting apple and Drupa slipped into her new role, the one of mothering a mother.

Her dreams alone were not sucked down that gaping black hole, not her heart alone that flew off handle. It flattered no end if concerned lover has only one dialogue to deliver:

'I.

Love.

You.'

An incredible experience for anyone with ears, she guessed.

Her mother had loved, had suffered. But what use was the proof of depth or hidden heights when passion was spent, firmly ensconced in the past, never to return except as blazing memory, a backdrop, a yardstick while reading a book or eavesdropping on newlyweds in a railway carriage? Hearts broke in the end, that was the truth, and with shrapnel hissing in damp souls, daughters sought their mothers' laps.

Drupa neatly pared the over-ripe apple; delicately she scooped out the rot, those browned edges like an old woman's toothless cackle, and handed her mother a rescued slice, 'Here.'

The sun sleepily stretched its arms in the sky before snuggling low into the warm backwaters that rippled about like a water-warm quilt. What the sun called a siesta, Drupa called end of the day.

Neighbours wiped feet on the coir mats at their door as they returned to their sleep. 'Shouldn't slurp up the stuff if he can't handle his drink.'

Keshavan weaved across the mud path, counselling all and sundry about salt contents in gruel, which he personally thought an uncommonly fine piece of advice. His wife, duly notified by the hubbub, had the three-fold duty of playing down her mortification, guiding his inebriated steps homeward while also gritting overdeveloped molars.

She waited till the door was latched and triplet sisters-in-law had taken their ringside seats before showering abuse at spouse.

'You do this to *me*?' she threw at him with a bucketful of question marks in lieu of the water the triplets had laconically suggested, not moving a muscle to fetch it themselves.

'Kkk...Kakana,' he squinted at what seemed to be Xeroxed copies of her multiplying alarmingly all over the place.

'He is drinking for he is sad.'

'He wants to be father.'

'You have to make him.'

Kanaka ignored the well-meaning advice in triplicate and left him confabulating with the curtain on his fours.

On the appointed day the Meledeth women got up auspiciously early, took a dip in the partially slushy pond in a corner of their one million and one cents of land, felt suitably cold and holy, plucked clean the branches of all floral adornment, embedded some spirally in their damp hair, arranging the rest in a flat steel plate along with tulsi leaves and other offerings for God.

'Hurry,' they bade each other, going through chores mechanically but speedily. The anticipation of a semi-wedding, all the more thrilling for its secrecy, permeated the Illam's worn walls.

In the kitchen reigned happy chaos; both cooks and pots harmoniously clashing in the battlefield. Vessels were borrowed from neigbours with suppressed excitement.

'What for?' they were pumped curiously as large vats changed hands.

And the triplets shrugged shoulders, giggling. 'Chumma,' they shifted from one foot to another impatiently, 'simply.'

Aviyal was a hotch-potch of over-cooked vegetable stems and the ripest mangoes were plucked and compiled into pulissery, a drop enough to tingle teeth unto death. Elissery and pachadi and olan, all sat in a row like the backbenchers they were, while turmeric seasoned the buttermilk a sunshiny yellow.

Today, they'd eat systematically; replacing the usual madness with method while serving and for that the availability of all ingredients was essential. Not a hint of the plaintain leaf's greenery was to peek out under the spread and swell of the multi-coloured cuisine. Their leaves were to burst with feasting today!

Kanaka, who came peeping, was hurriedly dismissed from the kitchen. The chaos gradually tapered off until only agreeable smells remained. Payasam sat sizzling on the stove, spewing hot globs of milk hissing onto ladled hands that came stirring. Deep-fried bits of golden-brown coconut were swimming in the payasam before the catering was finally declared done.

A spoonful of sunshine trickled down the sky and consequently rain was being freely forecast on the streets. A triplet aunt tripped over half-saree in her haste to pick up the drying clothes from the washing line. 'It is raining, it is raining,' she muttered.

'No, it isn't,' another triplet grumbled. 'Making double work for the rest of us.'

Mangala wagged a stained fingernail. 'You know what they say. If rain runs down a sunny sky, the fox must be getting married to the cat this very minute.'

The muted controversy over raindrops raged on while remnant domestic chores were performed in high haste. Kanaka was jabbed onto a stool before the only mirror in the house, handed a comb, and the long, laborious process of detangling her hair was commenced.

'Take it out,' she was bade excitedly and Kanaka bent to the iron box, which had carted in her trousseau so long ago, unlocked it and retrieved the crackling brocade of her wedding saree, fingering it absently with a semi-smile until a youthful sister-in-law snatched it from her hands and flattened the crescent of her lips.

The triplets unfurled the silk she was to wear, reverently helping her drape it around herself, prattling non-stop like pigeons, running for safety pins to secure pallu, pleats and gaping blouse-front. Mangala, into whose lap the freshest jasmine buds were haphazardly thrown, finished threading the floral crown that was to jut out like sun's rays from the bride's hairbun.

'Choti,' Kanaka's voice was muffled, lips clamping down on a safety pin. 'Come, choose my jewels.'

Drupa hunched silently on the bed, her fingers trembling over the box of yore, a box she had coveted and craved, before tilting it over completely. Out tumbled the treasures she remembered so well; the rubies, the emeralds and the turquoise and pearls that Kanaka steadfastly barred Keshavan from pawning or selling however lean the times and vacant the bellies.

In a crumpled pouch underneath the velvet lining was the ornament Drupa hunted for. Her hands settled on the heavily layered chain of the elaka thali, setting off its myriad leaves placed in frilly rows one under the other so that they shook and shivered like the minutest waves in a sea of gold. 'This one,' she said, holding it out to her aunt.

Kanaka nodded. 'Haven't worn this for so long...' she acknowledged before remembering, suddenly shooting up a piercing look at her niece.

Drupa beamed blankly at her aunt's left earlobe, so that Kanaka bent her neck for the shimmering choker to be wrapped around it. Instantly, the base of her throat began to buck like the backwaters; each time she moved, with every breath, the metal danced back and forth, now sheathing, now forking out its shiny implosions.

Kanaka moved her head this way and that, watching the rippling effect cast in her reflection. A strategic sprinkling of talcum powder, a determined dip into a vial of homemade kohl, the smearing of soot onto eyebrows and the synthetic beauty spot made to perch on her left cheekbone completed the ensemble. The beauty spot sitting blackly on the smooth white expanse of her skin would surely ward off the evil eye!

Amidst the urgent feminine humming around them, Keshavan and his brother benignly watched TV.

'Yes, yes, let's see,' Keshavan argued with a politican on screen. 'Your promises are one thing, your deliveries another.'

He shook a fist and his elbow dug sharp into a flabby spot on his brother's side. 'No use listening to these scumbags, Etta, best to go blank like you.' Suddenly he hollered, 'Girls, women, what are you up to? Look at the time.'

By late afternoon they were ready for the outing. Soon the motley procession set out, altruistically sweeping Kanaka like an army of ants lightly careening under a cockroach's carcass, to update God on the latest development and seek his general watch over things. Keshavan walked ahead, clearing the path, and the women followed through with their over-bright eyes.

Drupa, who had decided to stay back for someone had to tend to the bridegroom, watched them go.

Kanaka devoutly downed her eyelids, one hand curling into the saree pleats between her legs to raise them slightly so she could walk faster. She had already explained it to herself, this need to hoodwink husband. She well understood his compulsions, to act upon the spoken word, the spoken denial, to listen to a laundry-man and show her to the jungle. The best way out was to leave him no set mode of rebellion, to present him with fait accompli and offspring. It was enough that her own blood would flow through the baby's veins; didn't she belong to this family now? Open-ended blood corpuscles couldn't wrong Keshavan at all. The baby would grow in his house, his lap. His it would be, his alone.

At the temple entrance, devotees thronged in hundreds. Miracle-seekers from faraway places with faraway expressions were bustling in and out and the hurly-burly of worship was all around them. Through this stampede, Keshavan shepherded his retinue of women.

Someone behind them said with false heartiness, 'Is it the Namboodiri women?' before elbowing ahead without a backward glance. Though used to such slights, Keshavan still forgot to affect timely indifference, taking, for a moment at least, such comments for genuine greeting. Then, making a disgusted sound at the back of his throat, he carried on and the women followed through, maintaining their momentum.

At the stone stairs, Kanaka's feet began to drag as if weighed down by anklets of stone. Longer and longer she dwelt on each step, her foot slowing down in the rush, until the procession that bore her up had moved on and she, the impromptu deity of the day, lowered herself to a flattened boulder on the staircase, her gaze unseeing.

Someone nudged her in the hallowed maze and she moved an outstretched leg out of the way to let whoever it was behind her pass. It was... a man! A well-built six-foot twenty-something parcel of virility, bow-tied in muscles under the pristine whiteness of his sleeveless baniyan.

Kanaka couldn't help it, she simply sat there wonder-struck and looked. Sensing her intensity, he turned around and the eye she lent to roving, she allowed to embed itself electrically in his. Kanaka took a deep breath and then exhaled judderingly as the barren womb went whoosh in tandem.

The stranger stared sideways, contempt coating his eye before settling like spit in the bottom of a spittoon. Deliberately he strode away then, his disgust plain, snubbing all that she offered with casual sadism and she was left to struggle with the serpent of lust slithering about her, hissing and spitting.

Keshavan found his wife sitting on the temple steps, thus, with her eyes blinded by tear-damp tresses.

'My youth has indeed passed me by,' she murmured sadly.

Keshavan, catching the gist if not the words, hugged her to him. Everything will be okay when our baby comes.' He was bewildered by the dry, broken sobs that emerged from her throat, misread the context and wrapped big, clumsy hands around her, his gentleness unnerving her anew. 'It is all God's own will.'

God's will, she scoffed mentally. God's will was his impotence and thereby the lovelessness and empty lap that smote her! Then she heard the drums.

At home Drupa sat with Velyammavan, sponging him with lukewarm water, when he muttered feverishly in one of his defeatist flashes of lucidity, 'The fish brought her back on its silver scales. Do you know, Choti, she had found a baby in a seashell. That's all she dived for. She knew, she knew so much and I didn't know anything in the end.'

'She is back,' agreed his niece, giving him tiny sips of the tepid tea she had brewed. In vain she had searched for cardamom seeds, sweet cinnamon sticks, anything to mask the insipidness of the tea, but the kitchen had yielded nothing except the necessary ingredients to drum up mass meals.

Outside the sky rumbled ominously. Something had to wash out the stain in the sky, the sky had to be dyed blue again, the blue of the veins that had run softly down Ammooma's throat.

Into the tea Drupa added the one necessary ingredient, the pill that would pitch him out of his neutral gear into an impromptu honeymoon. It wasn't enough that a tabby-cat mated with a vixen, she smiled ruefully, consummation had to be facilitated. An over-the-counter pill was difficult to obtain. She was authorised to prescribe, but procurement posed a problem. Thrissur was as consumerist as it could be, but was still beaten hollow by Delhi. Less eateries, less acidity, therefore less chemists. This was all she could manage in town and the side effects she hoped would be as sumptuous as the blunt portrait on the counterfoil.

The old man lay back, licking his lips. She knew what he was up to. Arranging memories. She did it herself all the time; it was like a drug. If you edited out this sentence, that word, if you put that fact ahead of others or just reworked it a bit, then you were left with something palatable, something pliable, something you would want to recognise as your past and not break into a run. Memories formed a jail with implacable bars, and escape from that shitty dungeon was well nigh impossible for the convicts there of their own accord.

Drupa moved to a window sooty with twilight. The setting sun smudged treetops and left the sky full of dusty footprints from departing birds.

Meanwhile, unused to elbows digging into her side and the impersonal shoves of a sweaty population, whom she had previously noticed only at lipstick counters or when her hair was coloured too burgundy, Disha was trying her best not to recoil at this literal contact with commoners at the Golden Temple.

Hordes of sisters hugged her and she hunted for imprints of her bones on their fleshy frames, for identical 'same-to-same' sorrows in the flicker of their pupils, for an echo of her sobs. Frequently she came up flush with cashable stories in the emotional equivalent of an ATM machine. Insert card, hold hands, cry.

At the gurudwaras, they had initially dismissed her as Babaji's moll, called her the Sikh Scarecrow owing to those knifepoint collarbones that poked out farther than her wind-whipped nipples. But the sudden moans she emitted during prayers disconcerted even the devotees who tended to go wool-gathering.

Earlier testosterone terrorists used to take her hostage, engulf her in bliss, isolating her within that very bliss, setting her apart from the bliss-nots until, rocked by seismic spasms and dew-drenched from inside out, she flew up as light as the bubble in her aerated drink. Strangely, the same happened to her now at a spiritual level when she prayed. She became not the bruisingly beautiful piece of porcelain she saw in shop windows, but free, free from the shackles of her own torturous images of self. Light, almost airborne.

All those slim affections men bestowed upon her she had begun to suspect. That was boredom, crediting of a random erection. Let not my seed go to waste kind of logic that must have stood mankind in great stead when disasters and calamities threatened to wipe out the entire human race.

Disha eyed the vast sarovar around the temple and contemplated her new life. The beauty business had been rough. She had used all the products in phases. Ayurvedic whiteners, herbal under-eye cream, oil that strengthens hair to the point of rope, sunscreen lotions with the PH all balanced out for her beforehand, wet tissues that worked round the clock against her wilt, her ageing, her real rancid self. Only to be told she was out. Just like that. Despite the right soaps, creams, shampoos, oils, perfumes, deodorants, despite the banishing of dead cells from the bottom of her callused feet with a fierce pumice stone, regardless of the fact that she smelt well to her armpits. Displaced by a new, improved version with armpits one could eat. 'Duskier,' the clients had demanded in their clipped accents, 'More golden.' The definition of 'Asian' had tanned some more, her wheatish skin putting her out of the running or at least on discount. The scrapheap wasn't such a hot place.

Inside the temple, ornate feather fans swayed lethargically, and in the end the women gave in to Disha's urgent demand for attention by gingerly accepting lavish praise of selves and saints, keeping in balance the delicate mechanism that bound her sanity with theirs. Spiritually, almost in the slowest of motions, she was turning into a wisp of smoke before their very eyes; her kundalini was no longer drowsy, body decidedly celibate and the soul was rubbing its eyes. If they hurled themselves at her, they'd fall into that bottomless blur, they suspected. Despite the chemically brittle hair that suggested glassblower parents, despite the rigidity of her smiles, a sorority softly grew around her.

Most women had man problems; sons were missing, husbands were cheating. Sensible women that they were, they turned to chatter. The hush of deceit craftily exchan-ged for the voluble babble of gossip, voyeuristic peeps into other bedrooms where, goodness, they weren't getting it right either.

The Akaal Takht administration was considering her for treasurer's post and if the gauntness and Gucci seconds had initially thrown them off track, the sincerity of her penance and totally tuneless singing rallied them around. Piety had plucked out the cultured pearls and chiffons from her person as she gave herself as freely to faith as she had to fashion. The body elevated to a higher plateau, it almost spanned spiritual widths. No gropes, no faking of ecstasy, only rotations on pedestal.

Disha, just for the record, was still pretty, still as vulnerable as those skeletal collarbones suggested, still HIV negative. The slim-grim brigade with rigor mortis in their eye and the G-Spot Gym she barely missed. It was a relief to dry herself in the sun like Choti and not worry about a hardening, gnarled ginger of a face, about the ritual rutting, about discoloured vaginal discharge. Like sloughing off real self and donning a disguise. And if her adversaries thought her a bit skewed, she was merrily unaware of any estimate but her own.

When she shut her eyes and called to Vaahe Guru, she was back in her pre-Drupa Delhi home and she was walking on, leaving Papaji and Amma to their shouts. Unlike Choti, she remembered a life when she was the centre of her parents' existence, when the three were together as a family, before another baby came in to spoil everything. Disha liked to be other people some times, watch Kedar and Mangala from a distance and wonder what the two could fight about on a nice day like this, especially when they had her.

Babaji could do that just by looking at her. Transport her to that warm safe, place. Where nothing was saggy; not boobs, not soul.

Y ou think us fools?'

The gun's butt made a dull thud against Dave's head.

'I can make a difference,' he said in his heavily accented Hindi, moving encrusted lips with difficulty. 'I have a way with words and high contacts, you don't know. I can make the Prime Minister sit up and listen to you.'

'Yeah,' the man scratched his neck. 'A stenographer from Scandinavia make all the difference. If only you were someone who made everyone sit up. Woh kaun tha, that chap who came here waving a guitar bigger than him?'

The muddy water soaked into Dave's throat, settling in sediments along the way, so that he could only plough on in a duller voice, 'Bryan Adams...'

'Haan, haan. Chootiya-saala, with a circle of bodyguards—tiny kebab in the centre of onion rings.'

'But I am from here, I am Indian. Aren't I speaking Hindi?'

'Fashion hai ab. You all come here and learn Hindi and tabla, wear our kurta-pyjamas, but to be Hindustani you need to live and die for Hindustan. Kaleja chahiye.'

'Liver,' translated Dave with the dreary certainty of his doom and dictionary. The damp night had seeped into all his crusty bravado; he was tired and soggy with it until only the bondage of an accent remained.

Lately, he had begun to surrender to the surreal twist of fate. Fact was stranger than fiction for fiction sprang from facts, but facts had to constantly reinvent in order to stay a step ahead.

He knew the intrinsic truth about his own future for cement was seeping into the facial nooks and crannies of his escorts, and when he looked at them, all he saw was pale, empty air hardening. Mega migraines had established monarchy inside his head and a hollow scream was fast replacing where his throat used to be.

They laughed and the man tossed aside the bird's roasted leg he had been nibbling at with an air of finality. 'Marega tu hamare liye? Bryan Biriyani, banega Hindustani? Indian rope trick now is Indian gun trick, yaar. Listen to this.'

Dave listened. It was the last thing he did.

A tiny speck of blood mizzled on a sleeping cockerel. It crowed confusedly, heralding a whole change of season but the sky turned a deaf ear, shoring up its black clouds for the future.

In the temple courtyard drummers tattooed whole palms into the pelts they hit, thrumming the blood, and bodies offered themselves for flagellation under the cathartic whip.

Goddess Bhagwati entered the Velichapad in one smooth stroke, manifesting her spirit in his trembling limbs, staring out at her devotees through his enlarged eyes, amplifying her message via his lacerated tongue. The Velichapad swished the naked blade of the sword in his hand, sweeping it up, stabbing the air pointedly.

Kanaka stood transfixed, her eye longingly on the Velichapad's mesmerising visage. Suddenly, she cupped an ear with her palm and cried out in a frenzy, 'Endo,' like someone had called out her name.

She jumped into the fray of those in a trance, limbs convulsed under the threshing rope, inner music folding into the beat of the drum and heart, undulating to its insidious rhythm, thumps perforating eardrums. The Meledeth family unit watched in awe as she did them proud; she was the first among them to be divinely possessed.

With every cascading whack of the coir tip, Kanaka was remembering. Remembering each moment and man who spurned her, her grand design for life, thwarting every niche she carved out of the nothing she held in her hands; she heartily welcomed this wholesome mortification of flesh. And the fruitless mortality that dogged her steps went into exile for the while.

She spoke in tongue; her black tongue, bitten at the tip, darted rhythmically over crackling-dry lips as the rope came down again and again. She was a nail sinking into the wall of infinity under the blows of a hammer coming down again and again, to beat her deep down into nothingness, where bliss could cup her in its palms and blow softly at her brow.

'Ungghhh.' Rolling her eyes, she gave vent to the gurgles at the base of her throat, trapped words that broke free like secrets past their prime, speech patterns pouring out senselessly in an incessant purge until she fell down in a dead faint.

The commotion at the door alerted Drupa to the others' arrival. Mangala sauntered in gaily ahead of others, conch in hand, ululating. 'Ettan's bride is here.'

Velyammavan sat up, brightened, 'I knew. For the baby she went...'

'The Velichapad danced via her veins,' a Sambhaar Piece whispered with urgent pride to Drupa.

The bride entered the room then, her loosened hair streaming behind in frizzy halo, casting uneven shadows on the peeling wall.

17

KANAKA WAS BACK TO BEING A PHOTO OUT OF HER OLD wedding album, where she was captured in black and white crying piteously, heart and nose bursting full, with infinite joy simmering on a backburner.

Purged under the Velichapad's supervision, she had emerged sweat-shiny and plasma-soaked in energetic rebirth, malleable to an alien anvil, to a reshaping of future by spin-doctors; her own plans had gone so awry.

She smiled saucily in the direction of her brother-in-law, her bridegroom for the night, a thoughtful gift from the family to insure the future of the family. Sinking a tooth into her lower lip, drawing further droplets of blood, she focused on maintaining the sauciness.

'You are here,' he staggered up eagerly. 'They told me you were gone.'

Lukewarm gruel was served in chipped glasses to wash down the feast.

'It was one of those verbose sambhaars. More pieces than pulses,' Cheriyammavan pronounced, burping.

The three aunts began a countdown to the power-cut, that half an hour of pitch-black darkness the state government provided round the clock like other dysfunctional amenities.

'*Three minutes.*'

A new voice, the youngest in the house, took over the chant of 'deepam', another pair of hands guarded the flame from an adversary breeze as Mangala smiled coyly at the wall. 'You brought me water,' she said, looking at the man of mist bent to her, at the beads of condensation on the glass in his hand.

'*Two minutes.*'

'It will be sweet,' he swore, his face smooth as a facade, the tangy jamun juice mingling with the fresh water to dribble effervescent as thistledown down her lips. 'I can *never* leave you,' he'd say. He always did that, just before he yelled in another voice, a voice full of hatred and distrust, 'Take her away, dammit. Take her away.'

Drupa wiped spit off her mother's mouth, absently scanning the TV screen. Turbulent courtships conducted via elaborate costumes, sets, song and dance charmed her about as much as the opaquely mystifying 'rukavat ke liye khed hai' did during the Krishi Darshans over which she had no ophthalmologic choice as a child.

'*One minute.*'

An amorous couple jigged monotonously—one, two, three, kick—on a hillock enveloped in smoke.

Lightning shot across the window in a loud crackle, burnishing it momentarily like stained glass, and whacked the TV shut; the sky's throbbing veins had burst at last.

'Started.' A Sambhaar Piece ran to the window, putting her hand out. 'Monsoon.'

Trees bowed and scraped in obeisance as Rain God unbolted his optional eye and let the tears fall, sinking paper boats in rivulets, banging together hearts in ferries like so many pans; flowing, flooding, sluicing, overriding the thunder and lightning that ruptured the sky.

Candles, kept in readiness, were lit up with groping hands.

Mangala went bashful. 'There was thunder the first time our lips met.'

Drupa shrugged; the sky no doubt drooled like Amma drooled now, ladling steam, while Papaji swallowed her secrets alive. Gongs pounding in heads like sweet anticipation gone awry. All these pointless tinkles of passion were necessary or where would mankind be if it depended on everlasting love and fidelity?

No, it was in the sky all right, the hustle and bustle, Mangala ascertained, the ends of her eyes going conical. For she had been staring up until that very moment when view was necessarily blocked and could recall not a single cacophonic cloud poised to strike before the alien tongue sliced into her mouth, pickaxe in wake. Later she, too, had wondered at the thrumming static that their phlegm-flecked spittle, cobwebbed chin to chin, had crocheted to an incandescent cosmos, procuring breathless rain complete with rumbles.

'Your eyes are not black,' Kedar had huskily informed Mangala. 'They are coins of coir.'

'It is the lightning...' She closed them.

Drupa watched the eyelids clamp down. Perhaps Mangala was dressing up ho-hum hours to justify anxieties, to ward off mediocrity charges in retrospective, her daughter inferred. Just the southwest monsoons breaking wind, ma, no need to carry on so. Nature, mother of all dispersed seeds, taking credit for the ones doing nicely, thank you. But coincidences in intimacy do acquire shades of the supernatural and attributing ulterior motives to the weather was commonplace, Drupa was the first to agree.

'His dreams...'

'Are hollow jets of nothing now,' Drupa concurred wordlessly. 'The exact shade of air.'

Mother and daughter confronted each other, their eyes snarling up, doddering along the brink of...

'Amma?' Drupa dared to hope, going still.

'It is the monster with loose motions!' trilled Mangala then as the drops continued to fall tunelessly outside and the skies turned the earth over. 'Take your hand in, it will pull you into its mouth.'

'Amoeboic dysentry,' Dr Drupa obliged her aunts with a professional squint. *I can see us thirty years from now, less teeth, less of us, little old ladies slurping tea from plastic saucers.*

Two jittery feet had she and they shuffled her out, beyond roof or awning, Papaji's serenade or Amma's tabs on the weather, past the large rooms where raindrops plummeting into cement culverts tracked down patchy crevices in Meledeth Illam's steepled tiles, once brick red, and trickled into the barren nadu-muttam in resuscitation, sloshing it back into life. Outside, rotting gooseberries had ripped, their fermentation riding the wind like wine.

Thunderclaps helped infuse melodrama into her humdrum life, but real life with its stale air was closing in, too. Drupa felt the need for motion, to shimmer, to perambulate limbs, to break out from a bagful of squelched skin and Out-Foot right into someone else's puddle; anyone's, anywhere. Far away from the elsewheres cluttering up her path.

She crooned a lullaby into the darkness, downpour riding into mouth, curls and hands stuck to sides, the soaked sky sucking the air right out of her as Brighty Singh had till the horse thumped him with a panicked tail, dislodging his drunken kiss and textile Taj Mahal.

Tentatively, she poked out her tongue, hands interlaced on bulging abdomen, to taste a raindrop. Could her baby feel the rain, too?

'I am a suicide waiting to commit itself,' her lover had warned. Before his debilitation strapped his ass down on metal, he pledged he'd cold-bloodedly kill himself like she had been ordered medically to kill his child.

Apollo, she remembered reading as a child, was the cruellest of all gods, you couldn't worship the flaming disk *and* retain eyesight though some thought it a sign of good health to out-stare the sun's corona. Drupa squeezed her temples; the chariot was all hogwash, a one-seater without pillion, and the horses groomed for getaway. She had been his epidural, his shot of morphine, someone who rocked him to sleep so he could rest his eyes from his own intensity.

Thanks to him, she was thinking up sentences she never expected to think in a lifetime, rummaging among coincidences for something that made sense, was wearable, filling in blanks where happy-ever-after was; her chief role Fate's plaything, her chief regret the denial of post-coital bliss. Had barely got the geometry of sex right when eunuchs danced and docs asked her to furnish the fetus' gene map. To turn in amniotic fluid by inserting a traitorous needle that would pierce right through her belly and ferret out a sample from the low-lying placenta. She had signed those papers after all, for that fat needle to go chasing down the womb, tracking down, flushing out the fetus from its lair to gather incriminating evidence against it. *Anything you say can be held against you.*

'It will gasp for breath at birth,' the lab technician warned with barely suppressed relish. Behind her back, they called her Ashtavkra ki Ma; it was funny how love unbrained the Plain Janes. 'Will need incubator straight off. The disease won't let it live long, but you know that.'

If only, Drupa had yearned, if only I can pucker up for the Judas kiss, freak out on booze, bike, smash my brain against a convenient wall, if only I can stab the baby in its back and smile. The baby with wheeze on breath, death on DNA.

'Enema at five PM. Induce at six AM. Out by eight AM, if all goes well,' an orderly at that hospital far away had dispassionately scheduled.

If all went well for whom? No need to ask.

Just when she managed to fall asleep, she was brought brutally awake. The lab technician, the US doctor she then consulted over Internet who bounced cell maps back and forth, her one-time-lover, Papaji, Guddi Mausi, Badi, Amma, Ammooma, they had all begun to sneak into her head. At odd hours they woke her in the guise of relentless hiccups or acidic heartburn just so they could continue their harangue, shake documents and test reports at her. 'Look,' they sermonised, 'look,' burgling her very breath. She was wide awake at nights and lethargic by day, till her hours were no longer her own, but seamless sequences of mortgaged somnolence.

Global developments were afoot, experiments with mice were on; soon stem-cell research would triumph, genes with a double set of muscles may drop like manna from heaven, but her baby, it would be in a bin. What nurtured in her belly, what might nurse at her teat, it wasn't perfect; could wave no A-studded report card at her, would shake no rattle at her. There would be no cry of 'Amma', no meeting of eyes; wasted muscles allowed none of that. But evacuate it because it knew not where its next breath came from when, matter of fact, neither did its mother? To render it as unsafe inside her as it would be outside her...

During her house-surgency in a paediatric ward, she had seen many babies die in their mothers' laps and never enquired. Was cuddling the baby's little corpse therapeutic like, say, putting it to sleep in a crib had been? Did it become one with you then like the time it was in the womb? Could one heart beat for two, one nose breathe for two yet again?

'*Yet again*?' the thunder seemed to echo her.

When lightning lit a matchstick and illuminated a zigzag path, it felt like the flip side of darkness. But there her home was, the rains splashing up mud in pretend playfulness at its soaking hem. And then it was switched off, her home, but it was there playing hide and seek till the sky lit a torch again. It did not disappear because dark was not the opposite of light. It only concealed.

Nature, she hoped, would provide her with some clue. It was Nature, after all, that had loaded her with seed and set her speedily on the path of harvest season. Naughty, Drupa wagged a finger. Naughty, naughty Nature; rubbing two stones to make light, rubbing two bodies to make life. And then raining killjoy doctors with gloves to shove up her vagina. 'Reporting from battlefield,' they monotoned into their discreet microphones in white-white coats. 'The Gynaecological Government has ordered a closure of all commercial transactions and a quick evacuation of the PoW, who may or may not be dead.' Insert file pic of PoW sucking thumb.

A mockery of modern technology wasn't impossible, she knew only too well. Frizzy-haired godmen ran their whole industry on these freewheeling miracles. She could reproduce someone so-called normal despite serums and tests and labs and reports and self-assured shakes of head.

Locked in tipsy combat with self, Choti had sneaked out of the hush-hush hospice at sunrise, before they merrily came to administer the enema, to hunt for her baby, probably the only baby she'd ever conceive, and she had run like hell. Giving up on scouting for paradises around the corner and booking it a room right in her arms. Home was where you breathed, and when you breathed no more, it turned grave. She couldn't very well strangle it to premature death at site or shoot at sight, and turn her tummy into tomb. She shuddered in memorium. Even the Guru Granth Saheb was clear on bajar paap, killing of offspring; there was no greater sin in the world.

'You are having this...baby?' her dean asked disinterestedly, doodling on the note-pad nearest to him. She hadn't been his brightest student.

Drupa remembered Dasamma striving to keep the chick alive under a tin plate. To mother was just as jarring as to murder.

'Yes, sir,' she murmured.

He gnawed at the pen's tip with growing appetite. 'That isn't very...nice,' he had commented.

Nice! Condemned to eternal niceness, she had rebelled, bitten back the very mouth that articulated so delicately at her, 'How nice!' Cute can fall off face and Nice walks out of your soul, leaving gaps with fangs behind. Ask me, she wanted to say. Go ahead and just ask me.

The phone on his desk began to ring.

'No, sir,' she had intoned louder, the throb of milk in her chest.

Drupa inhaled now and the wet earth came up sticky in her nostrils as if with a straw. Then, when the breeze's breath grew foul, she retraced her steps back to Papaji.

Near the bed allotted to her, his retrieved skull beamed benevolently at her; wherever she went, he obligingly came along. He was the reason why she did not give out the stink Disha alleged she did, that stink of loneliness.

She looked into his eyes. The wind danced through the bare hollows with a whoosh, whipping up a vacuum, playing flautist till his dreams were airborne. No bare bones cluttered up her mantelpiece; she saw only his tranquil face, his smile, the resentment in his rhapsody...

Barely loving is
the language of love.

His verdict, her vindication, she lay down, but this time it was the lack of sun that stymied her; she who was used to praying passionately for dawn ASAP.

'I'm sorry I woke you,' her lover had whispered the night they spooned into each other, when he hadn't had his fill of her yet. 'Go back to sleep.'

But it was a different sleep now. You don't wake up mid-sleep to sleep the same sleep again or even wake up mid-dream to dream the same dream again. And now this newfound dream of the other woman! Her lover's wife, whose beauty hit her hard even in dreams, even when she was only a woman, a heterosexual woman.

'Must she unspike herself from that still warm penis and spill into my nightmares,' Drupa grumbled, wrestling with pillow and the moonlight spilling into her eye. Sighing, she sat up and padded across to the mask, ripping it off the wall and settling it on the skeletal mould. High time they met, her parents. She'd play matchmaker.

There was an amiable gurgle nearby, from the over-flooded nadu-muttam. A rainwater D and C, she surmised, so tomorrow it would sparkle clean, cradle a cerulean bud to match her cupid camouflage.

18

INSIDE THE ROOM THEY FACED EACH OTHER, THE FUTURE LOVERS, like two demons in a nightmare.

Kanaka took tiny, mincing steps, activating golden anklets, masquerading those tasselled women on celluloid that she had scrutinized for just such eventuality. She unwrapped her veshti, a finger worming its way into bellybutton under which the recalcitrant womb suddenly began to seethe.

'We have a job to do,' she whispered in desperate flirtatiousness, dispersing a newborn tic along a nerve. Her hands fluttered tentatively an inch above his shoulders, then she looked at him fully for the first time and her hands fell away.

His eyes were on fire!

Like he had a secret, an incendiary one, glowing like gunpowder kegs in his sockets. They blazed inward with blinding incandescence. A fierce desire to stroke them shut, those mad, ignited eyes of his, shot through her.

'I am wicked,' she babbled incoherently instead, slumping into the bed by the wall. 'I lied to them, to him, my husband, to her, your wife, that last time she was here. I said…you came to me,' she babbled. 'You understood—didn't you?—I was married to the wrong man…had prayed you were the groom the day you came visiting that first day. Oh, what can

I begin to tell you about my prayers?' She shivered. 'Wanted to be the real mistress of this home. Wanted to be Kutti. Wanted.' Eagerly, she turned to him. 'You *must* have come to me that day. I waited so long…'

A cool draught rifled her then, sprouting goose pimples along her exposed flesh and he settled on the bed beside her.

She almost felt the stickiness of phlegm where a highly recommended god-man had spat long ago to flush out the evil spirit he said he saw inside her as if she was made of transparent glass and it floated inside her like fish in an aquarium. She flinched anew from that stranger's visual devaluing at the temple stairway, the tin-drums on her wedding day, the muffled whimpers of her wedding night, the mute red mocking of the womb month after month, birthday after birthday, her sister's breathless breeding, the fabricated kisses and caresses of…this man and then every man.

She stole a glance at him; he looked like he had nothing else to do, nothing else to say in what remained of life. Ankles swollen and twisted. Eyelashes jagged clumps of baldness now. Eyelashes that used to be thick and long like rice grains. Gradually she grew mute, the deep calm by her side infecting her, enveloping her.

They sat together in silence, listening companionably to the rattle of reminiscences and the rain's chant and then the steadying catch in its breath like a tearful bride's tapering sniff, their chests rising and falling in tandem. It held a kind of ramshackle charm, their mothballed mouldering cache of memories, like the humming of human bones.

Eventually, she rose. It was when her hand brushed the door's wooden latch that he called out, so softly she almost didn't hear.

'Kutti.'

With a choked sob Kanaka turned around.

He was blinking at her like someone waking up from a deep sleep, remembering nothing but the sleep.

He swept his stubby eyelashes in formal invitation. His Kutti was too young a bride, he knew and yet he couldn't resist. He hardly had any time before they recalled him to sea. May be a baby would do the trick and his mind shimmied in perplexed pleasure at the thought. His bride! No longer kin, however strange and delicious the transition. But why did she hover so at the door, a frightened thing.

'Kutti,' he called again in the new way—man to woman —a cardamom playing pearl under his tongue.

Kanaka stumbled blindly across the room then to bunch brokenly in his arms.

'Shh,' he bade, embracing her, wiping incessant tears that fell on her cheek like the light rain outside. 'Shh.'

In the split second before her slumbers spluttered up with the mustard seeds of restless dreams, Choti fancied she heard someone sing. Snug under her heart, bang inside her belly sat the song. It was as if her whole body began to hum and suddenly she was in the plane that day when the sun in the comic book and the sun at the window streamed in their insanely smiling Siamese sunshine.

She yawned; the yawn took over her face, sealed her eyelids with duct tape, caramalised the dark clouds and brought with it the calm of unconsciousness. 'Sleep is a blessing from God,' Velyammavan's words floated along like a benediction and the pillow was suddenly a long-lost pal.

For Dr Drupa Ahluwalia, being diagnosed homesick had been the very devil.

Kanaka felt her chest tighten and feared it would burst with the ferocity of her grief and adoration; in gusty, ostentatious gulps, with tears and snot riding down her cheeks and chin, she wept copiously.

Tipping up her chin, palms cradling her face like it was the most precious scoop of water to the thirstiest man, his thumbs swabbed the soggy curls on her head, barricaded the rivulets down her cheeks. Gently, he dabbed at the telltale kohl, at a sooty beauty spot, until his gentleness sent her toppling to his misshapen feet in belated gratitude.

She didn't dare venerate though, nor touch even in worship, just lay prostrate at his feet for some innate inertia held her back. Mouth hovered tremblingly and long over a deformed, ingrown nail with unbearable reverence before he gathered her up in his arms.

His breath fairly whistling into hers, he bent her back so her scented hair could cast their spell upon his pillow; the jasmine buds had just begun to bloom along those locks, freeing their fragrance, fistful after fistful, along the way.

Kanaka's eyes migrated to his; this time those eyes leapt with twin flames from another fire, a hell she recognised, a hell of desire and grieving and greed and aching.

'Etta.'

He walked his fingers lazily down her spinal staircase and a hush pierced the bustle within her bosom at long last, surging deep into the Madman's kiss.

A kiss that began in the middle.